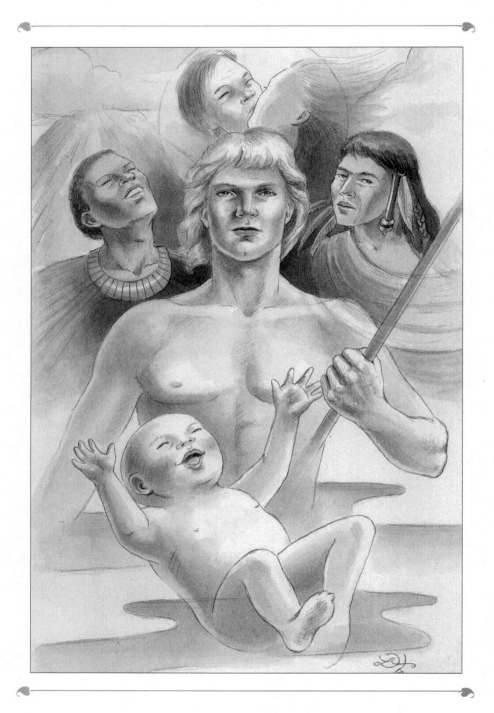

Llewellyn's World Religion & Magick Series

LORD OF
LIGHT & SHADOW

THE MANY FACES OF THE GOD

D. J. CONWAY

1997
Llewellyn Publications
St. Paul, Minnesota 55164-0383 U.S.A.

FIRST EDITION
Second Printing, 1997

Cover design: Anne Marie Garrison
Cover art: MoonDeer
Interior art: Lisa Hunt
Book design, layout, and editing: Jessica Thoreson

Cataloging-in-Publication Data
Conway, D. J. (Deanna J.)
Lord of light & shadow : the many faces of the god / D. J. Conway.
   -- 1st ed.
      p.   cm. -- (Llewellyn's world religion and magick series)
   Includes bibliographical references and index.
   ISBN 1-56718-177-5 (trade pbk.)
   1. Masculinity of God. 2. Paganism. 3. God--Miscellanea.
   4. Goddess religion. 5. Occultism. I. Title. II. Series.
   Llewellyn's world religion & magick series.
   BL215.3.C66   1997
   291.2'113--dc21   96-39222

Llewellyn Publications
A Division of Llewellyn Worldwide, Ltd.
P.O. Box 64383, Dept. K177–5, St. Paul, MN 55164-0383

ABOUT THE AUTHOR

I was born on a Beltane Full Moon with a total lunar eclipse, one of the hottest days of that year. Although I came into an Irish-North Germanic-Native American family with natural psychics on both sides, such abilities were not talked about. So I learned discrimination in a family of closet psychics.

I have always been close to Nature. Trees, herbs, and flowers are part of my indoor and outdoor landscapes wherever I live. I love cats, music, mountains, stones, ritual, reading, and nights when the Moon is full. I have studied every part of New Age religion from Eastern philosophy to Wicca. I hope I never stop learning and expanding.

I live a rather quiet life in the company of my husband and my six cats, with occasional visits with my children and grandchildren. Most of my time is spent researching and writing. Before I am finished with one book, I am working on another in my head. All in all, I am just an ordinary Pagan person.

TO WRITE TO THE AUTHOR

If you wish to contact the author or would like more information about this book, please write to the author in care of Llewellyn Worldwide, and we will forward your request. Both the author and publisher appreciate hearing from you and learning of your enjoyment of this book. Llewellyn Worldwide cannot guarantee that every letter written to the author will be answered, but all will be forwarded. Please write to:

D. J. Conway
℅ Llewellyn Worldwide
P.O. Box 64383, Dept. K177–5
St. Paul, MN 55164-0383, U.S.A.

Please enclose a self-addressed stamped envelope for reply, or $1.00 to cover costs. If outside U.S.A., enclose international postal reply coupon.

OTHER BOOKS BY THE AUTHOR

Celtic Magic
Norse Magic
The Ancient & Shining Ones
Maiden, Mother, Crone
Dancing With Dragons
By Oak, Ash, & Thorn
Animal Magick
Flying Without a Broom
Moon Magick
Falcon Feather & Valkyrie Sword
Astral Love
The Dream Warrior (fiction)
Magickal, Mythical, Mystical Beasts

FORTHCOMING

Soothslayer (fiction)
Warrior of Shadows (fiction)

LLEWELLYN'S WORLD RELIGION AND MAGICK SERIES

At the core of every religion, at the foundation of every culture, there is MAGICK.

Magick sees the world as alive, as the home that humanity shares with beings and powers both visible and invisible, with whom we can interact to either our advantage or disadvantage—depending on our awareness and intention.

Religious worship and communion is one kind of magick, and just as there are many religions in the world, so are there many magickal systems.

Religion and magick are ways of seeing and relating to the creative powers, the living energies, the all-pervading spirit, the underlying intelligence that is the universe within which we and all else exist.

Neither religion nor magick conflict with science. All share the same goals and the same limitations: always seeking truth, forever haunted by human limitations in perceiving that truth. Magick is "technology" based on experience and extrasensory insight, providing its practitioners with methods of influence and control over the world of the invisible before it impinges on the world of the visible.

The study of world magick not only enhances your understanding of the world in which you live, and hence your ability to live better, but brings you in touch with the inner essence of your long evolutionary heritage and most particularly—as in the case of the magickal system identified most closely with your genetic inheritance—with the archetypal images and forces most alive in your consciousness.

CONTENTS

	Introduction	xi
I	The Spiritual Mysteries of Mythology	3
II	The Sacred or Divine Child	9
III	Lord of Love & Fertility	29
IV	Lord of Creation & the Heavens	43
V	Lord of the Forest & Animals	55
VI	The Healer	63
VII	The Trickster	69
VIII	Lord of Judgment & Prophecy	79
IX	The Hero/Warrior	87
X	The Magician	93
XI	Lord of the Waters	101
XII	The Sacrificed Savior	107
XIII	Lord of Death & the Underworld	121
XIV	Recovering the Forgotten True God	133
Appendix I	Meditations	137
Appendix II	Gods & Their Attributes	145
Appendix III	God Symbols	167
Appendix IV	Cross-Reference	177
	Endnotes	189
	Bibliography	203
	Index	219

INTRODUCTION

Because of past experiences with the god of orthodox religions, I avoided the Pagan God for a long time. In my mind, He was the vengeful, judgmental orthodox deity whom no one could hope to please, and who particularly seemed to dislike females. To my surprise, I discovered I wasn't the only person who felt this way; even men were admitting to their discomfort in relating to the Pagan God.

Preconceived and force-fed ideas of the god created by Christianity and other orthodox religions were causing many people to shun the idea of connection with the Pagan God. The "accepted" religions still teach, as they always have, that the proper relationship between humans and their god must consist of begging, fear, blindly following religious commands, and transferring responsibility for individual actions to the deity in the hope of escaping punishment (karma). People are ordered to follow the rules laid out by the "spiritual representatives" of this orthodox god, primarily so they will keep these "representatives" in power, give up their money on demand, and not be curious about the real truth.

Unfortunately, this atmosphere causes most people, especially women, to remain disenchanted with the Pagan God and avoid connecting with Him. Until they discover the ancient truth of His being, aspects, and power, how can it be otherwise? Spiritual growth will remain one-sided and incomplete until this connection is made; for true spiritual growth, one must understand the Goddess, the God, and the companionship and working partnership between these deities.

The Pagan God is the powerful, original, archetypal entity hidden behind the pale, adulterated copy of the orthodox god. He is a being with the traits and aspects that women secretly desire in men, and men should desire to emulate. Although the patriarchal, orthodox religions changed His outward appearance (to a irascible-looking bearded male) and relationship to humans, they assimilated all His ancient spiritual stories, in one form or another, into their "scriptures" and "sacred" books. There was something about the God that could not be denied or destroyed completely.

Lest some should start yelling "foul" because of my speaking of matriarchies and patriarchies, please understand that I do not hold with making excuses for present problems and actions by laying blame on the past. Nor do I believe that all men are misogynists. Neither men nor women should use historical or personal mistakes as excuses, but take action right now to better themselves and their lives. Such discussion of history is merely used in this book as is necessary to put things into perspective, nothing more.

Are you ready for the next step in your spiritual growth? If so, journey with me through the ancient spiritual stories, following the thread of truth until we meet the reality of the Pagan God of many faces.

LORD OF
LIGHT & SHADOW

I

THE SPIRITUAL MYSTERIES OF MYTHOLOGY

The myths were originally spiritual teaching stories, a primer to help humans understand the Goddess and the God and the human relationship to every aspect of these deities. The myths were also stories of human spiritual development clothed in symbols. Those who were truly seeking spiritual knowledge would understand these symbols, while those who sought power and position would not.

Early humans knew and revered the position of the Great Goddess and all Her personalized aspects, but also knew and revered the position of the God as Her necessary and important consort/lover/son. Although the God was secondary to the Goddess in the beginning of human religion, these deities were both important in different ways. The God was a companion and partner, an essential part of the Goddess after She created Him. There are still hidden spiritual mysteries embedded in myths (teaching stories) that reveal this.

The patriarchies changed the original myths to condone what they were doing to civilizations and spiritual growth. After all, if the god condoned the actions of religious and secular leaders through his stories, obviously the priests were right and everyone else was wrong. With time and constant persecution, the people began to believe the lies and forget the truth. Unfortunately, this forced change in spiritual belief created profound problems. It brought about a disintegration of human self-confidence, self-value, and the relationship to the deity-powers and the world around them.

The deliberate changes of the God's identity in the myths further clouded the hidden stories of spirituality by concealing the path to the truth. If one does not know how to look for clues to follow, then one cannot find the way. This book is written to help you find the proper clues and discover your own path back to the true God. It is a journey that must be made individually; it cannot be a group effort, for spirituality is a personal experience. Finding this path is a personal responsibility, a spiritual endeavor which you can lay on no one else's shoulders. But it is such a pleasant, enlightening journey that I cannot imagine anyone not taking it.

DISCOVERING THE TRUTH OF THE PAGAN GOD

What humans know as "god" today is only a shadow of the true Masculine Energy of the universe, and an adulterated, twisted shadow at that. The roots of this deception began thousands of years ago.

The main reason for the drastic changes in the worship and understanding of the Pagan God occurred when the ruling matriarchies were conquered and reformed by patriarchal groups. Since all history is rewritten by conquerors, this deliberate fabrication should not be surprising.

In all probability, however, many of the conquests were not by the sword; some of the takeovers were very likely peaceful and, at first, supported by the women. But, as happens in the world today when religious institutions gain control of governments, things began to slowly decay from within these peacefully changed cultures. Wherever citizens become complacent about their government and religion, the fanatics and the power-hungry begin to carefully lay their plans to gain control.

In government this begins by enacting laws without the consent of the populace "for their good." These laws always take away control from the general people and place it in the hands of a special few. This is done so deviously that the citizens don't realize for a long time that they no longer have any say in what their government does.

This shift of control, to be effective, must include not only the ruling governmental body, but the judges and those responsible for defense of the citizenry. The judges give rulings to back the laws passed by the new government, and the military forcibly upholds the judicial decisions and the government's new laws.

The same thing happens in religion, in an even more insidious manner. The worshippers are carefully filled with propaganda that anyone who doesn't accept the "new ways" and believe as he or she is told is an enemy of the religion and the culture and is subject to open persecution. When religion becomes one with government, or dictates the laws from behind the scenes, the corruption is complete.

When a culture or civilization begins to decay in this way, it is easy prey for any other militant cultures. War becomes prevalent, with the younger men (the rivals for power against the older men) considered expendable. Women and children become no more than property to the men and war booty for the victors. The culture becomes dangerously lopsided.

What does this have to do with the truth behind the Pagan God? Actually, everything! In order to justify their actions, the conquering males had to rewrite the ancient teaching stories, the myths, to reflect a God in their image who would justify their actions: a God who was all-powerful with no competition from a Goddess; one who was devious and revengeful; a deity who could, and did, rape and kill and punish for the slightest infraction of impossible laws. This deity was given the power of creation, in reality something only held by females and the Goddess. The Pagan God devolved into a pale spiritual copy of what He had been and was totally foreign to His true nature.

In short, patriarchy created an atmosphere of Boy psychology, as Moore and Gillette call it,[1] based on fear of women and real men and promoting the dominance of others. By creating their "god" with this immature attitude and demanding that males emulate this "god's" nature, they attacked both true masculinity and true femininity, leaving both sexes hampered in their search for maturity.

Although the matriarchies were Goddess-oriented, they knew that the Goddess had a consort/lover/son, whom She created (along with everything else) to be Her partner and companion. Even though the Goddess was more powerful, She never considered Herself better than this consort. Each deity had specific responsibilities and parts to play in the lives of the people and all creation. She loved Her consort, as He did Her in return. She came to rely on Him as the trusted one who helped carry out Her decrees and uphold Her laws.

Suppressing the Goddess deliberately changed the role of the God. It ripped apart the spiritual values of humans, leaving a terrible void in their lives. Since each human is both male and female, women as well as men need to know how to relate spiritually to both the Goddess and God.

This new patriarchal image of the God gave men a false image of maleness. Those males who were born after the destructive rewrites of the myths and reforming of the God's nature tried desperately to model themselves according to this false deity image, thinking this was the ideal male image. Unfortunately, this brought internal and external chaos, a chaos that has brought nothing good with it down through the centuries.

By being bombarded with these false images of maleness, presented by religion, governments, the law, and the military, men have been tricked into becoming something that makes them uncomfortable, unhappy, and at odds with other humans and the world. More and more men are finding themselves opposed to this god's "male" image, and are wondering what to do about it.

Women have lost most, if not all, of their connection with and respect for the true God. Unfortunately, most of the world's women are afraid to open their minds to the truth of their spiritual feelings, following what is "acceptable," rather than go in a new and, to them, frightening direction. Even though they have been greatly abused by patriarchal ideals and control, they refuse to cast aside this false god, and have turned away from the God aspect. Trying desperately to find something in the patriarchal religions that speaks to them as females, they seek out the Goddess in the image of Mary, or non-sexist angels, in their search for a more compatible and real connection with spiritual power. However, this blindness leaves a hole in the spiritual life and growth of women, a hole that can only be filled by learning how to relate once more to the true God.

The original God was, and is, a complex deity[2] with more than one aspect. For centuries, the male-dominated religions have heaped a thick coating of lies onto the myths and spiritual stories, believing that these falsehoods would conceal the truth forever. However, if one knows what clues to look for and follows them through the myths of the world's diverse cultures, the truth about the God still exists. The patriarchies failed to remove all clues, either from laziness, lack of spiritual intelligence, or simply arrogance in believing that they could force people to believe their version of "truth."

The God first shows Himself to us as the newborn Child, the promising infant of possibilities and hope. He is the Lover who leads us to the beauty and joy of companionship, and the Lord of Creation and the Forest who reminds us of our connection with all Nature. As the Healer, He comforts us in times of sorrow, and as Hero/Warrior, gives us direction and protection when we feel under attack by the world around us. Under the guise of the Trickster, the God brings us up short when we have gone too far in one direction and are in danger of losing balance. He is the stern Judge who never lets us go too far astray without penalties. He is the keeper of the laws of the Goddess, the laws that affect us even though we may not believe in them. He brings what we call "miracles" in His role as Magician, just as He guides us onto spiritual paths back to the Goddess as Lord of the Waters. When it comes time for us to exit this life, the God reappears in His roles of Sacrificed Savior and Lord of Death to assure us that He took that path before us and there is nothing to fear.

It is impossible to include every world myth that fits into each of the following chapter-categories. I have chosen those that I thought were the most familiar and interesting. Because each deity is complex, a deity is often found in more than one category. The Divine Child later becomes the Sacrificed Savior, as often does the Son/Lover; the Lord of Judgment and Prophecy can also be the Magician and/or the Lord of Death.

Like Theseus following the thread into the center of the labyrinth, we will follow the clues of the true God through the myths until we at last face Him in the center of the inner temple, where He waits with the Goddess.

II

THE SACRED OR DIVINE CHILD

Although myths tell the stories of particular deities, they were meant to be much more than biographies. Myths tell us sacred, spiritual things about ourselves as well as illustrate the aspects and energies of deities for us. As Carl Jung and Carl Kerenyi point out in their book *Essays on a Science of Mythology*, the primary function of mythology is to reveal archetypes[1] in such a way that humans can understand them. Unfortunately, we have nearly lost the knowledge of how to interpret the myths, and usually read them only on a superficial level.

The images in myth correspond to inherited superconscious elements in the human psyche. This superconsciousness connects all humans and has access to everything known to our ancestors in every culture. We may not realize that we have access to these superconscious elements, but we do, and they affect us in our present life. Archetypes belong to all humans, not to just a few. We can't cut these ancient archetypes out of our lives any more than we can go without a brain or a liver. Whenever a person or a culture tries to excise spiritual archetypes, neurotic and psychotic disorders erupt.

Archetypes are living psychic forces that subconsciously influence our lives and how we view the spiritual, in whatever way we choose to practice it. Archetypes form an invisible, unbreakable link between every human and the God and Goddess, or Divine Source. Therefore, if we ignore or fear the archetype of the true God, we are like an engine not using all its cylinders.

Many people think that the myth of the Child-God was only an attempt by primitive cultures to illustrate the year-cycle of the Sun, particularly when it begins its rise during the darkest season of the year, or to explain the growth and death of vegetation. The stories of the Divine Child are more than this; they are stories of the God-potential in every human, the potential that can be born again and again.

The God's aspect of the Sacred[2] or Divine Child is remembered by most people today through the Christians' Christmas scenes. However, as the myths of this aspect unfold, we shall see that the whole Christian story of the Child at Christmas (Winter Solstice) and His death at Easter (Spring Equinox) was copied from much older myths.[3]

What many of us have not realized, though, is that the Divine Child existed in more than the Winter Solstice stories. This Child-God can be found in a great many myths of miraculous birth, abandonment, exposure, and danger, which is followed by triumph over great odds and dark forces. The father in these stories is usually dead, missing, or an actual threat to the Child. The maiden-mother may have a mortal husband, but he doesn't consummate the marriage with her until after the birth of the firstborn Child.[4] The mother may be in great danger along with the Child, have died in childbirth, or in rare cases have abandoned the Child herself.

The firstborn Divine Child in every culture was sacred and usually had a special preordained fate—that of the later Sacrificed Savior,[5] the one who dies for the betterment of the people. This Child also had within his nature a touch of darkness or death; consider Hermes in his role as Psychopomp for dead souls, Apollo in his dark aspect as Vediovis connecting him with the Underworld, Dionysus and his wild Maenads, and Zeus Zagreus from Crete who was fed by bees (souls) and was sacrificed by the Titans.

This Divine or Sacred Child is a creation born of the Goddess (even when the mother is supposedly human), Her future companion in infant form. Even if a human mother is present, the Child is always connected in some way with an aspect of the Goddess. Unfortunately, some of the myths have been so mutilated that we no longer know which goddess was connected with the Child.

This Divine Child is the Pagan God at the beginning of His power and cycle of life. In terms of human spiritual symbolism, the Sacred Child is the Goddess' gift of newness to us, Her children: new life, new hope, new opportunities, new beginnings.

This Child must evolve toward a type of independence in order to fulfill His destiny. The Goddess brings the Child into existence, as She does all creation. She gives all Her creations the gifts of life, awareness, and sometimes certain abilities with which to grow in special ways. She does not dictate to Her creations, but watches over them as they develop in unique ways. Unlike humans, the God never deviates from Her path. Any myths that show the God in a threatening or negative role toward the Goddess were most certainly matriarchal stories rewritten by patriarchal clans.

The Goddess has given humans the ability to create on the physical, mental, and spiritual levels. Hopefully, we put much thought and love into creating a physical child. But it is mental and spiritual creation that puts humans above the level of Her other creations. We can create mental children in the forms of ideas, art, books, and projects. We create spiritual children as we strive for higher goals, discovering new pathways back to the Goddess. However, as we create these "children" of the mental and spiritual, we must learn to let go when it is time for them to be born. The Child cannot grow and develop unless we allow it to separate from us; in other words, it must come into existence and stand on its own merits.

By rereading and interpreting myths of the Divine or Sacred Child, we can learn more about the true aspects of the God and our own spiritual journey toward Him. His stories are directions to the possible pathways for our own spiritual growth. They are signposts along our journey, with the stories of the Divine Child marked as "begin your search here."

In ancient Egypt, the Divine Child was the god Horus. After Isis retrieved the body of Osiris, who had been killed by his brother Set, she performed powerful magick on her brother/husband's body and conceived a child. When it came time for Horus to be born, Isis was attended only by the cobra goddess Buto in her hiding place in the swamps of the Nile Delta. She knew that Set would surely destroy the rightful heir to Egypt's throne if he should learn of the birth. Isis made a bed for Horus out of a mass of papyrus reeds.[6] The Divine Child Horus was portrayed as a child with one long lock of hair on one side of his head and his finger in his mouth.[7]

While very young, Horus was exposed to many dangers. He was attacked and bitten by wild beasts, stung by scorpions, burned, and suffered intense intestinal pains. The god Thoth drove out the scorpion's poison; his mother's great magickal powers saved him at other times.

One day while Isis was away, Set found the body of Osiris, cut it into fourteen pieces, and scattered the pieces throughout Egypt. After gathering all the pieces, except the phallus (which was eaten by a crab), Isis, along with her sister Nephthys, her nephew Anubis, Thoth, and the child Horus, performed the first embalming. Osiris then ascended to the immortal world and became king of the dead.[8] However, as the Child Horus grew, Osiris came often to teach him the use of weapons so Horus could reclaim his inheritance and avenge himself on Set.

The Divine Child as the very young God is born from the love of the Goddess to be Her son/companion and the hope and inspiration of all life in the world. Horus, whose eyes were called the Sun and the Moon, represents the God's ability to lead us along the proper spiritual paths in times of joy (light, day) and sorrow (darkness, night). Although He is attacked by those who do not believe in Him or who want His power destroyed, He can never be killed. The Goddess protects Him through Her own great powers and through the other ancient archetypal energies She can call for assistance. He succeeds over great odds and against terrible dangers.

Through what appears to be death, the Goddess can bring forth new life and shows us by example how to create something fresh and renewing out of the darkness in our lives. This creation can be physical, mental, or spiritual. As with all new life, in whatever form it takes, we are personally responsible for what we create. We must protect it, nourish it, and keep silent about it until it is strong enough to withstand the negativity thrown at it by jealous and envious people.

The birth/creation of new life, new projects, or new ideas also helps us bury the "dead" for which we still feel sorrow. When someone close to us dies or a relationship ends, we can lessen the emotional impact by getting involved in deeper spiritual seeking or a physical project. Instead of trying to erase the memory of the loved one (which is impossible anyway), pull out all the positive things learned from the relationship and use them in new ways. If a favorite project dies on the vine, use what you learned in working on it to create a new and better project. If a way of life has "died," take what you learned and create a different life-path for yourself. Embalm the rest of the emotional ties and bury them.

Like Isis, keep silent about what you are doing. Invite help only from those who are sympathetic and willing to work for your good. As the Great Goddess does with all Her creations, recycle experiences in your life, changing them into something fresh, productive, and positive.

The Osirian Mysteries[9] retold the story of Osiris' death and resurrection as well as the birth and rise to prominence of his son Horus; they honored the power and importance of his mother Isis. The child Horus was pictured as young boy with a finger in his mouth, this gesture being both a symbol of innocence and an admonition to keep silent among the uninitiated about the spiritual wisdom of the Mysteries. It is possible that Horus as Heru was the same as the Far Eastern "Lotus-Born" Heruka.

There are a great many myths similar to the story of Mithras throughout the world. The Persian cult of Mithras remained the leading rival of Christianity for centuries, probably because a great deal of Christianity was based on the story of the god Mithras.[10] In fact, a great many of the ceremonial details from the Mithraic Mystery Religion were stolen outright by Christians to form their own ceremonies.

The conception story of Mithras has two versions. In one, the mother of Mithras was a mortal virgin who was impregnated by a deity. In another, a female rock, the *petra genetrix,* was made fertile by the phallic lightning of the Heavenly Father.[11] After this conception, however, the two stories merge, giving the same details. Mithras was born in a cave of "the Rock,"[12] where shepherds and Magi brought birth gifts. The festival of his Epiphany, which marked the arrival of the Sun Priests (astrologers) or Magi,[13] was adopted by Christians in 813 C.E.[14] The birthday of Mithras was celebrated on December 25 (Birthday of the Unconquered Sun),[15] and his triumph over death and ascension to heaven occurred at the Spring Equinox.

This myth has been heavily overwritten by patriarchal powers, particularly to eliminate most of the references to the Goddess. However, Cumont[16] states that certain parts of the religions of Mithras and the goddess Anahita had a close connection. (Anahita was the Great Goddess' name in that region.)

Birth in caves was an important part of the mythology of several deities and semi-deities who fit into the Divine Child-Savior category: Apollo, Bacchus, Hermes, Jupiter/Zeus, Mithras, and Krishna. Even the Persian prophet Zoroaster was said to have been born in a cave on December 25; the Persians called Zoroaster the "Ram of God who takes away the sins of the world." In the Persian sacred drama to celebrate this birth, they used candles, incense, and holy water.

In various cultures around the world the name of the mother of the Divine Child-Savior is very similar. These names are all variations of the name of the Goddess. Maia/Mary comes from the root word meaning "water," symbolic of the waters of the abyss from which the Goddess created everything.

Mother	Son
Maia	Buddha
Maia	Hermes
Maya	Agni
Myrrha	Adonis
Myrrha	Bacchus
Maya Maria	Sommona Cadom (Siam)
Mariama (title)	Krishna
Mary	Jesus

Wise men bearing gifts also played an important part in the Divine Child myths. Prophets brought Krishna gifts of gold, frankincense, and myrrh. When Confucius was born, five wise men came and heavenly music was heard. Magi came to honor Mithras,

Zoroaster, and Osiris. Greek writings even say that Magi came to the birth of Socrates, bringing gold, frankincense, and myrrh.[17]

The Pagan God makes His appearance as a new creation of the Goddess, a helpless child. He comes from the cave (Earth womb) because He is to have His strongest impact upon the Earth and its inhabitants. Those who learn of His existence through their spiritual studies go with their personal gifts to welcome Him. To better understand His aspect of Light, they celebrate His birth as the Sun begins its rise again at the Winter Solstice. (Some spiritual systems associated the Winter Solstice with the death of the God and the Spring Equinox with His birth.) At the Spring Equinox, they acknowledge His influence over all Nature as plants once more begin to grow and animals bring forth their young. His youth, vigor, and productivity are honored at the Summer Solstice, while His death as the Sacrificed Savior (Grain God) is acknowledged at the Autumn Equinox.

Like the God, we each have a personal rise and fall of circumstances within our lives. As each new Child of ours is born, we should rejoice and celebrate the beginnings of life, projects, and/or turning points in spiritual growth. When the importance of this Child is seen, by ourselves and/or others, the birth is acknowledged with joy. Then we must learn to let go and let our Child develop, for holding too tight will warp and strangle its ability to develop.

In 376 C.E., Christians seized the Mithraic cave-temple on the Vatican Hill. They stole the title of the high priest of Mithraism (Pater Patrum) and gave it to the Pope in Rome, and took over the meeting day of the followers of Mithras: Sun-day. They also began to require baptism[18] for their followers, as did Mithraism.

Divine Child stories from Greece and Crete have many details similar to the Horus and Mithras myths. The Cretan myth of Zagreus, the "Goodly Bull," is probably the oldest. The Greek writer Hesiod told this story as part of his work on the family connections among the Olympian deities. Zagreus, as the Cretan bull-god, was associated with both Dionysus[19] and Zeus. Zagreus, Dionysus, and Zeus all were sometimes pictured with horns on their heads. The bull and/or horns are common symbols connected with the Divine Child in many cultures. Horns and antlers were the earliest sign of the Consort of the Goddess, a sign of masculine divinity.

The beginning of the original story of the Cretan Zagreus is much the same as the later Grecian Zeus, but tells of Zagreus' sacrifice by the Titans, his ascension to heaven, and his rebirth through Rhea. He died at the Winter Solstice and was reborn at the Spring Equinox.

The sanctuary of Zagreus in Crete was a cave on Mount Dikte. The Cretan stories describe this Divine Child as a beardless youth who rode a dolphin. The words *dolphin* and *Delphi* are related to the root word for "womb." The sea-dwelling dolphin symbolized the sea-womb from which humans and animals arose. Delphi, on the Isle of Delos, the birthplace of Apollo, was considered to be the womb of "sacred places."

Early in his life, Zagreus fulfilled the role of Sacrificed Savior, returned to the Goddess, and was reborn in another form. The fact that he was said to have died at the Winter Solstice and was reborn at the Spring Equinox negates any connection with the Sun, but rather places Zagreus into the category of Lord of the Forest and Animals.

The later story of Zeus shows a much more aggressive, strictly male-oriented deity, who began his life in the traditional circumstances of the Divine Child. The ancient god Cronus mated with his sister Rhea, producing several of the divine Olympians. However, Cronus swallowed each at birth because of a prophecy that his children would supplant him. To save her last child, Zeus, Rhea hid in Crete[20] and at his birth, gave the newborn baby to Gaea. When Rhea returned to Cronus, she presented a rock wrapped up like a baby, which the ancient god promptly swallowed.[21]

Gaea kept Zeus hidden in a cave on Mount Ida on the island of Crete. There the nymphs Adrastea and Ida cared for the Divine Child. Bees brought him honey, and the goat Amalthea supplied him with milk. Afraid that the baby's cries would be heard by Cronus and the child discovered, Rhea instructed her servants, the Kuretes, to make noise by dancing and clashing together their shields and swords continually. When he was grown, Zeus found a way to make his father Cronus regurgitate his siblings.

This story has many of the same symbols as in the myth of the Egyptian Horus. The birth of the Child is kept hidden, in this case because of danger from the father instead of the uncle, both of whom represent anti-Goddess and anti-Pagan forces. The Child is placed under the care of Nature and its creatures, which is to be His future realm. Lest the negative forces in the world find and destroy the Child before it is time for Him to make His appearance, He is protected by special guardians, the Kuretes, whose activities mask his existence until He is strong enough to act. When the Child-God does gain strength and wisdom, He finds an ingenious method of "freeing" the gods from patriarchal and anti-Pagan control.

The mountain in myth represents a spiritual place or higher plane of consciousness. By placing our thoughts in a spiritual framework, we can dip into the primordial sea or "idea-womb" of creative energy. We can draw strength and learn helpful knowledge through communication with the gods and our own ancestors (the dead).

Although the later Greeks called Zeus "father of gods and men" and said he was the ruler of all the deities on Olympus, there was a hymn composed to Zeus around 300 B.C.E. and later engraved on stone in Crete[22] which calls him the "biggest boy." This is a reference to his Divine Child status, under the name of Zagreus. In other words, Zeus was the "biggest" or most important of the Divine Children in the Mediterranean area.

Hermes, the Greek god of magick, letters, medicine, and occult wisdom, was far older than the Grecian culture. "The Ram-Bearer" was the son of Zeus and a mortal maiden named Maia, daughter of Atlas. He was born in a cave on Mount Kyllene[24] in Arcadia. Scarcely a day old, he was able to leave his cradle and steal the sacred heifers entrusted to his half-brother Apollo.

The cave where Hermes was said to be born was considered to be a place of primeval Chaos. This type of chaos does not mean confusion; it refers to the swirling abyss of creative energy from which all creations, even ideas, must come. He, too, came from an Earth-womb (cave) on a mountain (a high spiritual plane). When he was very young, he jolted the gods out of their staid way of thinking by doing something they thought to be impossible.

In the same way, sometimes our spiritual lives go along in a staid manner and we don't realize our thinking has gone into a rut. Out of our spiritual seeking is born a new idea or way of looking at the spiritual. At first it seems to be quite ordinary, with no surprises.

Then this idea or thought suddenly reveals itself as much more powerful than we had imagined, jolting us into deeper thought on the
subject. We are shocked and amazed at what power and possibility
lie within this new creation. The Child has turned into the Trickster
and taken us unawares.

The goat-foot god Pan is sometimes said to be the son of Zeus,
at other times the son of Hermes. In the Homeric hymn to Pan, the
baby Pan was considered so ugly that he was abandoned at birth by
his mother and nurse in the mountain forests. His father Hermes
discovered the child, wrapped him in a hare's skin, and took him to
Olympus.

Pan is a very ancient deity, sometimes called the most primeval
of procreative forces. He is the sexual and creating force behind all
Nature, including humans. To some, he may appear ugly; the Greeks
looked upon the procreative act with women as an evil necessity, as
do many religions today. To others, his beauty is found within the
mystic power of his music and dance, the original dance of life; to
them, nothing created by the Goddess is ugly. Some of our spiritual
seeking, particularly when we are making a change from patriarchal
to Pagan religions, will at first appear repellent. This is because we
are still looking at our "find" in the old frame of thinking. If we are
wise enough to look deeper, we discover a hidden beauty that will
raise us to new spiritual heights.

We may abandon an idea, project, or relationship because we
feel it has mutated into something we do not like. We see it as a
strange being in a form we didn't plan. The God takes up this idea,
project, or relationship, sees the worth within its strange form, and
takes it to the Goddess on a higher spiritual level. Oftentimes this
abandoned "child" will reappear in our thoughts or lives, revealing
its true inner beauty and worth so that we work on helping it mature.

This often happens on spiritual journeys. We take a path that
we feel will be beneficial, then abandon our attempts when we feel it
is too difficult, or objectionable to others, or even because we
become frightened (because of orthodox programming). We throw
aside the "newborn child." But the Goddess sends Her most trusted
messenger to make certain this "child" does not die. The beginnings
we made are not destroyed, but lie temporarily dormant within our
subconscious minds. At some time in our lives, this "child" will

again make its appearance; we will then see its true beauty and worth, and joyfully help it to grow.

Pan is also the deity of freedom: freedom of expression; freedom to choose the way we will live our lives; freedom to follow whatever spiritual path we feel we like best. He is also a deity of sexual freedom. We can choose to love indiscriminately, taking our chances with physical diseases and unreliable (possibly dominating and violent) lovers, or we can choose to experience love wisely and carefully. The key lies in the knowledge that sex is not sinful or dirty, but a gift from the Goddess.

Eros, or Cupid, was never pictured as anything other than a very small child. Modern interpretations erroneously list Eros as the god of love; instead, he was the deity of "demanding love,"[24] which is very different (more on this in the next chapter). Originally, Eros was not the son of Aphrodite but her companion and consort. In later myths, he was usually listed as the son of Hermes and Aphrodite. However, still other stories say his father was Ares or even Zeus himself. Eros and Aphrodite had a child of both sexes named Hermaphroditos.[25]

The Greek Orphic religion said that Eros was hatched from an egg laid by the goddess Night in the womb of Darkness. In this myth, Eros was of both sexes, winged, and had four heads.[26] The Goddess in triple form lived with Eros in a cave, while the mother goddess Rhea sat at the entrance. Although the Orphics believed that Eros set the universe in motion and created Earth, sky, and Moon, the Triple Goddess still ruled the universe itself.

Demanding love in spiritual terms is much different from the human emotional meaning. Like those struck with the arrows of Eros in the ancient myths, we can find ourselves in a higher state of spiritual consciousness (love) or we can turn our backs and walk away (hate). We can't be fence-sitters in spiritual matters; we must make decisions. Spiritual love formed the universe and everything in it. We must exit the cave-womb of Darkness and grow in the Light, or we can die a slow, spiritual death because we are afraid to be separated from what we consider to be security.

Demanding love in human terms can be a smothering form of emotion. It can kill friendships and relationships, turning real love into a form of emotional "murder." Some parents practice demanding love, trying to control their children through the thin guise of "protecting" them even as adults. This type of emotion can warp a person for a lifetime unless he or she is strong enough to break away. Humans also practice a more insidious and deadly form of demanding love through the guise of religion. Millions of people have been murdered to "save their souls."

However, in myth Eros symbolizes the demanding love of the Goddess, not the smothering emotions of humans. It is part of the God's responsibilities to awaken humans to the need of acknowledging a higher power than themselves. The arrows of the child Eros reawaken the planted seed of spiritual striving within each human. We can turn away from Her love, which demands that we acknowledge Her and Her consort in some manner. Or we can respond to Her love and seek Her and Her consort in a spiritual way. In the world today, the God is trying to reawaken humans to the existence of the Goddess, something that has been buried for a very long time. In His appearance as a non-threatening little Child, the God can draw us to know Him, and through Him we can discover His Mother.

The god Dionysus is primarily known as the deity of wine and sexual freedom, but he is also called Dithyrambos ("double-birth" or "twice-born"). Dionysus, a Divine Child, was given this title because he was born after the death of his mother, Semele.

Zeus developed a lust for Semele, daughter of King Cadmus of Thebes. Disguised as a mortal and never allowing the girl to see him, he had an affair with her. When Semele was six months pregnant, Hera, also disguised as a mortal, advised that the girl make her lover reveal himself to be sure he was not a monster. Zeus, in his usual way of overdoing things, appeared as thunder and lightning and Semele was burned to death. Hermes saved the unborn child, sewing it into Zeus' thigh until it was time for Dionysus to be born.

The Titans found Dionysus and, at Hera's orders, tore him into pieces that they boiled in a cauldron. His grandmother Rhea rescued him. He was then raised by the Queen of Orchomenus disguised as a girl. Hera discovered where he was, but Hermes temporarily changed him into a baby goat. The Divine Child was raised in Thrace, suckled by goats, and tended by satyrs and nymphs.[27]

The Iliad says Dionysus had a strong connection with the sea through the sea goddess Thetis, who was one of his early nurses. One of the Orphic hymns said that the Nereids or water goddesses were the first to celebrate the mysteries of Dionysus.

Sometimes spiritual thoughts are born ahead of their time according to human standards. They come under immediate attack by those who fear or are jealous of them. The Pagan God, as He appears at the beginning of each new age of human spirituality, stands in danger of being torn apart. If this should happen, He will regenerate Himself in the Chaos-cauldron of the Goddess and reappear once more.

Sometimes the Child-God will at first disguise Himself in a non-threatening form as a soft, gentle entity. True, this is part of His power and form, but only part. When He has been nurtured and loved by those who have already discovered the Goddess in all Nature, the Child-God will reveal His other side: all Nature has opposites. Those who turn away from Him and the Goddess for whatever reason will find themselves filled with unhappiness and negative thoughts (madness). He simply shows us both sides of the Goddess and Her laws: ecstasy and despair, spiritual heights and hopelessness, positive and negative results from our actions and thoughts.

Like Dionysus, every human who discovers the beauty of the spiritual path has a double birth. We are born into human form (the first birth) just as Dionysus was. However, when we willingly seek out and follow a true spiritual path, we are granted a second birth, the inward birth of the spirit.

Christians liked this idea, adopted it, and promised this second birth through their baptism, ignoring the fact that baptism was only an outward sign—a ritual used earlier by the Pagan Mysteries. To the Christians, a person was baptized with the hope that someday he or she might discover spiritual truths (defined by them, of course). To the initiates of the Mysteries, baptism (initiation) was a sign that a person was already diligently seeking and had made progress in this search.

The Eleusinian Mysteries celebrated the birth of a Divine Child to the goddess Demeter, namely Dionysus under the names of Brimos, Triptolemus, Iasion, Elenthereos the Liberator, or the Holy

Child Iacchus.[28] The name Eleusis meant "advent." The reenaction and celebration of this birth were a vital part of the Eleusinian Mysteries until they were destroyed by the Christians. These Eleusinian celebrations were held in an underground temple and a symbol of Iacchus placed in a winnowing basket *(liknon)*. The birth was symbolized by the silent reaping of an ear of corn. The sacred basket representing his cradle was carried in all processions of Dionysus. These Mysteries had one basic theme throughout: death was not the end of life, but only part of the cycle of eternal life through reincarnation.

The Hindu deity named Prajapati is mentioned only in the most ancient books called the Brahmanas and the Rig Veda. He is a mysterious deity who comes into being by hatching from an egg. This egg floated in the waters of the abyss or void. After hatching, he rested on the backs of sea monsters and floated about in a cushion of water flowers.

The God in His Child-form has domination over all positives (flowers) and negatives (monsters). These powers were given to Him by the Goddess; in this myth Her name has been obliterated and we have no way now of determining which aspect was once connected with Prajapati. From the Child-God we can learn how to float through the ups and downs of our lives, confident that we are not forsaken by the Great Mother and Her companion. In the realm of our spiritual selves, we learn not to fear the abyss for it is only the vehicle to another "hatching." In the mental realm of ideas, we learn also to value the abyss, for it is the bottomless cauldron of creative energy.

The Hindu god Krishna is far older even than the Persian Mithras; it is possible that Krishna's birth story was taken by the Persians and retold as that of Mithras. Many of the Christian ideas for their Divine Child-Savior come from the myths of Krishna.

An incarnation of Shiva, Krishna was born to Devaki ("the Goddess"), sister of King Kamsa. His birth was announced by a brilliant star and angelic voices. Shepherds and wise men brought him gifts. He managed to survive a Slaughter of Innocents ordered by his uncle, King Kamsa, because his parents hid him.[29] He was called Firstborn, Sin Bearer, Redeemer, Liberator, and the Universal Word (Logos).

In all stories of the Divine Child's birth in which His arrival is announced by spiritual voices and bright stars, only those who are prepared and ready know of His birth. The God does not make His appearance to everyone; He appears only to those who are spiritually prepared to receive Him. He can survive any attack on His existence, for the Goddess will not tolerate His non-existence. He is vital to Her; He is the trusted one who carries out Her laws of universal order, the opener of the way for Her children who desire to know the highest spiritual thoughts.

Buddha ("Enlightenment"), whose original name was Siddhartha, was conceived and born in a miraculous manner according to the legends. His mother, Queen Maya, dreamed that a snow-white elephant[30] entered her womb; another story says she dreamed of a six-rayed star; still another legend says the Bodhisat came to her, holding a lotus. After ten months, she gave birth while leaning against an udumbara tree. However, the birth was highly unusual, as Buddha emerged from her side without causing her pain. After six days, Maya died, went to the heavens, and was made a deity. Siddhartha's father kept the boy isolated from the miserable part of humanity so he would not become a world savior. Siddhartha was in his twenties before he knew that people got sick, grew old, or died. When he discovered this, he left the palace and his family, giving up material wealth and comfort to seek spiritual enlightenment.

Buddha, as the Divine Child, is born without pain to himself or his mother, because he is secure in his place in spiritual matters. If we can learn how to place ourselves in such a state of spiritual oneness through our communion with the God, we need never fear experiencing or causing pain in our spiritual growth. In the beginning, our life circumstances may temporarily keep us isolated from the very things we need to grow in a spiritual manner, but there will come a time when we are strong enough to make our own decisions. If we are responsible enough to make those decisions, then, like Buddha, we will step out in confidence, leaving behind all hindrances in our search for enlightenment.

The Polynesians of the Pacific Ocean also had a tale of a Divine Child. Maui was born prematurely to a goddess, and was left on the sandy shore covered with a jellyfish. One of his god-relatives, Tama-nui-ki-te-Rangi, happened to come walking along the beach. Seeing this strange lump on the sand, he removed the jellyfish and found the human-looking Maui.

The Child-God can manifest Himself in strange forms and even stranger ways to us. He will do what is necessary to draw our attention but He will not force us to acknowledge Him. We must take the first steps, whether out of curiosity or desire.

Sometimes we find our spiritual guidance in the strangest places and forms, totally unforeseen and unannounced. We never know what out-of-the-way discovery will propel us forward on a spiritual path or a material project. We must train ourselves to be aware and curious about everything around us.

Even King Arthur of Camelot can be considered a Divine Child, as can his son Modred. Arthur was born through magick performed by Merlin, then taken away at birth to be raised in secret. Some writers said that Arthur had no father, but was born like the Norse Heimdall of the Ninefold Sea Goddess. The ninth wave brought Arthur ashore at Merlin's feet.[31] Likewise, Arthur's son Modred, by his half-sister Margawse, was born and raised in secret. When Arthur heard of this birth, he ordered that all children born on May Day (Beltane) be gathered and put on a ship, which was sent out to be wrecked at sea. However, Modred survived this Slaughter of the Innocents.[32]

The stories of Arthur have become so Christianized that it is difficult to dig through the morass to the original truth. It appears to be a retelling of Krishna's story, except for the dalliance with the half-sister. I believe that this episode was added to pound home Christian ideas, for in many cultures the term "sister" referred to a priestess. In other words, if you have dealings with Pagans, you will come to grief.

TWIN BIRTHS

There are also several world myths of Divine Twins. The Greek myth of Apollo and Artemis is probably the best known. Leto, the mortal mother of the twins Apollo and Artemis by Zeus, fled the wrath of Hera and was carried by the South Wind to Ortygia. There Artemis was born. When she was only a few hours old, she helped her mother across the straits to the Isle of Delos where Leto gave birth to Apollo. When he was only a few days old, Apollo fought with and killed the Python, then purified himself and went to Olympus.

This is one of the few twin myths in which the children are not opposite in temperament or morality, but are of the opposite sex. On the physical level, each human has both male and female chromosomes within them; it is only a predominance of one set of sex chromosomes which makes us male or female. On the spiritual level, we need both male and female responses and ways of looking at things to make us balanced in our spiritual seeking. When we are balanced, we no longer have to fear the ill-wishes of others and can take our rightful place in the spiritual pattern where we belong.

From the Persian religion of Zoroaster[33] comes the myth of the Sacred Twins Ahura Mazdah and Ahriman. These deities were born simultaneously from the womb of Zurvan, the primal Mother of Infinite Time, at first a goddess with two faces, then a bisexual deity.[34] There was rivalry between these two Divine siblings from the moment of birth, for Ahura Mazdah was the Heavenly Father of Light and Ahriman the Spirit of Darkness. Even though Ahura Mazdah was wholly good, he was not considered superior to Ahriman, who was wholly evil and whose influence upon the Earth was greatest because he had created the material world. Later religions took the idea of Ahura Mazdah and made it into the "one God theory"; they also turned Ahriman into the devil. The concept of the Holy Spirit comes from the idea that Ahura Mazdah was said to express his will through Spenta Mainyu, or the Holy Spirit.

In this Persian story, the Sacred Twins are born of the Great Goddess out of the abyss of Chaos, Time, and Spirit, the source of all creation. Zurvan is portrayed with two faces: the Mother of Life and the Crone of Death. She brings forth at the same time both positive and negative energy, the necessary ingredients for all life; neither is considered better than the other, as Ahriman is not considered inferior to Ahura Mazdah. Although the Persian patriarchy called Ahura Mazdah "the Father of Light" and Ahriman "the Spirit of Darkness," they realized they could not eliminate Ahriman, for he represented the physical powers and creations of the world. Without the physical, Spirit would have nothing against which to compare itself and no meaning for existence.

This story continues on to the end of the world, when Ahura Mazdah will triumph and cast Ahriman and his followers into a kind of hell. However, no one will stay in this "hell" forever, only until the negatives are destroyed. Then the Earth will end and all will go to "heaven."

The Pagan God exhibits what we see as both "positive" and "negative" traits. However, He is acting totally within His nature, for He, as companion of the Goddess, loves, disciplines, and, on Her orders, sees that all the energy that makes up life and the existence of everything eventually returns to Her for recycling.

On a personal level, we are always plagued with moral and spiritual decisions: "Should I do this?" or "Should I do that?" Even though we make what we call "good spiritual decisions," we should never forget the physical side of life. The Goddess never demands asceticism from Her followers, and definitely not useless self-sacrifice. She brought us into this physical world to learn, to progress, and to be joyful in our surroundings. She does not demand that we be poor, suffer bad health, or be miserable as part of Her worship or our spiritual growth. That is a patriarchal "law," not Hers. Through many incarnations, we each will burn away the negatives that hold us back, until we can become one with Her again.

The Iroquois and Hurons of North America have a similar legend of Divine Twins. The maiden Breath of Wind was impregnated by the Master of Winds, a spiritual entity. The twins formed within her hated each other so much that they fought fierce battles in the womb, finally killing their mother in one of these fights when they were born. Ioskeha represented positive energy and goodness, while Tawiscara represented complete evil.

The mother Breath of Wind symbolizes Spirit, the Creatress Goddess of all creation. Although She creates us, She gives us free will to live our physical lives and develop our spiritual paths as we choose. Fierce mental, emotional, and spiritual battles over what is good and what is evil are being fought constantly within the human mind and spirit. Unfortunately, this battle over the personal interpretation of good and evil can extend into the physical, where we are trying to force our spiritual views on others, or they on us. We can "kill" or cut our connection with the Goddess by trying to force others to think like we do instead of working on ourselves and not worrying what someone else does or thinks.

UNDERSTANDING THE DIVINE CHILD

In these myths we see an attempt to divide good and evil into separate categories. You must remember that the cultures from which these myths came were predominantly patriarchal. Patriarchy has always tried to categorize everything into either positive or negative. Twins, and those of other multiple births, have closer mental and emotional ties than other siblings; often they also have very different personalities. By looking at these myths as the stories of one being with the normal opposing sides of good and evil, one can understand these stories better.

The Divine Child appears as a helpless being who must face fearsome opposition, great danger, and attack by the powers of Darkness. However, appearances can be deceiving. The Child-God has inborn powers which help Him defeat Darkness, as baby Apollo did with the snake. He has great wisdom, like baby Horus when he helped Isis embalm his father. Helpless, He is not. He is born fully knowing His place beside the Goddess and His role in the growth of humans.

The Child-God began His existence as a small creation of the Goddess, as do we all. However, He was born consciously knowing His responsibilities as upholder of Her universal laws, co-parent of humans and their struggles toward the spiritual light. Like the Goddess Herself, the God is not found by looking outside ourselves, but by looking deep within. He will first reveal Himself to a seeker as a child, then gradually reveal His other aspects as we are able to understand and acknowledge them.

We need to find and acknowledge the Divine Child within each of us. Without this acknowledgement, we can never realize and grasp the opportunities of newness when they enter our lives. Without finding Him, our spiritual growth will be imbalanced, perhaps even stunted.

III

LORD OF LOVE
& FERTILITY

In this aspect of the God, the Divine Child has grown into the Lover/Companion of the Goddess. He has progressed beyond the appearance of helplessness into the stage of mature Lover: One who can give and not just take; One who learns to go beyond His own needs and truly care about the needs of another; One who has taken up the robe of responsibility and is willing to do His part.

Unfortunately, some humans do not progress beyond the child. They spend their whole lives demanding attention from others, and if these others continue to give in to this self-centered attitude, they become slaves to a demanding ego. There is also the opposite side of the child, which is the parents refusing to believe their children have progressed beyond the child and no longer need their direction. Both ways of thinking are self-defeating and detrimental to spiritual growth.

When humans reach the early stages of the Lover aspect, we call it puberty, that stage of life when hormones begin to rage through the body. A lot of humans, though, seem to think growing into the Lover means to get as much physical sex as possible without responsibility. The gentle Lord of Love and Fertility becomes the over-balanced, lustful, and phallus-proud God of Sex.

Under patriarchal influences, males have been encouraged to indulge in penis-pride, and are excused for their sexist behavior. On the other hand, females have been vigorously condemned and punished for thinking in the same manner. The fact is that both extremes laid down for males and females are destructive to human spiritual growth. Both sexes must be responsible for their sexual behavior and any children created by such acts.

The Lord of Love and Fertility, under His true nature, has a rightful place in this world. Sexual love is needed to keep humans and animals alive; offspring are necessary to continue the species. Sexual love also has its place in the appropriate stage of human emotional development. It was given to us by the God and Goddess as a means of enjoying a deeper bond with a companion with whom we share deep affection. If properly used, the sexual act can be a stepping stone to higher emotional and spiritual development.

The Lord of Love is necessary to the Goddess, for a mingling of His masculine energy (semen) with Her feminine energy (the egg) is needed for Her creations. Oftentimes, the God is said to "die" after this union. In physical terms, this symbolic "dying" can be related to the deflated penis after intercourse. The God withholds nothing in His offering to the Goddess. Only in this manner can a true creation be formed. Because of this unrestrained offering, the Lord of Love and Fertility is connected with other aspects of the God, especially the Lord of the Forest (vegetation and animals) and the Sacrificed Savior.

However, the word *fertility* has a meaning seldom applied to it these times. Fertility means to be fertile, to bear fruit easily, to produce something. Setting aside the most obvious definition, that of producing children, this leaves us with the concept of producing other things. On a mental level these can be ideas, inventions, new methods of doing things, etc. In other words, our knowledge of, and relationship to, the Lord of Love and Fertility can influence our creativity.

We also find this Lord on a spiritual level. Our relationship with Him determines whether or not, and how much, we are fertilized with the incentive to seek spiritual understanding and knowledge. If we allow it, He will fill us with a deep love of the Goddess, and through Her, of Him. We will instinctively know what spiritual paths are not right for us. We will not be taken in by the "sideshow" religions, but bypass them to find the truth behind the ancient archetypes.

Some of the best-known myths of the Lord of Love, the ones that are truest to His nature, come from the Middle East and India. These cultures originally looked upon sex as something natural and sacred. It took them a lot longer than the Greeks and Europeans to change their thinking on this point.

The cult of Adonis came to the Mediterranean civilizations out of the Semitic cultures of the Middle East. In Jerusalem, Adonis was known as Tammuz, where amazingly he was said to have been born in a cave in Bethlehem of the Virgin Myrrha.[1] He died at Easter time, when the red anemone (his symbol) flowered.[2] Adonis was also associated with the goddess Asherah in Syria, and he came to be the companion of both Persephone and Aphrodite in Greece.

According to the Greek myth, Adonis was the offspring of King Cinyras and his daughter Smyrna, through the manipulation of Aphrodite in retaliation for Smyrna's mother bragging about her daughter's beauty. When Cinyras discovered what he had done while drunk, he tried to kill his daughter, but Aphrodite changed the girl into a myrrh tree. Cinyras struck the tree with his sword, and out fell the baby Adonis. Aphrodite grabbed the child and hid him in a chest, which she gave to Persephone for safekeeping. (Because of her relationship with the volatile Ares, Aphrodite could not take Adonis to her palace.)

Persephone was curious about the contents of the chest and soon opened it to find a beautiful child inside. She raised him in her Underworld palace and made him her lover. Soon Aphrodite showed up to claim Adonis and was furious that Persephone would not give him up. The goddess of love took her claim directly to Zeus, who seeing that the dispute would likely turn nasty whatever he decided, turned the matter over to the Muse Calliope. The Muse decreed that Adonis would spend one-third of the year with Persephone, one-third with Aphrodite, and one-third by himself. Aphrodite loved the youth too much, so she slyly used her magick love girdle to persuade him to give her his share of the year and avoid going to Persephone at all.

Away went Persephone to Thrace, where she told Ares that Aphrodite had thrown him aside for Adonis. Ares was furious. Changing himself into a wild boar, Ares waited until Adonis went hunting on Mount Lebanon. There he attacked the youth, goring him in the thigh and killing him. Adonis' blood spilled on the ground, forming blood-red anemones, and his soul went straight to Persephone's realm. In desperation, Aphrodite took her problem back to Zeus and asked that Adonis be allowed to spend at least the summer months with her. Zeus agreed.

On the surface, this is a tale of the growth and death of vegetation. However, hidden underneath is a spiritual story of another part of the God's nature. At first Adonis is the Divine Child, born of a virgin and threatened by the father. The Child is rescued and allowed to develop in safety (the Underworld). He becomes a man, sexually active and responsive to the Mother aspect of the Goddess, in both Her positive and negative energies (Aphrodite and Persephone). But Aphrodite's constant drain on his energies during lovemaking put his life at risk; in other words, there must be a cycle, a rise and fall, in all things, and Adonis was allowed none. Ares as a boar gores him in the thigh (castrates him), thus sending him to the Underworld (a time of rest). Only when Aphrodite offers a reasonable cycle of existence is Adonis allowed to return to her.

The Goddess cannot and will not go against Her own laws. Everything in the universe lives and dies by cycles. There are high and low times of all energy. The God must abide by these cyclical laws. Although He is an independent entity, He draws His power and reason for existence from the Goddess Herself.

In human terms, we must also abide by the cycles of life and energy. If we push too long and too hard, we will find our lives seriously threatened and our plans crashing down around us. We must go into a state of withdrawal or rest. Only when we learn and agree to live by the cyclical laws of the Goddess can we go on with our projects and/or our everyday lives. If we refuse, our energy will be cut off (castration). Our projects will remain "dead"; our spiritual progress will stop; our physical lives may even be forfeit.

Later Adonis and Aphrodite had a son, Priapus. Priapus was always shown with an oversized phallus, a symbol of carnal lust.

Too much of a good thing can become a grotesque caricature and a detriment. Priapus was a deity of lust, an energy devoid of affection and concerned only with self-satisfaction. However, Priapus carried a pruning knife, the symbol of castration and the necessary rest before another cycle can begin.

Tammuz was the Hebrew version of Adonis;[3] another of his names was Dumuzi. He came to Jerusalem from Babylon, although his cult was much older than Babylon. His mother and bride was Ishtar, sometimes called Mari. Like Adonis, Tammuz died and went into the Underworld. However, in this myth Ishtar herself went after him. To be able to pass each of seven gates (symbolic of the chakras), Ishtar had to leave behind one piece of adornment—jewelry or clothing. When she finally reached the Underworld palace of her dark sister Ereshkigal, she was naked and defenseless. Ereshkigal imprisoned and tortured her. The god Ea sent a messenger with magick words which freed Ishtar from Ereshkigal's power. He also took pity on her love for Tammuz and decreed that he could spend part of the year with Ishtar, but had to return to the Underworld for the rest of the time.

The symbolic language of this myth reveals how the Goddess is willing to use Her energy to "rescue" each human from the Underworld or the abyss, in order for that person to be reborn into a new life. As the deflated penis is the "little death" for men during intercourse, so the point of giving birth is a kind of "death" for a woman. Through the God (Ea, in this case), the Goddess (Ishtar), and the use of magick words (the creation process), all created forms are drawn up from the abyss (cauldron) and into the light (rebirth).

The cult of Attis and Cybele originated in Phrygia. There, Attis was said to have been born of the Virgin Nana, who conceived by eating an almond or a pomegranate. His birth was celebrated on December 25 and his death on March 25. The story says that when he became the lover/priest of the goddess Cybele, Attis took a vow of chastity, that he would love no one except Cybele. However, Attis soon broke his vow by having an affair with a mortal woman. When Cybele found out, she was both angry and hurt. The goddess cast a spell of frenzied madness on Attis, who ran into the mountains. There, under a pine tree, he castrated himself, and his blood poured on the Earth. However, Cybele took pity on him as he lay dying and changed him into a pine tree.

The almond and pomegranate have long been symbols of fertility in the areas where Goddess worship had an ancient history. In this story, the God takes a vow of chastity, not to abstain from all love, but to adhere to the Goddess. His sexual energy gets out of balance and He involves Himself with worldly attachments. He really isn't aware of this imbalance until the Goddess brings Him up short and threatens to withdraw Her support. Then He falls into depression at Her abandonment, causing Himself harm by going the other way into imbalance (castration). He only survives because the Goddess takes pity on Him, changing His form into a new creation.

Spiritual love, like physical love, can have a fanatical side if it is allowed to get out of control and balance. Neglect of responsibilities, family, and even the physical self in favor of a "religion" is not spiritual. The practice of austerities and/or immolation of any kind is not spiritual. True spirituality is balancing all your responsibilities and realizing that a true spiritual being does not require, or even like, blood, pain, or physical excesses.

Other fertility deities from the Middle East were Aleyin of Phoenicia, Ba'al of the Semitic regions, Ba'al-Hammon of Carthage, and Hay-Tau of Phoenicia. Aleyin was the son of Ba'al and a rival of his brother Mot. A god of springs and rain, he had seven constant companions and eight wild boars. In the fragmented myth we now know, the goddess Anat appears to have been the source of their battles. Ba'al himself was called the son of Asherat-of-the-Sea and the consort of Asherat. Ba'al-Hammon wore ram's horns. Hay-Tau of Phoenicia is a little known deity, similar to Adonis.

Several Hindu gods are connected with the aspect of Lord of Love and Fertility. A few of these deities are Indra, Shiva, Kamadeva, and Krishna. Prajapati was father of the gods and humans and protector of all humans who procreate.

Indra was known as *sahasramuska*[4] ("thousand-testicled") and often behaved like a rutting bull. He drank huge quantities of *soma* (Goddess-energy), not to stay alive, but to just get drunk.

Although Shiva is primarily known as the Lord of the Dance and the Lord of Yoga, and practiced asceticisms, his prominent symbol is the lingam (phallus). Throughout India, phallic pillars represent the lingam or penis of Shiva; these pillars are reddened with ocher or blood to simulate the menstruation blood of the Earth Goddess. A large area around each of the lingams was said to confer remission of sins.

In his love aspect, Shiva was accompanied by the Ganas (Vagabonds), which are similar to the Greek satyrs of Dionysus and the Celtic bird-footed Korrigan. The Ganas disliked city life and chose to live in harmony with Nature.

Shiva was a deity who saw no need to conform to human-imposed regulations which are against spiritual nature. Shiva's shakti[5] was Mahadeva (Great Goddess), who was also known as Jagan-Mata (Mother of the World).

One story tells of Shiva going in disguise to the forest home of seven sages. Because the sages were so engrossed with their spiritual practices and had been neglecting their wives, the god found it very easy to seduce the seven women. The sages were furious when they found out, cursing Shiva with castration. When Shiva's phallus fell to the ground, the universe was plunged into darkness. Horrified, the sages realized who Shiva was and begged him to undo what they had done. Shiva agreed, but only if they would worship his linga.

This is really another lesson in the importance of staying balanced. The sages were too engrossed with what they deemed to be spiritual matters, and were neglecting their physical lives. When they had this brought to their attention (the seduction of their wives), at first they were furious and reacted in a violent manner (cursing). Things became even worse (the universe became black). The sages recognized the God and His importance and worked to bring themselves back into balance. However, the God pointed out to them that they had to worship His love aspect: the creative power that runs through everything and every task, from the physical to the spiritual.

Shiva had three wives—Uma, Durga, and Parvati—who represent the three aspects of the Triple Goddess.[6] Therefore, this god would be a trident-bearer, one with a triple phallus who could fertilize all three aspects of the Goddess at the same time. The symbol of the trident was associated with many of the fertility gods. Sometimes the trident was replaced with the symbol of a triple key. This idea of three led to the association of three-leafed plants with the god of the trident, as well as with the Triple Goddess. In ancient Ireland, the god Trefuilngid Tre-Eochair had the shamrock as his emblem.

The thunderbolt or lightning was also a phallic symbol of the God's power to fertilize the Earth Mother. The Tantric-Buddhist wand is called the *dorje* (*vajra* in India); this tool represents the thunderbolt which penetrates the Earth and leaves drops of the God's semen (gems).[7] The *dorje* is also called "diamond-holder," meaning that divine spirit can be sensed through orgasm.

Krishna was raised by "holy women" in a sacred grove, but was primarily a god of sexual delights. An incarnation of Vishnu, Krishna was a truly carefree deity when it came to sharing his loving attentions. He enticed several cowherds or shepherdesses (Gopi girls) into his dance of love, satisfying each of them. However, only one Gopi, Radha the Insatiable (the She-Elephant), could satisfy and hold this lover-god. She became his mistress.

Krishna's loving attention represents the seductive call of the God to immerse oneself in the spiritual, as well as the physical; to give oneself up to the senses, inner and outer, when involved in something. The sound of Krishna's flute is said to entice every woman who hears it. The flute symbolizes the celestial music that reverberates within each soul; the God calls to the feminine part of every creation, drawing it to Him, that He may teach each soul to balance the masculine and feminine energies.

Kama or Kamadeva[8] was called the god of desire and love. Another of his names was Ragavrinta (the stalk of passion). Myth says that Kama carried a sugarcane bow strung with humming bees and a flower-tipped shaft of desire. He was associated with Rati (passion) and the Apsaras (love nymphs).

Although the Hindu god Vishnu primarily was a sacrificed deity, his name meant "the expander," "he who excites men," and "he who penetrates," all titles belonging to a fertility god.[9] The Kiakra, an emblem composed of a (male) cross and a (female) circle, belonged to Vishnu.[10]

In Egypt, the best-known god of fertility was Seb, also known as Geb. He was the brother/husband of the goddess Nut and father of Osiris, Isis, Set, and Nephthys. Seb and Nut spent so much time copulating that the god Ra commanded that their father Shu separate them. Nut (a sky goddess) was pushed up into the heavens, while Seb (an Earth god) was forced to remain on the ground under her. Seb is pictured in ancient Egyptian drawings with a very long, erect phallus pointing toward the arched body of Nut.

Although the spiritual and physical are necessary for human growth, they should not be in constant contact. This only leads to obsession instead of balance. Periods of separation are needed.

Osiris, besides being god of the dead, had an aspect of fertility and sexual love. A symbol of his sacred marriage with Isis was the *menat;* in hieroglyphics, this was a phallic-shaped vessel pouring fluid into a wide pot.[11] The oldest festival celebrated by the initiates of the Osirian Mysteries was the Sed, where Osiris was represented by the phallic obelisk.

The Egyptian deity Khnemu was known as a creator god who was worshipped with his two wives, Sati and Anqet, both fertility goddesses. Khnemu was called the Divine Potter because he was said to have created through his wheel (the Wheel of Life).

Min (Lord of Foreign Lands) was always portrayed with an erect phallus in his primary role as fertility deity. The Greeks identified him with their god Pan.

The Egyptians had one god who looked different from all the others. Bes (Lord of the land of Punt) was a leopard-skin-clad dwarf with a huge head, prominent eyes, a curly beard, and a tongue protruding from his open mouth. A guardian against all evils and dangers, Bes was also the god of marriage and childbirth. The protruding tongue in ancient sculpture is almost always a symbol of sexual intercourse. Many of the features of this god remind one of the Greek Pan.

Ancient Greek myths are full of fertility and love gods. The first to come to mind is probably Eros, the companion of Aphrodite. However, the Greek Eros, known as the God of Bringing Together, personified the more negative type of love: demanding love. The Romans knew him by the name of Cupid; in Roman myth, Cupid had a much softer side to his energy, as the Roman Venus did.

The Greek Eros had a nasty habit of shooting his flaming arrows into the hearts of unsuitable people. Without a thought, these people would go chasing after the object of their affection, always someone who was not the least interested in being chased.

The initiates of the Orphic Mysteries said that Eros was the firstborn of Mother Night, a primal creatress. Even Plato believed that Eros was the oldest of the deities and the one who gave the souls of the dead strength to ascend to heaven.[12]

Dionysus also was more a deity of frenzied lust and ecstasy than a god of affectionate love. His priestesses were called the Maenads (Roman, Bacchantes), who celebrated his rituals with orgies, wine, and nakedness. The Greeks and Romans frowned upon this sexual freedom practiced by women, but dared not interfere; the few times men did interfere, they were torn to pieces.

In rebellion against the typical Greek male attitude, Greek females eased their psychic wounds by taking part in Dionysian rituals, where divine madness was allowed. There, they indulged their repressed sexuality as well as their deep angers. Since divine madness could not be punished, Greek males were afraid to interfere with these rituals. By law, no woman who killed while in such a frenzy was put to death.

Dionysus was usually shown naked, other times wearing a saffron-colored robe. Called the Liberator, Dionysus carried a thyrsus and sometimes rode a panther. The touch of the thyrsus wand was said to be capable of turning water into wine.

The problems we have with this aspect of the God arise from the patriarch cultures of Greece. We like to say Greece gave us our laws and civilization. Unfortunately, we also got some of their negative attitudes toward females. The phallic symbol of the God became a weapon in classical Greece. Females were treated as slaves and property, and were subject to rape at any time by their "owners" (husbands or brothel keepers). Too much of this attitude of females as second-class citizens still exists today.

To the Romans, Dionysus was known as Bacchus and Liber Pater. As the ever-young god of wine, Bacchus was accompanied by satyrs, centaurs, and female Bacchantes (the milder Roman equivalent of the Maenads).

The woodland god Pan symbolized the all-powerful procreative force of life that resides in every procreating creature and cannot be totally denied. Pan, as a symbol of Nature, denotes the basic vitality of the life force against all odds.[13]

In the ancient myths of the Etruscans, the predecessors of the Romans, the god Mars (Maris) was a fertility god rather than a deity of destruction and war. A fragment of this fertility aspect can be found in the fact that prayers were offered to Mars as well as to the grain goddess Ceres in May when the farm lands were blessed. The ancient Persians had a similar god named Martiya.

Angus mac Og of the Celtic myths was a young god of love. Other versions of his name were Angus of the Brugh, Oengus of the Bruid, and Angus mac Oc. He had a golden harp which made irresistible sweet music, while his kisses became birds carrying love messages.

The Arthurian legends are full of god-symbol figures, but none that fits into the typical pattern quite like Lancelot. The interpretation of Lancelot's name ("Big Lance") shows his connection with the ithyphallic consort of the Goddess. His original name in the Celtic legends may have been Lanceor (Golden Lance), who was the consort of Colombe, a version of the Dove Goddess.

Among the Norse, the god Freyr, brother of Freyja and son of Njord, was a fertility deity. He was pictured as having a large erect phallus, symbol of his fertility powers. The Norse called him the Lover. So powerful and necessary was Freyr that he was worshipped as part of a triad along with Odhinn and Thorr. He was the consort of the Giantess Gerda.[14]

Once, when Odhinn was gone from his great hall, Freyr crept in and sat on Odhinn's throne, from which he could see anywhere in the Nine Worlds. As Freyr stared north into Jotunheim, land of the Giants, he saw Gerda, daughter of Gymir. She was so beautiful that Freyr fell instantly in love with her. He told no one about his desire, but he refused to eat, sleep, or talk. Njord, Freyr's father, became worried and asked Skirnir, Freyr's servant, what troubled his son. Freyr finally told his childhood friend, but said he feared to go because the Giantess would surely refuse him. Skirnir agreed to go to Jotunheim to get Gerda. Riding Freyr's horse, Skirnir galloped all day and night until he at last passed through a curtain of magick flames and found Gerda's hall.

At first, Skirnir offered Gerda eleven apples of youth to promise herself to Freyr, but she haughtily refused. Next he offered Odhinn's magick arm-ring, but she refused that also. In desperation, Skirnir finally threatened her, first with Freyr's mighty sword (which didn't impress her, either) and then with a terrible curse of losing her beauty and never having a lover.

Gerda at last agreed to meet with Freyr in the beautiful Barri forest nine days later. Skirnir returned with this promise, and Freyr set forth to woo and win the beautiful Giantess Gerda. Gerda was so taken by Freyr's gentleness and true love that she became his consort.

Sometimes the God Himself will not approach human consciousness directly because we, like Gerda, have preconceived ideas and would reject Him. Instead, He sends a messenger bearing gifts. However, the God is persistent; if we continue to refuse to see His true Nature, often we are maneuvered into at least meeting with Him. Like Gerda, when we see His beauty and goodness face to face, we make the choice to be with Him.

Chimati No Kami of Japan was a phallic deity, who ruled over the Positive Force of life; he was also the god of crossroads and footpaths.

Atea/Atea Rangi of Polynesia was a deity of the regenerative life-force. It was believed that he was the god who began all life.

Daramulun of Australia was the god of fertility and creation. He had an exaggerated phallus, a mouth full of crystals, and carried a stone axe. The bull-roarer was said to imitate his voice at the male initiation ceremonies.

The Aztecs called their fertility rain god Tlaloc. As Lord of the sources of water and "the one who makes things sprout," Tlaloc was a very ancient Nature and fertility deity.

The rain and fertility god of West Africa was Xevioso, who carried a thunder axe.

UNDERSTANDING THE LOVER

If we are ever to be capable of love, both specific and unconditional, we need to connect with this aspect of the God and learn from Him the true depth and meaning of this emotion. We cannot think that sexual love is dirty and to be avoided, neither can we use it as a weapon or a substitute for genuine, caring affection.

With overpopulation the most polluting human-caused problem on Earth, we must choose wisely with whom, when, and how many children we will produce. We should not continue creating little bodies that are wracked with inherited diseases. We must open our eyes and see the truth of character in those with whom we get emotionally involved. This aspect of the God can teach love, but love with responsibility for all one's actions.

Mentally, the Lover can teach us to channel our energy into creative projects and goals. We can learn from Him that one does not need a great amount of talent to create, that a person with minimal talent in an art or craft can create to please themselves, thus creating contentment and happiness within.

Spiritually, the Lover opens the way for us to experience and learn about spiritual love. Through His caring, He gently guides us to the knowledge we need to acknowledge and accept the Goddess, with whom He created us.

IV

LORD OF CREATION & THE HEAVENS

The Lord of Creation and the Heavens is an aspect of the God most recognized because of the current orthodox beliefs that their god lives in the heavens. Even the past patriarchal gods, for some reason, mainly tended to be sky deities. Perhaps because the sky appears to be the highest point in human observation and it is over everything on the Earth, they thought that making their god a sky deity showed his power.

This aspect of the true God is something different, however. The Lover has grown into the Father and co-parent and nurturer of all creation, along with the Goddess. He has moved into the position of cooperative partnership with the Goddess, willingly taking on the responsibility such a position requires. Although He is now Father, He still upholds the Mother's decrees. His energies of creation are blended with Hers at Her discretion, and, like fathers everywhere, He makes certain that the creations live by Her laws.

The Father of the Heavens (high spiritual planes) shows humans that spirituality does not come free nor is it a frivolous game, but has certain rules and responsibilities that must be followed and obeyed.

We are never forced to seek spiritual growth along a particular path or even at all. However, if we do start a spiritual search, no one (God or Goddess) will stand over us to be certain we do not abuse the powers we develop. If we get out of control, the immutable universal laws will see that we are put in our place.

The myths of deities of the heavens, creation, the planets, and the weather are numerous and varied around the world. The Celtic Irish Sun god was known as Bel, Belenus, or Beli Mawr. As the "Shining," he was similar to the Greek Apollo and was called on for fertility and purification.

Bel/Belenus was honored at Beltane, or the first of May. Cattle were driven through the bonfires at that time for purification and fertility. At Beltane, Bel's spirit is still honored in the Beltane cake, which is sometimes made to look like a human. This dough "victim" was also used in certain Far Eastern celebrations, rather like the Christian host.[1]

On August 1, the Celtic peoples celebrated Lughnassadh or Lunasa, a harvest festival, in honor of Lugh of Ireland and Lleu Llaw Gyffes of Wales. These Sun deities were considered "harvested" at that time of year.

The Celtic harvest deity of Ireland and Wales, also known as "the Shining One," was Lugh, a Sun god. This deity had several variations of his name: Lugh Lamhfada, Llew, Lug, Lugus, Lug Samildananch, Lleu Llaw Gyffes, and Lugos. The son of Cian and Ethniu, Lugh's celebration was at the harvest festival Lunasa.

Ogma of Ireland was called "Sun-face" and was similar to the Greek Hercules. He also had several variations of his name: Oghma, Ogmios, Grianainech, and Cermaid. Ogma presided over eloquence, poetry, inspiration, and magick.

Greek legends tell of the Titans who first ruled the heavens. Uranus (Heaven) was the consort of the goddess Rhea and father of the Titans, one of whom was Cronus. Because Uranus locked up her children, Gaea talked Cronus into castrating his father and freeing his siblings.

Cronus mated with Rhea and became the father of the twelve Olympian deities. Because of a prophecy that his children would supplant him, Cronus swallowed each at birth, except Zeus, whom

Rhea hid in Crete. When grown, Zeus, with the aid of Metis the Titaness, made Cronus vomit up his children. Then Zeus chained Cronus in the depths of the universe.

The masculine universal energy combined with the feminine universal energy to bring the universe and all the heavenly bodies into existence before humans were created. The masculine energy became a temporary chaos, eclipsing nearly everything for a time. The twelve children would be the twelve zodiac signs, eleven of which were hidden until the chaos was brought under control. They became visible once more through the energy of the one sign (Zeus) not swallowed by the chaos.

In spiritual terms, we create a spiritual path through the combination of our personal masculine and feminine energies. We begin to produce "children" (both psychic talents and spiritual traits). Along the way, we arbitrarily decide that we will only allow further development of one of our "children," thus making us out of balance (chaos). Eventually, that one "child" forcefully brings to our attention the necessity of the others, and we have to bring them into the light again (vomiting). When we do this, the chaos of our life is chained, and we move on to more advanced things.

Zeus (Greek) and Jupiter (Roman) were basically the same sky deity. Jupiter/Zeus is always shown with a thunderbolt, crown, and his familiar, the White Eagle. Zeus, like the Norse Odhinn, ruled humans; although he was divine, he was still subject to the will of the Fates. This god held dominion only over the heavens, while his brother Pluto/Hades ruled in the Underworld and another brother (Neptune/Poseidon) ruled the oceans and all water.

Jupiter's name may have come from the Sanskrit *dyaus pitar*.[2] Known as "the Smiter," "the Best and Greatest," and "Stayer," he was a sky god wed to an Earth goddess, Juno. Rain was considered to be his seminal fluid fertilizing the Earth. Thunder was his voice, lightning his weapon.

Although Apollo is sometimes called the Sun god, he actually represented the principle of Light, not the Sun. The Greek god Helios was the actual Sun deity who drove his Sun-chariot through the heavens each day. Apollo had such titles as Phoebus (brilliant), Xanthus (the fair), and Chrysocomes (of the golden locks). He was the son of the god Zeus and the mortal woman Leto and was born on the floating isle of Ortygia. His twin was the goddess Artemis. Themis herself fed Apollo nectar and ambrosia instead of milk, which gave him great strength, even as a newborn baby.

Like Apollo, if we feed ourselves on spiritual ideas, we can have the strength to do whatever is necessary. Our physical life may be hard and filled with negative circumstances, but we can rise above all this by turning to spiritual strengths.

The thunderbolt or lightning was considered by the Greeks to symbolize supreme creative power and illumination. Jupiter had three thunderbolts, representing chance, destiny, and providence, all forces that can mold the future.[3] The thunderbolt was a symbolic tool of the God's ability to fertilize (or make fruitful) the Goddess. In Tantric-Buddhist practices, the *dorje*[4] (*vajra* in India) represented the God's phallus which penetrated Mother Earth, leaving drops of His semen (gems) there.

The *vajra,* or Tibetan thunderbolt, was symbolic of the world axis, the connecting link between all realms of existence. It is also connected to the Hindu god Shiva, whose glance from his third eye is said to destroy all material forms in preparation for their reforming.

Indra, King of the gods and Lord of Storm, held the *vajra* with which he released rain; he was the consort of Indrani. At the Autumn Equinox, Indra was the deity who won back the Sun.[5] Like the Norse god Odhinn, Indra was beyond good and evil. Many things he did appeared to violate cosmic order, although they did not. He was said to always befriend the outcast, the weak and oppressed, and those physically handicapped.

At one time, all the gods abandoned Indra, leaving him to battle and defeat a terrible dragon alone. His mother thought of him as a curse; he had to eat a dog's intestines before he was allowed to drink the soma. Although Indra had to fight the other gods on occasion, he was also the destroyer of demons and evil. The Rig Veda says Indra was the only god strong enough to conquer the darkness with the Divine Word.

Whenever we choose to follow a spiritual path that is different from the ordinary, we may find ourselves ridiculed and perhaps disowned by family and friends. We may even feel we have to walk through fire to get where we want to go. However, if we persevere, in the end we will discover spiritual knowledge that will enable us to dispel the darkness and rise above criticism.

In India, Brahma was known as father of the gods and humans, creator of the universe, and guardian of the world. He was connected with the goddess Sarasvati. Brahma was one of a trinity of Hindu gods: Brahma the Creator, Vishnu the Preserver, and Shiva the Destroyer. The Gandharvas were deities of the air, rain clouds, and rain; they were skilled horsemen and musicians.

Vishnu was a Sun deity; some of his other titles were the Preserver, Conqueror of Darkness, Lord of the Principle of Light that permeates the entire universe, and Jagganath (Lord of the World).[6] Another of his titles was Three-stepper or Wide-strider; he was supposed to have taken three steps to measure out the universe. Vishnu was connected with the serpent Ananti and the goddess Lakshmi.

The Norse god Thorr, known as the Thunderer, was considered to be a champion of the gods and an enemy of the Giants and Trolls. He was very popular among the Norse people as a protector and friend. Symbols of his magick hammer Mjollnir[7] are still worn today. Some historians believed that Thorr's hammer Mjollnir is the same as the double-axe or labrys of the Cretan and Hittite thunder gods. His daughter was the Earth goddess Thrud ("Strength").[8] His wife Sif, with her golden hair, was a grain and harvest goddess. Thorr drove a chariot pulled by two giant male goats. He was pictured with wild red hair and beard and dressed in battle clothes.

Although he was known to be hasty sometimes in judgment, Thorr was always a reliable friend. He ruled over storms, weather, crops, trading voyages, courage, strength, and protection. Legends say that he struck the clouds with his hammer to release the rains needed for crops. His home in Asgard was called Thrudvangar, "Thrud's Field."[9]

The Norse god Balder, the son of Odhinn and Frigg, was called the "Bright One"; he was a Sun deity, as well as a sacrificed savior. The only remaining major myth of Balder is of his death.

The Finnish-Ugrian cultures had three major sky deities. Ilma was god of the air and the father of the goddess Luonnotar or Ilmatar. Jumala, also known as Mader-Atcha, was the supreme god, a creator deity who also ruled over thunder and the weather. Ukko was the "ancient father who reigns in the heavens"; he controlled the clouds, rain, and thunder.

In the Mesopotamian creation epic, legends say that everything began with watery chaos. The god Apsu (the sweet waters that produce springs and rivers) and the goddess Tiamat (the sea or salty waters) combined their forces to create the universe and the gods. Apsu plotted to murder their children because they were troublesome, but the god-children found out about this. They sent the god Ea to kill their father Apsu. Tiamat had not supported Apsu's plans, but at his death she fought against her children.

First, Tiamat chose a second consort, Kingu, by whom she gave birth to thousands of monsters to aid her. The god-children were afraid of their mother, until Marduk,[10] son of Ea, decided to go against her. In return, the god-children promised that Marduk would be king of the gods. Using a net, Marduk caught Kingu and the monsters and chained them in the Underworld. Then he killed Tiamat. He used half her body to make the sky, and the other half to make the Earth. He created humans out of Kingu's blood. He also created a dwelling place for the gods in the sky, fixed the stars in the heavens, and regulated the length of the year. Marduk also took control of the tablets of sacred law.

One interpretation of this myth is purely spiritual. Each of us starts in life with numerous karmic imbalances, positive and negative, which can cause confusion and resentment when we finally have to deal with them. Many times these imbalances revolve around family, who seem to do their best to impede our progress. Only by cutting these family ties and creating a new life for ourselves can we get control of our destiny.

The Middle East had many gods of the heavens and creation. In Babylon, there was Addad/Haddad, the Crasher and Master of Storms, whose symbol was forked lightning. His consort was the goddess Shala.

The Assyrian god Asshur was a Sun deity, the Supreme God, Self-Created, Maker of the sky and Underworld. His main consort was Ninlil.

The Middle Eastern god Sinn was the Moon god of Mount Sinai, "Mountain of the Moon." He was said to have been born to Inanna or Nanna, the Queen of Heaven. This Moon deity was also Lord of the Calendar and the enemy of evildoers. Sinn was the father of the Sun god Shamash and the goddess Ishtar;[11] he may have originally been a Sun deity, but was replaced by Shamash. Sinn was the consort of Ningal.

In his original form, the god El (known in Canaan, Phoenicia, Akkadia, and Babylon) was called the Supreme God and the Master of Time. He wore bull horns and was the consort of the goddess Asherah, in her form of the sacred cow. When the Hebrews chose El as their only deity, they enlarged upon his attributes of benevolence and war and dispensed with the goddess Asherah. The Assyrian name for their bull-god was Shedu.[12]

The Hittites had a weather god named Hupasiyas. In their story of creation, this god slew the dragon Illuyankas. Another Hittite weather god was Teshub, who carried a thunder hammer and a fistful of thunderbolts.

In Syria, a major sky god was Rimmon/Rammon. The pomegranate, a symbol of life and death, was sacred to him. He was the god of weather, storms, and thunder.

Ba'al ("the Lord") of the Semites was the consort of the goddess Astarte, but he fought annually with Yamm, Lord of Death, over her favors. It is quite possible that Ba'al became Bel among the Celts; Ba'al became known in Ireland through the Phoenicians who traded out of their Spanish colonies.[13] His name may have come from the Sanskrit word *bala* or *bali,* which means a sacrificial offering.[14]

In the Zoroastrian religion of Persia, Ahura Mazdah was called the Great God, the Lord, the Illumined Divine Being, who was master of heaven. He gave the Asha, or universal law, to humans. As the Sun or sky god, Ahura Mazdah was known also as Ormazd, Ormizd, or Hormizd. He was the twin brother and rival of Ahriman. The brothers became bitter rivals after Ahura Mazdah's sacrifice was accepted by an older deity, but Ahriman's was rejected.

The Slavic cultures had a pair of opposing deities representing sky and Underworld, Light and Dark. The White God was Byelobog, a good deity who would fight his evil brother Chernobog, the Black

God, in a great final battle at the end of the world. Byelobog represented the positive half of the spiritual. These deities were similar to the Persian rival gods.

In the Slavonic-Russian regions, there were several summer festivals for sky gods. The Slavic deity Kupalo/Kupala was sometimes referred to as a god, other times as a goddess. He/she was the deity of the Sun, treasure, and fertility. His June festival may also have been Svantovit's celebration. Another Sun summer festival was for Khors, whose symbol was a flaming wheel.

Summer was also sacred to the god Perun, god of thunder and lightning. Perun or Pyerun was a thunder deity, similar to Jupiter and Thorr. Called "Lord of the Universe," Perun held an axe or hammer. He continued to be worshipped in parts of the Balkans until the eighteenth century.[15]

The Slavic god Svarog ("Bright, clear") was a deity of the Sun, sky, and fire. His son Svarozic was similar to Hephaestus.

Ra, known as "the Creator," "the Supreme Power," and "the Only One," was the Egyptian Sun god and Great Father. Later myths list Ra as the creator of heaven, Earth, and the Underworld. At his temple in Hieropolis, he was worshipped in the form of a giant obelisk, which represented a petrified Sun ray. He was the destroyer of night, darkness, wickedness, and evil.

Ra the Sun god was said to be the father of all the pharaohs through mating with the queen mother.[16] In the beginning, Ra was believed to have been born of the Mother of the Gods, and it was not until the Ptolemaic period that he was declared to be self-begotten.[17] A later legend says that Ra castrated himself to create a race of beings from his blood.[18]

After Ra sent the goddess Hathor to punish humans, he grew tired of the world and yielded his throne to his son Shu, who then yielded to his children, Seb and Nut. Isis, daughter of Nut, wanted Ra to share his great magickal knowledge, but he refused. Finally, she made an invisible snake to torment the god. In return for her releasing him from this annoyance, Ra transferred the magickal knowledge directly from his heart to hers.

Sometimes we become stagnant in our spiritual seeking. We do not want to share what we know, nor do we seek anything new. We grow "old." The Goddess, in Her wisdom, breaks us out of the rut by allowing us to get ourselves into negative situations from which we have no escape. We must be willing to open ourselves to higher sources so that we may begin a new, different, and better existence. Part of this process is sharing our knowledge with other true seekers.

Egyptian mythology says that the god Khnemu/Khnum was a potter-god who made the World Egg on his pottery wheel. Out of this World Womb he brought forth all creatures. Pictured as a man with a ram's head and long wavy horns, he was called the Molder and the Divine Potter. He was associated with the goddesses Sati and Anqet.

Amen/Amoun/Amun was called Great Father, an Egyptian god similar to Jupiter and Zeus; he was also known as "the Hidden God." Some myths list him as a creator of the universe.

The Egyptian scarab beetle in deity form was Khepera or Khepra. This god was "He Who Becomes," the god of transformations and a symbol of creative energy and eternal life. Although some of the myths speak of Khepera as a creator, later pictures show him emerging from a lotus blossom, a yonic symbol of the Great Mother.[19]

Although we may consider ourselves self-made in this life, our source and power come through the Divine. If we desire to change, we must retreat into the lotus blossom, or the spiritual womb, and be initiated, or reborn. In the spiritual womb, we learn to combine our masculine and feminine energies to produce a new life.

The god Shu was an early god of the sky, similar to the Greek Atlas. Shu was the consort of his twin sister Tefnut. As the god of air, he symbolized divine emptiness, the nothingness that is necessary for inspiration.

The Chinese culture had the Jade Emperor, or Lao-Tien-Yeh, who was known as Father Heaven. In Japan, Izanagi was the creator god, the Great Father; he represented the Male Principle of creation.

Akshobhya (Imperturbable, Witness) was one of the Cosmic Buddhas of Tibet. His symbol was the thunderbolt, and he ruled over enlightenment.

The Lugbara of Zaire and Uganda in Africa had a sky god called Adroa. As "God in the sky and on Earth," Adroa was acknowledged as a creator god who was both good and bad. He particularly held power over the law and social order.

The Aboriginal cultures of Australia had a bisexual Great God and Life-Giver called the Great Rainbow Snake or Julunggul. Among the Polynesians of the Pacific Ocean, Tangaroa was the creator god.

There were several sky gods among the Native American cultures. Many tribes worshipped Kitcki Manitou (Kici Manitu, Manitou); he was the Father, Master of Light, the Great Spirit, the spirit in everything. Asagaya Gigaei of the Cherokee was a thunder deity. The Pawnee had Atius Tirawa, god of the Sun, Moon, and stars; they also revered Tirawa, a creator god of fire-making, hunting, agriculture, and religious rituals. Hahbwehdiyu of the Iroquois was a good creator god and twin brother of Hahgwehdaetgah, an evil deity.

The Mayas of the Yucatan Peninsula had three deities who could be classified as sky or heaven gods. Gucumatz (Feathered Snake) lived in both heaven and hell; a shapeshifter, he was a god of agriculture and civilization. He was closely associated with the god Hurukan. Hurukan (Triple Heart of the Universe) was an ancient deity who created the Earth, animals, humans, and fire. However, Itzamna was also called creator of humans and father of the gods; he was the Lord of night and day and the consort of the birth-goddess Ixchel. The Aztec culture tended to have deities of death and sacrifice, but they did revere Mixcoatl (Cloud Serpent), god of the stars.

The storm and weather god Illapa of the Incas ruled over thunder and lightning, while Inti was the Sun god and consort of Mama Quilla, the Moon goddess. Viracocha/Huiracocha (Foam of the Lake) was the Great God, the Creator, and Being Without Beginning or End. Among the Incas, whose Winter Solstice fell in June,[20] they celebrated the Feast of the Sun to honor their god Inti Raymi and the harvest of the maize. Inti was the deity of the ruling dynasty and was represented by a great golden disk with a face.

UNDERSTANDING THE SKY GOD

Like the gods of the heaven, air, creation, and storm, we must learn to withdraw for periods of time, sinking into the stillness and silence (air) of meditation where we can access the superconscious mind. In this silence, we will be given the guidance (heaven) we need when facing certain problems. We will know instinctively when we should speak out and when we should remain silent, when we should go in a new direction and how to go about it. Ideas (creation) will come to fruition through divine inspiration (rain). By understanding this aspect of the God in spiritual terms, we can rise above limitations.

V

LORD OF THE
FOREST & ANIMALS

Robin Hood, the Green Man, the May King, and the Horned God are all variations of the Lord of the Forest aspect of the God. This aspect symbolizes the secret laws of Nature and the unending ability of life energy to reproduce itself. This aspect also represents the unity needed between the Lord of the Forest, the Earth Mother, Nature, and humankind before there is any exchange of deep spiritual knowledge.

In many Celtic legends, the Green Man (Lord of the Forest), or Jack in the Green, is the Fool, similar to the figure shown on tarot cards. Outwardly, he appears to be simple and childlike, while behind the mask he wears, the Lord is the complex challenger to all initiates, the one who reveals the deepest Mysteries. His realm appears to be the Land of Enchantment, where time and space mean nothing. The vegetation spouting from the mouth of the traditional Celtic Green Man symbolizes the creativity in all its forms that is possible when the initiate learns to use the "keys," or words, of power and formation.

The Roman deity Terminus was the god of land boundaries. On February 23, sacrifices were made at the boundary stones between neighboring farmlands. There must be boundaries on all levels of life in order to ensure a sense of individuality. Everyone needs his or her own private place, whether it be twenty acres of forest or a single room, to maintain a sense of self. Even the Eskimos, whose igloos are the home of more than one generation, have designated corners or areas which are considered inviolate without invitation. Neither humans nor animals interact, grow, or respond well to conditions where there are no boundaries or privacy.[1]

Faunus was a gentle Roman deity of fields, woodlands, shepherds, and prophecy. In general appearance, he somewhat resembled the Greek Pan, with his short horns, pointed ears, and hoofed feet. Ancient descriptions say that Faunus had the legs and tail of a deer and the smooth-skinned body, arms, and face of a handsome youth.

His followers, the fauns, were beautiful young men with tiny horns and pointed ears, but not necessarily hoofed feet. Unlike Pan and his followers, Faunus and the fauns were gentle creatures who liked to dance with the woodland nymphs. They were no threat to human women. Faunus, the grandson of Saturn, played the pipes and filled the woodlands and fields with his haunting music.

This Greek god's Roman name was Lupercus; he was honored at the Roman Lupercalia festival when his priests performed the rites naked. The Lupercalia was a joint festival with an aspect of the goddess Juno and showed Faunus' strong connection with the fertility of the land, animals, and humans. He is the very ancient, primal force that is necessary to fertilize and balance the Great Goddess.

There was always a purpose behind the actions of Faunus. He did not indulge in uncontrolled sexual exploits simply to see how many partners he could have. He did not squander his powers, but used them wisely and to good advantage. At the same time, Faunus saw the joy to be experienced in life, not only through sex but through music.

There was another side to Faunus, as there was to Pan. He could fill humans and animals with the dark, terrifying emotions of mindless panic when they trespassed uninvited into his special areas. The word "panic" comes from this fear generated by Pan, who was said to use a magick yell to fill his enemies with fear and take away their strength.[2] He often fulfills this role when an unprepared seeker pushes into Otherworld realms. The blind panic and fear such a person feels will cause him or her to swiftly withdraw. These emotions are created to protect seekers who would not understand or benefit from the mystical experiences, or who seek such experiences for the wrong reasons.

Pan was one of the oldest deities in Greece. He was known as the Horned One of Nature and the Goatfoot God. As ruler of all Nature spirits, Pan was considered to be the positive life force in the world. He was associated with healing, agriculture, animals, fertility, music, dance, medicine, and prophecy. He also had a dark side, if provoked, and was said to cause panic and even temporary madness.

The Arcadian (Greek) woodland deity Pan was an amorous god who liked nothing better than to chase down and seduce females. He was a wild-looking deity, half-man, half-goat. As a symbol of his frequent sexual adventures, he was shown with an erect penis. Although Pan came to be portrayed as a lecherous being by the patriarchies, originally he merely represented the masculine forces of Nature. As a son of the Earth, he was a fertility deity and the Little God. In matriarchal times, Pan was not an oppressor of women, but their loving companion.

One later Greek myth tells of Syrinx, the daughter of the river god Ladon, who walked along the riverbank near Pan's woodland domain. When Pan saw her, he set out in pursuit, chasing the frightened nymph. When Syrinx felt Pan's rough hand and heard his heavy breathing, she screamed for her father Ladon to protect her. Ladon changed his daughter into a clump of reeds along the river's edge. Pan waited a long time for Syrinx to change back, but she never did. Finally, he plucked some of the reeds and fastened them together in a horizontal line with stopped ends. When he blew across the open ends, he made beautiful music. Pan called the musical instrument the syrinx, or pan-pipes.

If we pursue spiritual things too intently, they can slip away, leaving us with only a shadow of what we sought. We must learn to entice gently and be willing to wait patiently. If we do find ourselves grasping at a spiritual idea, only to have it turn rigid within our hearts, we need a time of quiet and meditation until we can create an appropriate atmosphere for its return. When it does return, we usually find it has presented us with another aspect of its appearance, one which we then can learn to use in a beautiful manner.

In the Mediterranean areas, the Summer Solstice was a time of Pan and the Forest Goddess. Pan, with his pipes, enticed nymphs and human maidens to rendezvous with him in the green woods for love and pleasures.

Pan is often associated with Dionysus and the Maenads. Very old legends say that he coupled with Athene, Selene, and many other forms of the Great Goddess.[3] Pan's sacred drama of death and resurrection was the original "tragedy," from the Greek *tragoidos,* "Goat Song."[4]

In ancient Roman art, the first Mediterranean Green Man, or Lord of the Forest, appears in connection with the Dionysian Mysteries. Since this deity's followers often wore beards of leaves and daubed their faces with wine, this was very likely an early depiction of Pan. Later, the followers of Dionysus used a bearded mask covered with ivy or vine leaves during their initiation ceremonies. In the Eleusinian Mysteries, which concerned the baby Dionysus, a phallus made of figwood was placed in a winnowing basket to represent the god.

The Roman god Vertumnus, known as the Changer, was a shapeshifter deity; his name probably comes from the Latin *vertere* ("to change").[5] His features and gentle nature were much like Faunus, but he was primarily associated with fertility and the proper return of the seasons.

The goddess Pomona, deity of rural fertility, was courted by many gods, including Vertumnus, but she rejected them all. Vertumnus was quite smitten with her, so he decided to present himself to Pomona in a variety of shapes to ease her distrust. First he took the form of a farm laborer, then a vinegrower, and finally a harvester, but the goddess only turned away. At last, he shapeshifted into an old country woman and won Pomona's heart.

In order to get humans to acknowledge His existence and learn about Him, the God will use every avenue of human interest. He will present His aspects through any activity or train of thought, wooing us to follow Him on a spiritual path.

In Northern Europe, especially in Celtic countries, the Summer Solstice was considered the time of the Faery Queen and Cernunnos or the Green Man. The Green Man and the horned god Cernunnos may well be Celtic versions of the ancient Pan.

The Green Man can still be found in old carvings in Britain. He is portrayed as a face peering out from among leaves and vines; sometimes he is shown enclosed in the trunk of a tree. He is a mysterious woodland deity who cares for the forests, all kinds of trees, and all forest plants. He is said to be of a human man-form, green in color, and dressed in leaves and bark. Green George, Leaf Man, and Jack-in-the-Green are other names for the same deity.[6]

The great Horned God of the Celts was known by several names: Cernunnos or Cernowain; Atho in Wales; Herne the Hunter in Windsor Forest;[7] Hu Gadern to the Druids. All these were aspects of one deity and his powers. Whatever name and form he took, he had one common feature: antlers or ram's horns on his head.[8] The name Cernunnos probably comes from the word *cerna* (horn);[9] on the Gundestrup Cauldron (second century C.E.) he is shown with antlers on his head and wearing or holding the Celtic torque. Cernunnos and all other Nature and forest gods were representative of the stag-god,[10] who was sacrificed annually. He was considered a consort of the White Moon Goddess.

Cernunnos was known in various forms throughout Europe. He was called the Horned God, God of Nature, God of the Underworld and the Astral Plane, the Opener of the Gates of Life and Death, the Lord of all Nature, and the Horned One. He was often pictured sitting in a semi-lotus position and had long curling hair and a beard. He was naked except for a neck torque; sometimes he held a spear and shield. His symbols were the stag, ram, bull, and horned serpent. He ruled over virility, fertility, animals, physical love, Nature, woodlands, reincarnation, crossroads, wealth, commerce, and warriors.

The famous chalk-cut figure of the Cerne Abbas Giant in Britain may represent Cernunnos, or an aspect of him. This figure is two hundred feet long, from the top of his club to his feet. His phallus alone is thirty feet long.[11] No one is certain which deity this figure represents. He could be an ancient image of Cernunnos, Sucellos (Good Striker) with his mallet, the Irish Dagda with his mighty club, or the club-wielding giant in the Welsh story Lady of the Fountain.

The medieval stories of Robin Hood and his band of Merry Men is simply an offshoot of Cernunnos, dressed up in such a way as to make it acceptable to the secular authorities. In these tales, Robin is particularly devoted to the Virgin Mary, a Christianized aspect of the Goddess; one form or another of the name Mary has been used for the Goddess in a great many cultures. (See Chapter 2.) The title "Merry Men" very likely originally was "Mari's Men," meaning a group of men devoted to the Goddess and Her priestesses.

Most of Robin's activities took place in, or very close to, great areas of ancient woodlands. He protected this domain and the animals within it, with the same devotion and vigor attributed to the Green Man and other woodland deities.

The stories of Robin Hood teach us respect for Nature and other creatures. Outwardly, like Robin and his men, we humans are allowed to harvest plants, trees, and animals for our use as long as we keep the balance needed for Nature to repair and replenish Herself. Inwardly, we are symbolically instructed to keep a balance in our mental, emotional, and spiritual levels of life. We should cultivate balance in all areas and activities. Fanatics (those out of balance) are an aberration of the Goddess' will and laws, for fanatics have little or no self-discipline. They take a shortcut to satisfy their warped sense of "right," rather than work patiently to achieve a more positive result which will benefit all, instead of just their own little group.

The Hindu god Rudra was a wild, unpredictable deity; besides his identity as a sacrificed savior, he was also connected with the meditating, beneficial Lord of Beasts.[12] Another Hindu god of the woodlands was Vajrapani, who was similar to Pan.

Rudra used his great archery skills to send both humans and animals into the Otherworld. Even the gods were afraid of this tempestuous, unrestrainable deity, for Rudra used his death-arrows to hand out punishment to all who broke spiritual laws. Once the god Prajapati developed a lust for his own daughter Usha (the dawn); the girl changed herself into a gazelle to escape him, but Prajapati raped her. Rudra saw what happened and considered the treacherous act a mortal sin, a vile breaking of spiritual laws. Prajapati was terrified when he saw the god and promised to make him Lord of Animals if he would withhold punishment. Rudra shot him anyway.

The Lord of the Forest and Animals has direct responsibility over Nature and the results of procreation. Procreation taboos were set in place for a good reason, as were all of the spiritual laws. If we break one of these natural laws, especially with the deliberation shown by Prajapati, we can be certain that this aspect of the God will exact payment. We cannot upset the balance of Nature or procreation without penalties.

The Finnish-Ugrian mythologies tell of Tapio (Dark Beard), who was the god of water and woods. He was the consort of Mielikki, the goddess of the forest and animals. Tapio was said to wear a hat of fir and a moss cloak; he was invoked by the ancient Finnish people to supply an abundance of game for hunting. There are also stories of Pellervoinen, the god who protected the fields, trees, and plants.

The Slavic regions had three prominent animal/forest gods: Krukis, Leshy, and Volos. Krukis was the protector of domestic animals, but also the patron of blacksmiths. Leshy was a deity of the deep, wild forests; he was very dangerous. The god of horned animals of all kinds was Veles/Volos. He may have been a form of Cernunnos, for he was also associated with oaths.

The patron god of Hawaii was Lono, god of the woodlands and agriculture. His five-day festival was a time of games, sports, pageantry, the hula, surfing, and feasting.

Tekkeitsertok, an Eskimo deity, was considered to be the most powerful of the Earth gods; he ruled over deer and hunting.

The Aztecs primarily had gods of death and sacrifice. However, they did have one prominent god of Nature and fertility, who was called Tlaloc. They also called him "the one who makes things sprout" and "Lord of the sources of water."

UNDERSTANDING THE LORD OF THE FORESTS

The Lord of the Forests is the original prophet and poet, the one who teaches us how to reconnect with the deepest source of inspiration. By following Him back to Nature and becoming sensitive to Her once more, we can learn the relationship between humans and deities, the microcosm and the macrocosm. He stands at the gate to the superconscious, that connecting link between all humans, past and present, and all divine powers.

VI

THE HEALER

This aspect of the God is one of compassion and healing on all levels, but also of exactness regarding the degree of healing decreed by the Goddess. Humans primarily think in terms of the physical when contemplating the healing God. However, some injuries and illnesses of the mind and spirit can be more deadly and devastating than any physical ailment. The healing God has the power to heal on these levels also. To initiate any healing, we must first ask straight from the heart, not give lip-service to satisfy appearances. Some people don't really want to be healed of their ailments, for healing would rob them of the control they exert over family and friends. So, to receive the healing we desire, we must believe and truly want a complete healing. The healing God can instantly distinguish truth from falsehood in our request.

Although the Greek deity Saturn is usually thought of as a god of judgment and sometimes of the Underworld, he was also revered as a healer. The original sigil of Saturn is our present-day medicinal symbol *Rx*. This was often written on paper and given to the sick to eat; this was thought to bring about a cure.[1]

Apollo was known for his healing powers, although his arrows were said to both heal and kill. Like the elf-shot of Britain, Apollo's arrows were said to curse with paralysis, wasting sickness, and stroke. As the far-shooting god of the bow and arrows, he was similar to the Vedic Rudra. As a bringer of plague, Apollo was called Smintheus; this word comes from *sminthos* (a type of rat). He was the god of medicine and magick.

The God uses His supernatural "arrows" in accordance with cosmic laws and karmic balance; there are more positive encounters than negative with this aspect of the God. However, His healing comes within the mind or the soul, more often than the physical body. We speak of being "heart-sick" or "soul-sick," both conditions for which there is no human cure. These are the times the Healer God can cure us of an affliction, or at least kill off the desires and/or stresses that are causing problems. However, for the cure to be lasting, we must make every effort not to repeat the situation that caused the problem in the first place.

Asclepius, a healing deity, was the son of Apollo and Coronis, daughter of the king of the Lapiths. When Coronis married someone else while she was pregnant with Asclepius, Apollo caused her death, then repented and rescued the unborn child from the funeral pyre. Asclepius learned his healing skills from the centaur Chiron. Harmless snakes were used in his healing temples as part of the healing dream therapy. There were also great libraries in these temples. Asclepius inherited the title Paean (Giver of Light) from his father Apollo. His followers were called *paeoni* because they sang hymns of thanksgiving for his healing miracles. Asclepius also knew how to use certain herbs to raise the dead. Because this interfered with the order of Nature and the laws of karma, Zeus killed him with a thunderbolt.

Dreams are powerful things. They speak to us in symbolic language of our present problems, past hurts, and sometimes of things to come. Dreams can truly be Givers of Light if we take the time to understand them and listen to what they are telling us. The God, as the Eternal Dreamer within the heart of the Goddess, can show us how to cure the ills of our minds, hearts, and souls. But first we need to acknowledge His true character and seek His advice.

Strangely enough, the phallic Priapus also had healing temples where the sick came for sleep treatment. Priapus was called the Pan of Asia Minor and worshipped especially at Lampsacus. Abandoned at birth and raised by shepherds, Priapus had power over fields, flocks, bees, fishing, and the raising of vines for wine (like the god Dionysus). His phallic image was placed in orchards and gardens to protect and increase the fertility of plants. Bacchus, the Roman version of Dionysus, was said to have "healing in his wings."

Hermes carried the caduceus, a symbol of healing powers. As far back as Mesopotamia, the healing god Ningishzida (a lover of Ishtar) carried such a wand; there was only one snake on this wand, however, and it was double-headed and double-sexed.[2]

The caduceus of Hermes symbolizes the rising kundalini making its way up through the seven chakras or light centers of the astral body. If we strive to force the kundalini's rise before we are spiritually prepared, we will only cause ourselves mental and spiritual harm, and will meet the Trickster instead of the Healer. Originally, the caduceus symbolized the dual effects of healing: the actual treatment of ills, but also the release of torment through death.

The Egyptian Thoth was acknowledged as a great healer and magician. In the the battle between Horus and Set, Thoth healed them both from their wounds. A great supernatural serpent (perhaps the forerunner of the snakes in the temples of Asclepius) was said to guard the Book of Thoth; this book was hidden in an underground (some sources say underwater) palace.[3] Its contents were so sacred that only certain initiates were allowed to see this book. Another ancient Egyptian healer god was Imhotep (he who comes in peace); a son of Ptah, he was similar to the Greek Asclepius. He was associated with medicine, healing, magick, study, and knowledge.

The most famous Celtic healer deity was Diancecht of Ireland, the physician-magician of the Tuatha De Danann. He was associated with healing, medicine, regeneration, and magick. During the battle between the Tuatha De Danaan and the Formorians, Diancecht brought the Celtic dead back to life by submersing them in a special cauldron or well, a symbol of the Goddess' cauldron-womb of primal energy.

Diancecht was the grandfather of the hero-deity Lugh, who won admittance to Nuada's hall by his wisdom and skills. Once Diancecht destroyed a terrible baby of the Morrigan. When he cut open the child's heart, he discovered three serpents that could kill anything. He killed these, burned them, and threw the ashes into the nearest river. The ashes were so deadly that they made the river boil and killed everything in it.

Sometimes, to be cured of a spiritual ailment is a painful process. The three serpents could be likened to arrogance, greed, and lying, three traits that are deadly to spiritual development. Arrogance comes when a person thinks he or she is the greatest psychic or spiritually developed person on Earth. Greed arrives when a person uses his or her psychic talents and arrogance to swindle others. These people lie to themselves about their right to do such things. However, there is always a day of reckoning. The Healer God usually waits until physical death to read the karmic sentence, but I have known it to happen within one's lifetime. Like the Egyptian Otherworld court where the heart was weighed for truth, the Healer God rends the heart of the offender for the truth and then gives His recommendation to the Goddess. Karmic debt is added to whatever is owed, and the person struggles with the debt until he/she can balance the scales.

The British Celtic god Nodens was said to be a healer who could take on the form of a dog. This canine form was often the disguise of a god who accompanied the Great Mother.[4] His main sanctuary was at Lydney, Gloucestershire, where special accommodations were available for temple sleep and dream therapy, very similar to the sleep-temples of Asclepius.

In the Hindu pantheon, the twin gods of the morning were the physicians of the deities. Called the Asvins, these golden-colored deities were also known as the Horsemen. Another of their names, the Nasatyas, comes from the Vedic root word which means "to save" and is descriptive of their role as great healers. They were known as beneficent friends of the sick, healers of the blind and lame, and restorers of youth to the old. Their father was Sudhanvan, "the good archer," a title similar to that of the healing Apollo.

Shiva was considered the greatest of physicians, for he knew all about poisons, although they could not harm him. When the world was formed, both nectar and poison appeared. Shiva drank the poison to save the world; his neck turned blue from the poison, thus giving him the name *nilakanta* (blue-necked god). He wore poisonous snakes as a necklace, linking him with the Greek Asclepius who also used snakes in his temples.

Like Shiva, we need to learn how to transform negative energy into positive energy. When we find ourselves confronting negative energy, either from ourselves or others, we need to take it in fearlessly and transmute it to higher spiritual energies from which we, and others, can benefit. Sometimes we must wrestle with it in ritual (Shiva's drinking the poison), while other times we must work on transmuting it during dreamtime (the poisonous snakes worn as a necklace).

Chinese mythology mentions two healing gods: Shen Nung and Yao-Shih. Shen Nung was a god of medicine, pharmacy, and agriculture; along with Fu His and Huang Ti, he was part of a triad of medicine gods, but was considered to be the actual King of Medicine. Yao-Shih was a master of healing and psychic abilities. In Japan, O-Kuni-Nushi, the Earth God and Great Land Master, was associated with medicine and self-realization.

The Zuni of North America called Yanauluha the Great Medicine Man. He was connected with civilization, agriculture, animals, healing, and knowledge.

The Underwater Panthers were known to many Native American tribes (primarily the Ojibwa, Menomini, Potawatomi, and Eastern Dakota). These deities, also known as Great Horned Snakes, were pictured as enormous panthers with bison horns and short yellow hair or coppery scales. They were evil gods of water, but a great source of wisdom and healing power, especially with herbs that grow underground.

UNDERSTANDING THE HEALER

The Healer God is a teacher as well as a physician. His work is done on the soul more than the body, the heart and mind more than on actual physical events. He is compassionate, yet a firm teacher; often he assumes the guise of the Trickster, veiling his wisdom in difficult symbols and words with double meanings. The wisdom shared by the Healer is never meant to be taken literally; it requires deep thought and spiritual seeking to understand the true hidden revelation. Once correctly understood, the wisdom learned from the Healer can help us balance karmic debt and aid us in avoiding another painful cycle of rebirth filled with further suffering.

VII

THE TRICKSTER

The Trickster has been an important mythological character as far back as paleolithic times, according to Joseph Campbell. He is a liar, cheat, joker, and fool. He is frequently cruel and lecherous, without pity on his victims. A shapeshifter, he often disguises himself in many human and animal forms. Although the Trickster epitomizes disorder and destruction, he is also known as the Culture Bringer, for he often gives illumination of one kind or another.

The Trickster brings conflict and death into the world, but often restores life and hope after chaos has caused great calamities. He can appear both cunning and stupid. In later European culture, the Trickster became the Fool or Jester.

This aspect of the God is difficult to understand, for until this time we have found the God to be a compassionate, understanding companion of the Goddess, with concern for the learning processes of humans. Now we see the first of His "dark" faces. The Trickster God is rather like the drill sergeant in the army. When we need His teaching, He expects us to work at our spiritual growth, not dally around and be lazy.

The Nordic god Loki was a Trickster with a human form, as was the Middle Eastern deity Enki and the Greek Hermes. In Africa, we find Rabbit (the animal form), who became part of American culture through the story of Brer Rabbit. Mantis was another African trickster. In China, Fox was the greatest shapeshifter and trickster; in Japan, it was Badger. Throughout Europe, we also find many tales of Reynard the Fox.

However, the Trickster was not only an extraordinary animal, but a shapeshifter who often used a human form; this is seen in such African deities as Eleggua, Legba, and Exu, and the well-known Norse god Loki.

The name Loki may be related to the Sanskrit Loka, which was a spirit of the seven celestial planes. To the Norse, Loki was known as the Father of Lies, the Trickster, and the Shape-Changer. Although he was a blood-brother of Odhinn, Loki was known for his malicious revenge, cunning, deceit, evil, and dark magick.

Loki was bisexual, but was the father of several offspring, most of whom were troublesome to the gods. In Nordic-Germanic myths, Hel was the daughter of Loki and the Giantess Angurboda. Loki also fathered Jormangund the World Serpent, Fenris the great wolf, and Odhinn's eight-legged horse Sleipnir.[1] Unlike Sleipnir, who was a benign being, Fenris and Jormungand were treacherous, dangerous, and of malignant energy.

Fenris symbolizes the dangerous potential all humans have deep inside, the negative energy that, if not controlled, can break out to cause physical, mental, and/or emotional harm, usually to others; however, the self feels the backlash in one way or another. This Fenris-energy can best be described as the temper and the desire to harm another person. Used properly, this energy can help in self-defense.

Jormangund, also known as the World Serpent, represents an energy that clings to and controls a situation or person. This can be best identified in relationships, whether intimate or pertaining to a career. Lovers, and often parents, will use whatever constricting manipulations they can to avoid releasing a person or children. The more the other person struggles to live his or her own life, the more the lover or parent tightens the coils. It becomes a battle for control and power. Jormungand-energy is appropriate if used to fight for personal freedom against the malicious control of others, maintain a hold on life in trying circumstances, or hold to goals that are beset with many obstacles.

Norse myth describes the goddess Skadi as the beautiful daughter of the Giant Thjazi. Loki was caught snooping by Thjazi and, in return for his life, helped the Giant capture Idunn, keeper of the golden apples of Asgard. As soon as the gods were aware of Idunn's disappearance, they turned on Loki and made him tell the truth, then forced him to lure the Giant back to Asgard, where the gods slew him.

After her father was killed by Thorr, Skadi came to the gates of Asgard and challenged the gods to fight, in retaliation for her father's death. In an attempt to dissipate her anger, Loki took a goat and went out to greet her. Since he had caused the problem in the first place, the gods thought this was only just. Loki tied one end of a rope to the goat, the other to his genitals. Then, the goat pulled one way and Loki the other, until his genitals pulled loose. Loki fell bleeding into Skadi's lap, bathing her with his blood. However, Loki used his magick to repair the castration and went on to be as lecherous as ever.

Although the goddess considered this payment enough from Loki for her father's death, she was also determined to have a husband to fill her time in her lonely castle. Skadi had her eye on the beautiful Balder, who was already married. The trickster Loki again came up with a sly solution: Skadi should choose her husband only by seeing his feet. The gods stood behind a curtain with only their feet showing, and Skadi chose Njord, the sea god. This marriage didn't last long, as Skadi hungered for the snow-covered mountains, while Njord refused to leave his sea home.

The Trickster will not allow us to avoid the payment of karmic debts. Sooner or later we have to make some form of restitution. Once we have done this, we can rebuild our lives and move on. Often the payment is painful, and hopefully we will not continue to repeat the actions that brought about the need for payment. If, like Loki, we continue on the same path, we will be forced to pay a very high price, as in the tale of Loki's final punishment.

As a death spirit, like Shiva the Destroyer, Loki was periodi-cally sacrificed to the goddess Skadi,[2] but he always returned to life. As final punishment for his malicious tricks, the gods chained Loki to an Underworld rock with a poisonous serpent hung over him. His wife Sigyn catches the dripping poison in a bowl, but when she goes to empty the bowl, Loki writhes in torment and makes the Earth quake. At Ragnarok, or Doomsday, Loki will break free and lead the evil ones in a death battle against the gods,[3] thus setting the stage for the end of this world and the beginning of a new one.

There never was a time when Loki was not scheming to cause some deity embarrassment or trouble. In the beginning, when Asgard had no walls to keep out the Giants, the gods made an agreement with a strange man (a Giant in disguise) to build impreg-nable walls around their domain. The man asked for the Sun, the Moon, and Freyja. Following Loki's clever instructions, the Aesir agreed. Loki proposed that they lay out a set of rules for the builder to follow that surely he could never meet: the man could only use his stallion and take no longer than six months, the time from the first day of winter to the first day of summer. However, they soon realized they had been tricked—the builder was a Giant and the walls would go up in time. Odhinn warned Loki that his life was forfeit if they had to send Freyja to the Giant.

Loki waited until the night when the Giant and his stallion Svadilfari went toward the rock quarry. He shapeshifted into the form of a mare and enticed the stallion away with him. The Giant could not finish the walls in time. When the Giant protested, Thorr finished him off with his mighty hammer. Loki and the stallion, however, had disappeared.

When Loki returned months later, he brought with him a colt with eight legs as a gift to Odhinn. This horse, Sleipnir, was the off-spring of Loki and the stallion.

This myth is symbolic of the misuse of powers and the making of promises to the God and Goddess. Think carefully before you make promises, either to humans or to deities, for the payment for breaking them will be high. Also, keeping such promises may require sacrifices.

The Greek god Hermes was a trickster from the day he was born. He was called on for cunning, good luck, profit, travel, commerce, and as an aid for thieves; he was also a deity of the crossroads and messenger of the gods. The Roman Mercury was similar, but was more of a messenger than a trickster. However, Mercury was said to be the patron of merchants, smiths, and alchemists, even though he was often considered to be untrustworthy. The most common depiction of this deity shows him wearing winged sandals. Hermes was associated with the Triple Goddess.[4]

Hermes was only twenty-four hours old when he played his first trick on his half-brother Apollo. Apollo was the keeper of a herd of sacred cows for the gods, but Hermes sneaked away with fifty of them. The young god made the cows walk backward into a cave where he hid them, then sacrificed two of them to the Olympians. The little boy hurried home and lay innocently in his cradle. Apollo knew immediately who was responsible, but Hermes denied it. Furious, Apollo carried the child to Zeus, who made him return the heifers. Reconciliation finally came when Hermes invented the cithara (a musical instrument) and gave it to Apollo. In return, the god gave Hermes the caduceus and entrusted him with the sacred herd. Hermes later became the messenger between the gods and humans. (There is a similar Hindu story of Indra tracking down cattle and freeing them after an enemy stole and hid the Aryan herds.)

The Trickster God is adept at hiding His actions. We seldom realize what He is doing until we suddenly find ourselves facing a drastic new situation. If we learn the lesson He is trying to teach, we can reconcile with Him, thus gaining his friendship and usually an unexpected gift. If we learn to understand the Trickster God's unusual teaching methods, He will gladly be the messenger of spiritual truths.

After Rhea reformed the baby Dionysus, who was torn to pieces at Hera's orders, Hermes temporarily transformed the young man into a ram. He then took him to Mount Nysa and gave him to the nymphs to raise.

Another time, Hermes aided Zeus by stealing the beautiful mortal Io, whom Zeus had turned into a white cow to hide from Hera's wrath. Hera claimed the white cow and placed her in the keeping of

Argus Panoptes of the hundred eyes. Hermes was a clever thief and trickster, but he knew at least one of Argus' eyes would see him if he tried to make off with Io. So Hermes played his flute until Argus fell asleep, then crushed Argus' head and cut it off. He then brought Io, in her white cow disguise, to Zeus.

This aspect of the God may seem capricious and troublesome most of the time, but He does have another side—that of protecting us from dangerous situations through the use of camouflage. That is, He uses His trickiness to deceive those who would harm us in any way. While out on the astral plane during trance, meditation, or astral travel, the Trickster can disguise our comings and goings. On the physical plane, He can shield us from negative and/or dangerous people by drawing their attention elsewhere. For the Trickster God to work with us in this manner, however, we have to learn to accept the unexpected and often jolting surprises He puts in our path and gain positive experiences from them.

The Greek god Pan was also considered to have a trickster aspect, among other attributes. Like his father, Pan was a master trickster, an impish deity to his followers, but one who brought discord and problems to others. His worshippers met only in caves and grottoes.

The Hindu god Krishna had many characteristics of the Trickster. Once, he even tricked Indra himself. The herdsmen were preparing to give an offering to Indra as god of the rains, when Krishna appeared and told them they should be honoring the mountains that fed the cows, and the cattle themselves who gave milk. Then Krishna appeared on the mountaintop, shouted "I am the mountain," and proceeded to take the offering for himself. Furious, Indra caused a flood of rain to pour down. Krishna just laughed as he raised the mountain on one finger to provide shelter for the herdsmen and their cows. He held the mountain there for seven days and nights. This amazed Indra, who descended from heaven with his wife Indrani to speak with Krishna.

It never pays to get too complacent about our presumed stage of spiritual growth, or the Trickster will pull us up short. He never allows us to get too conceited about our position on the spiritual path. If we do, He will show us in an embarrassing way that we are not as advanced as we thought we were.

Legba, a god of both Voodoo and Santeria, as well as ancient African religion, is similar to Hermes the Trickster. He was ithyphallic and androgynous like Hermes. During certain dances in Legba's honor, he was sometimes portrayed by a girl wearing a wooden phallus. Like Hermes, Legba was thought to be the embodiment of the Word or Logos.[5]

In Japan, the trickster god was Susanoo, who was similar in temperament and morals to the Norse god Loki. He was a mischief-maker and god of storms, thunder, agriculture, earthquakes, and snakes. Susanoo's idea of a joke was always in poor taste, according to the ones who were on the receiving end. One time he showed up in heaven to visit his elder sister Amaterasu, the Sun goddess. Having seen his prankish behavior before, she grabbed her bow and quiver to meet him. Susanno pleaded innocence, saying he had come to say goodbye because he was going on a long journey. As proof of his good will, he and Amaterasu created three goddesses and five gods through magick.

But Susanoo got carried away and dropped a dead horse into Amaterasu's house through a hole in the roof. One of the goddess' women was so frightened that she stabbed herself with a weaving shuttle and died. Amaterasu was very upset; she hid in a cave and refused to come out. Because she represented the Sun, the world was plunged into darkness. The only way the other deities could get Amaterasu out of the cave was for the goddess Ama-no-Uzume to do a lewd nude dance. Susanoo was not the least ashamed of his actions.

By not being realistic about Susanoo's behavior, Amaterasu opened herself up to more pranks. If we deliberately "blind" ourselves to the negative character of friends and/or lovers instead of seeing them as they really are, the Trickster will set us up. He will create such a situation that we can no longer avoid the truth, but have our noses rubbed in it. The Trickster God forces us to face the truth and make decisions, whether we like it or not.

The best-known trickster among the Polynesian cultures was the god Maui. Although he was a great hero-god, Maui was also a shapeshifter who enjoyed doing malicious magick.

When Maui went fishing with his brothers, he always jerked their fish off the lines because he could not catch any of his own.

They finally refused to take him along. After a string of bad luck expeditions, they gave in and let Maui join them. He brought a special hook, called Manai-ka-lani, with him that would catch all the fish they needed. They went far out to sea but caught nothing but sharks for some time. Then Maui chanted magick spells over his hook and promised to catch a huge fish. The hook caught, the ocean moved, and all the brothers had to pull on the line. This went on for two days. Finally, land began to rise from the water, and the islands of New Zealand popped to the surface.

This story of the Trickster illustrates a point in the use of magick—be careful how you use magick, because you might get something you didn't want. Maui's brothers were willing to take him fishing only because he had a magick hook, and they wanted the biggest fish ever caught. If we are greedy, the Trickster will give us a wild ride, all the time providing the illusion that our request is being granted. Then the ride stops, and what we get is something totally different. The Trickster has His methods of teaching us not to be greedy, just because we have learned to magickally create desires.

Coyote and Raven were trickster deities known to many Native American tribes. Among the Aztecs, Coyote was known as Huehue-coyotl (old, old coyote); this mischievous prankster was honored by festivals where gaiety and unrestrained physical sex abounded.

UNDERSTANDING THE TRICKSTER

The Trickster aspect of the God breaks us out of ruts, gets us to think beyond conventional lines, and makes us question outer "realities" against inner truths. Without Him, we would fail to see the humor and joy in many things around us. We would be overly serious, never realizing that not only life but spiritual matters are not all staid and dull. He also keeps us from being too gullible and accepting someone else's word on spiritual matters.

Like the Trickster, the personalities we call "mavericks" are the ones who suddenly present us with new ways of looking at old concepts. The Trickster keeps us on our toes, flashing reality and falsehood at us like things seen in a strobe light. By learning how to dance around His traps of illusion and trickery, we learn to trust our intuition. When we learn to treat our intuition as a natural event instead of some abnormal occurrence, we instinctively are opening ourselves to spiritual guidance and wisdom.

VIII

LORD OF JUDGMENT & PROPHECY

Judgment and prophecy are closely connected aspects in the true nature of the God. In judgment, we present reasons for doing or wanting to do something; we may only do this on the subconscious level, without fully realizing what is taking place. The God keeps a record of positives and negatives. This record is the Akashic Records, like the Tablets of Destiny, which the Mesopotamian god Marduk held. We are not cajoled into or forcibly prevented from doing anything. Through free will, each human builds a record of past lives and actions.

As Lord of Prophecy, the God sends messages of future events to receptive individuals, who may or may not share the messages with their fellow humans. The God consults the Akashic Records to determine which humans have listened to divine wisdom or had such gifts in previous lives. We may be surprised by who receives prophecy in any of its varied forms, but however much we do not understand the selection, it is never a random event.

If we are to be open to the development of psychic talents, we must connect with the God in His true form. By learning through Him how to look into our past lives, we can begin clearing up old debts and emphasizing and relearning old talents. Once a connection is made with the God, we can receive divine guidance in all our affairs.

The Greek Apollo, twin brother of the goddess Artemis, ruled over lawful punishment of crimes. He was also a strong god of prophecy, poetry, music, the arts, and magick. Apollo was so gifted with the large lyre that wild animals gathered at his feet when he played. The satyr Marsyas challenged the god to a musical contest; the judges were the Muses, who were Apollo's constant companions, and King Midas. Apollo won the contest and killed Marsyas. Midas, who voted against Apollo, got a permanent pair of donkey's ears.

Talents, whether spiritual or physical, can be used in such positive ways that the benefits seem almost miraculous to us. These talents can be enhanced through connection with the God and Goddess. If, however, we refuse to be truthful in the use and the estimation of these talents, we can end up looking like fools. The God does not tolerate any deviation from the truth.

The Greek god Apollo was originally a Sun deity,[1] but later became a god of prophecy, music, magick, healing, and poetry. Under the title of Apollo Python (in a serpent-form), he took over the ancient Goddess center at Delphi. The laurel became his sacred plant because it created a poetic frenzy in the prophetic Delphic oracle. The ancient definition of the word *ecstasy* was "divine madness or inspiration." The rites of Dionysus and Pan brought ecstasy to their initiates, much as did the rites of Cybele, the Muses, and even Mars and Odhinn.[2]

The Greek god Dionysus was called the Lawgiver, among his many titles. He was often shown holding two stone tablets upon which the laws were engraved.

Prometheus was called He Who Foresees and Forethought. He was the Titan who stole fire from the forge of Hephaestus and gave it to humans. One of four sons of the Titan Iapetus,[3] Prometheus saw that the war with the gods would fail and kept neutral. A cunning Titan, he held a secret grudge against the Olympians for killing his people. A very old legend says that Prometheus was the actual creator of humankind, making them out of earth and his tears; Athene breathed soul and life into these creations. His creation of humans and his gift of foreseeing make the later stealing of fire for humans understandable.

The supreme god of judgment in the Greek pantheon was Zeus. He was a deity of the law, justice, and oracles. The oracle school at Dodona was his. Ancient writers considered Dodona to be the first oracle and prophetic center.[4] Prophecies were said to come from the sound of the wind through the leaves of the sacred oak grove.

The Roman god Saturn was honored at the Saturnalia,[5] beginning December 17 on the old calendar and lasting seven days. His consort was the goddess Ops, a harvest goddess. He gave his name to Saturday and is associated with the seventh planet.

Saturn is a lord of judgment,[6] symbolizing time, which eventually destroys all its creations. His other titles are Father Time, the Great Lesson-Giver, and Ruler of the Golden Age. He represents the law of limitation set upon all creation by the Goddess. He is related to the Ouroboros (the serpent with its tail in its mouth). The Babylonian name for the planet Saturn was Ninip, also a name of their Underworld god of the dead.[7]

As all things begin and end, so do they have a continuation of existence in one form or another. As the Lesson-Giver, Saturn forces us to learn life lessons and balance karmic debts.[8]

The Roman deity Janus had two faces or heads looking in opposite directions. Since his faces look into the past and the future, Janus is a god of prophecy and a deity of the reconciliation of opposites. He had no Greek counterpart.

The God sees into the past as well as into the future. He knows the truth of all past events and actions, and also can see and interpret all future possibilities. Nothing is hidden from Him. The further we advance along our spiritual path and strengthen our connection with the true God, the more we too are granted glimpses into the workings of prophecy, time, and cosmic guidance.

The fat little elephant-headed god Ganesha remains one of the most popular Hindu deities. Legend says he was formed by the goddess Parvati from the sweat of her beautiful body mixed with dust. At the time of his creation, Ganesha had a face and form like the other gods. Parvati appointed Ganesha as guardian of the gate to her abode. The god took his job very seriously. When Parvati said she wished to see no one, he tried to turn away the god Shiva. Shiva was in no mood to be kept out and had Ganesha beheaded. Parvati refused to have anything to do with Shiva until the god replaced

Ganesha's head. The first animal to come by was an elephant; Ganesha was given its head.

Ganesha is the Hindu Lord of Obstacles and rules their removal. He is also known as the God of Scribes and Merchants. His festival is during the August Full Moon. It is said that if Ganesha is worshipped at this time, wishes will come true. Because Ganesha is thoughtful, wise, and knows the scriptures, he is invoked before every undertaking to bring success. He represents the combination of force and cunning.

Ganesha also creates the difficulties that are part of human accomplishment, to lead humans to spiritual enlightenment and to seek the God. This deity was considered to be the master of initiation and mysteries and the guardian of the gates to self-realization.

The Hindu god Chandra, sometimes called Soma (a masculine name in Sanskrit), was the god of the Moon; he ruled over psychic visions and dreams. Born from the churning of the sea, Chandra/Soma was known as the source of all inspiration. The sea is a symbol for the primal waters of cosmic energy that are used by the Goddess and God for creation. Water is also symbolic of human emotions. A sensitive person, one who is not afraid of emotion, will be open to guidance through dreams and meditative visions.

Varuna, god of the Sun, was the deity of cosmic law and order; he judged human actions. This deity is a remote, mysterious god who sets snares to catch those guilty of perjury, oath-breaking, and lying, among other sins.[9] There appears to be a link between the Hindu Varuna and the Persian savior Mithras. His Iranian counterpart would appear to be Ahura Mazdah.

Yama, god of death, was the judge of all the dead. Also called Samana the Leveller, he judged over human dharma (duty), truth, and righteousness. The King of the Underworld and judge of humans was also known in Tibet as Yama the Restrainer. There was also a wrathful and protective Buddha called Hayagriva (Horse-Necked One) who represented the terrible aspect of spiritual powers.

The Egyptian god Thoth was called the Lord of Books and Learning, the Elder, and Lord of Holy Words, among other titles. He was self-created and the inventor of hieroglyphs and numbers. Thoth had greater powers than even Osiris or Ra, making him the first and greatest of magicians. He had an ibis head and held the writing reed and palette of a scribe. As judge of the gods and humans, Thoth was the consort of the goddess Maat, who judged all souls for truth at death.[10]

As Lord of the Dead, Osiris was also a judge of souls. All the deceased had to come into his courts where their hearts were weighed for truth. Legend also says that the head of Osiris was preserved in some manner in the temple at Abydos.[11] There, the head provided prophetic knowledge of the afterlife. This shrine had a sacred well called Pega; some of the priestesses of this well later went to Pirene in Corinth, where they tended a similar well.[12]

Amen of Egypt, who was connected with the goddess Mut, was a deity of prophecy; his priestess-oracles founded schools of divination in Libya and Greece. Later, this deity was combined with Ra and given the name Amen-Ra.

The Egyptian god Anubis is primarily thought of as a Lord of Death. However, he was also an important judge. Abandoned at birth by his frightened mother Nephthys, Anubis was raised by Isis and assisted her in the first embalming, that of his father Osiris. As protector of the souls of the dead, Anubis guided souls to the judges and then helped judge them. Portrayed as a jackal-headed man, Anubis had an important role to fill, even though his looks were against him.

We must recognize that everyone has a role to play in the events of life. By being ourselves, whether in physical life or when seeking a spiritual path, we are true to the divine spark within us.

The Norse god Odhinn judged all creatures in the Nine Worlds from his throne. To gain wisdom, he sacrificed one of his eyes in order to drink from Mimir's Well, a fountain of wisdom. He also disguised himself and stole the sacred cauldron of "wise blood" from a cave where it was guarded by a Giantess.[13] When Odhinn appeared on Earth, he was usually seen as an old wizard with a gray beard and one eye; he leaned on a staff and wore a broad-brimmed hat.[14] His ravens, Hugginn (Thought) and Munnin (Memory), brought Odhinn news from all places in the Nine Worlds. This deity produced two frenzies: the well-known battle frenzy and the frenzy or madness of the seer in trance and the poet in creativity.

The Norse god Mimir/Mimr was known as a very wise god, whose head was kept at the Fountain of Wisdom after he was killed. The gifts of foresight and prophecy were so strong in this fountain that even Odhinn made a physical sacrifice to drink from it.

In the Scandinavian pantheons, severals gods were connected with judgment and prophecy. Forseti, son of Balder and Nanna, was associated with good laws, justice, and arbitration. Tyr,[15] "The One-Handed," was the patron of the assembly or law court. He pledged to hold his hand in the mouth of the great wolf Fenris while the creature was chained; when the chain held, Fenris bit off Tyr's hand. Odhinn, leader of the Wild Hunt, was the ultimate judge for the Goddess in Her aspect as Crone.

The Celts in Wales honored Bran the Blessed, brother of Branwen; he was associated with ravens and prophecy. After rescuing his sister Branwen from her cruel husband, Bran died of his injuries. He ordered his head be cut off and buried on the White Mount in London with his face toward France, promising to give warning of any invaders. Lugh of both Ireland and Wales was also a god connected with ravens and prophecy.

The Persian heaven deity Ahura Mazdah was a type of judge, as he gave humans the Asha, or universal law, and judged their obedience to it. The Sun god Shamash was known as Protector of the Poor, Judge of the Heavens and Earth, and Lord of Judgment; he was the consort of Aya. The Babylonian god Shamash gave the famous code of laws to Hammurabi.[16]

The Persian prophet Zoroaster was said to have prayed on a high mountain and received the Persian laws from their god; these laws were the Zend Avesta, or Book of the Law.

The Sumerian god Kingu was both the firstborn son of the goddess Tiamat and her consort. When Tiamat entrusted the Tablets of Destiny to Kingu, she also gave him the authority to sit in judgment over all the gods and humans. He held this position until he was overthrown by the god Marduk.

Enlil of Sumeria, Babylon, and Assyria was called the counselor of the gods, the dispenser of good and evil, and lord of all regions. As the god of destiny and order, Enlil judged by the Tablets of Destiny, deciding the fates of humans and gods. The son of Anu, he was the consort of the goddesses Ninhursag and Belit.

Marduk of Mesopotamia was the oldest son of the god Ea and the consort of Sarpanitu. After he killed the goddess Tiamat, Marduk held the Tablets of Destiny. His son Nabu was the god of destiny and writing; a serpent-headed dragon was his symbol.

Assyria and Babylon had a god whose task was to sit in judgment over unscrupulous judges; this god was Gibil/Nusku. He was also said to destroy dark magick.

Several Chinese deities ruled over judgment and prophecy. Kuan Ti was not only associated with justice and protection, but with fortunetelling, divination, and dark magick. Lei-King punished the guilty who managed to escape human law. Shou-Hsing, god of longevity, was the keeper of the books that listed the lifespan of humans. T'ai-Yueh-Ta-Ti (Great Emperor of the Eastern Peak) saw to it that the payment of good and bad karma was carried out. Ti-Tsang-Wang-Pu-Sa was a god of mercy who tried to arrange for a good reincarnation. One of the ten Lords of Death and ruler of hell was Yeng-Wang-Yeh (Lord Yama King); he ruled over judgment, punishment, and karmic justice.

In Japan, Kannon Bosatsu, the male version of the Chinese goddess Kuan Yin, was a deity of mercy and compassion, who was called upon to temper karma.

Australian cultures knew of Gidja, god of the Moon,[17] dreams, and prophecy, while many Native American tribes honored the Thunderbirds, who carried guiding messages between humans and deities. Kulkulkan of the Mayas was a form of Quetzalcoatl and a god of organization, order, and law. The Incas of South America had a god of miracles, oracles, and the arts; his name was Pachacamac (Lord of the Earth). Among the Dahomey of Africa, Fa was the god of destiny who ruled over the personal fate of each human.

UNDERSTANDING THE LORD OF JUDGMENT & PROPHECY

When we learn to identify with the Judge and Prophet aspects of the God, we become sensitized to our environment: both places and people, both positive and negative. We learn how everything is bound together in a mysterious fashion, how all is one with everything and the One, yet each is separate in an individual manner. Those who learn to reach for and submerge themselves in this aspect are psychics, mystics, Pagan Nature followers, and creative people.

IX

THE HERO/WARRIOR

The Hero/Warrior aspect of the God is not what many men imagine Him to be. This aspect is not the macho man who struts through life, trying to prove how brave or how strong or how male and virile he is. He is the caring, concerned man who faces reality and does what he can about situations in a positive manner. The Hero can also be a woman who exhibits the same traits.

The Hero can be both positive and negative, when applied to human behavior. This aspect can describe someone who will aid humans and other creatures as the need arises, never waiting for praise, or it can describe a person who takes unnecessary chances or seeks martyrdom.

Like the Hero, the Warrior can also be positive or negative. The positive Warrior protects the weak and those in danger, regardless of personal cost. The negative Warrior likes violence and the terror generated from such action. Because of their experiences of being victims of the negative side of the Warrior, many women are uncomfortable with this aspect of the God.

The hero who is following the will of the God and Goddess is seldom harmed in the ancient tales. In nearly every world hero legend, when the hero does die, he is transformed into a deity or semi-deity and taken to heaven.

Most of the Finno-Ugric legends are contained in the Kalevala. In the beginning, this book says, Ilmatar, who was the virgin daughter of Air, came down from the sky into the sea. As she frolicked over the water, the East Wind made her pregnant. The goddess floated on the water for seven centuries, unable to give birth because there was no land. Finally, the god Ukko, the highest of gods, sent a teal to build a nest on her knee. With the eggshells, Ilmatar created the Earth, sky, Sun, Moon, and clouds. Even though dry land was now available, the goddess carried the child for another thirty summers. Her son Vainamoinen had to struggle for another thirty-one years to reach the mainland and begin his life.

We may take a long time to find the way onto the spiritual path that is best for us (being born). We may also have to struggle for a long time afterward before our lives appear to improve.

The Norse god Heimdall was the champion or hero of the goddess Freyja. After Freyja obtained her famous necklace Brisingamen from the four dwarves, Odhinn was jealous and got Loki to steal it. When she discovered the necklace missing, Freyja was devastated. She called upon the shining god Heimdall, guardian of the bridge to Asgard, for help. Heimdall's magick powers were as potent as those of Loki. He chased the Trickster over great distances and through several shapechanges, finally cornering him on rocks in the ocean while both were in the forms of seals. There was a great battle, but Heimdall won and returned the necklace to Freyja.

If anything of great importance is stolen from us—our reputation, our freedom to choose a spiritual path, even material possessions—the God can return it. If we have a true, strong connection with Him, we can ask for His help and guidance, and expect a positive result.

Thorr was also a hero/warrior for the goddess Freyja. Once the Giant Thrym stole Thorr's magick hammer. In exchange for its return, he demanded that the gods of Asgard give him Freyja as his wife. Thorr offered to go to Jotunheim in her place, dressed as the veiled bride. The ruse worked, and when the hammer was put in the "bride's" lap to bless the marriage, Thorr grabbed it and slew the Giants.

The mysterious Nordic god Tyr or Tiw was similar to the Roman deity Mars. Loki's offspring Fenris or Fenrir, the terrible giant wolf, was growing more dangerous and unpredictable each day, and the gods decided that he must be chained. However, Fenris broke every chain and restraint with which they bound him. Then a magick chain was forged, but Fenris, fearing the innocent-looking chain, refused to cooperate. The god Tyr volunteered to put his hand into the wolf's jaws while the others chained the animal. When the bindings were tight, Fenris struggled but found himself caught fast. Before Tyr could remove his hand, the wolf bit it off.

Often, the only way evil can be bound and/or destroyed is by self-sacrifice. The sacrifice can be devastating at the time, but the long-term outcome can only be positive. If evil is allowed to exist and grow, it eventually harms everyone.

One of the greatest Celtic Irish hero-gods was Cu Chulainn. He could also be considered a Divine Child and Sacrificed Savior, for he was begotten by a "father that was not a man,"[1] and later in life died bound to a sacred pillar after being cursed by the goddess Macha; he was pierced by arrows and his blood fertilized the Earth.

The Dagda, an Irish god, was a hero-deity. He was called the first among warriors because of his immense size and strength. During the battle with the Fir Bolgs, the Dagda's strength and Lugh's cunning gave victory to the Tuatha De Danann.

In the later Arthurian legends, Galahad, son of Lancelot and Elaine the Lily Maid, was a hero figure. The story of Galahad's reigning for a year and then suddenly dying before the altar is a form of the sacred king story.

The Greek god Ares was a typical warrior of the negative aspect. The Greeks thought of him as a tough, blood-thirsty liar who was greatly concerned with his male image. He was the god of war, terror, uncontrolled anger, revenge, and brute strength. As the blood-thirsty warrior, Mars once went so far as to attack Athene, who symbolized wisdom; she cracked him in the head with a boundary stone.

The Romans softened him somewhat by combining him with an earlier Etruscan god Maris; they named him Mars.

One of the later Greek heroes who became the god-object of the Orphic Mysteries was Orpheus. The son of Apollo, Orpheus was noted for his musical abilities rather than his fighting techniques; his music and singing tamed even savage beasts. When his wife, the nymph Eurydice, died, he went into the Underworld to bring her back. By looking at his wife before he reached the surface, he lost her permanently to death. At the end of his life, Orpheus became a sacrificed god when the Maenads of Dionysus tore him to pieces[2] (some said this was because he refused to love another woman other than his deceased wife). His head was set in a fissure of rock near Lesbos, where it gave predictions.

The Egyptian god Menthu/Mont sometimes was portrayed with a bull's head and carrying a *khepesh* (a very curved scimitar). He was a hero-god of war and protection. The bulls kept in his temple at Hermonthis in Upper Egypt were sacred to him.

Wepwawet of Egypt (Opener of Roads and God of the Underworld) was pictured as being wolf-headed. His image was always carried at the head of the processions for the Osirian Mysteries. Dressed as a soldier, Wepwawet was a deity of war, protection, defense, and martial arts.

One of the Hindu hero-gods was born to the Seven Mothers after Agni had sex with them while they were menstruating. This solar hero was born surrounded by a red cloud penetrated by lightning. Later, this hero was killed by a spear in his side. From his dead body sprang another hero just like him, his own reincarnation.[3]

Once a spark of true spiritual fire is planted within a soul, it cannot be killed. That spark will run from lifetime to lifetime.

The Chinese hero Fu Hsi was said to have received the fourfold concept of the Primal Arrangement from a dragon-horse who lived in the Yellow River.

Ogun/Ogoun of the tribes of the Volta area in Africa was the god of iron and warfare.

UNDERSTANDING THE HERO/WARRIOR

The God in the aspects of Hero and Warrior shows us the way to honor the connectedness between ourselves and the rest of creation. He also points out spiritual virtues to be courted in our search for spiritual growth and enlightenment.

The Hero/Warrior is a man or woman who has learned self-achieved submission to the work of the God and Goddess. It is through our own victories in life that the works of karma are brought about. Through these victories and the balancing of karma, we are regenerated.

X

THE MAGICIAN

The magician deities are sometimes thought to be the same as a specific type of sorcerer, those who personify the evil demiurge, such as the Gnostics believe in.[1] The Greek culture put giants and the Titans into this category. By attempting to shift the magician's role from the benevolent to the malevolent, the patriarchies attempted to create a false image of magick and its uses.

The positive aspect of the Magician is the human who has learned to use the cosmic laws of magick to create better conditions for her/himself, as well as for others. The negative side of the Magician is the manipulator who uses the same magickal powers to control other people for selfish and non-spiritual reasons.

The Magician aspect of the true God has many traits of the Trickster in Him, although in this stage of development, the God has chosen to use His powers in more gentle ways. According to Joseph Campbell, the Magician and the Trickster aspects oppose each other.[2] However, I believe they do not oppose as much as blend into each other, as will be shown. The Magician will sometimes use his powers to trick, while the Trickster can use magick.

The God as Magician shows us that using magick is not wrong, unless our motives are negative. He and the Goddess expect us to do everything we can to solve or change a situation before we call on Them. This applies to both spiritual and physical aspects of life. Nothing comes from sitting on our hands, be it spiritual wisdom, material comfort, love, or health. When we have exhausted ordinary physical measures, the God and Goddess provide magick as a supplement.

Although the Welsh bard Taliesin is not considered to be a deity, his story epitomizes the role of the magician to the Goddess. The goddess Cerridwen was the great Crone of Wales. She was connected with the Moon, the magick cauldron, and grain. All true Celtic Welsh bards claimed to have been born of her; in fact, as a group they called themselves the Cerddorion (sons of Cerridwen). Drinking from her cauldron was said to confer the greatest inspiration and talents. The journey into the cauldron was part of a bard's initiation; this was a dangerous journey, as seen in the tale of Taliesin.

Taliesin began life as Gwion Bach. As a young man, Gwion Bach wandered through northern Wales. Suddenly he found himself at the bottom of Lake Bala where the giant Tegid and his wife Cerridwen lived. The goddess had two children, a beautiful girl and an ugly boy. Cerridwen was brewing a potion for her son that would make him very wise. She imprisoned Gwion Bach and set him to stirring the cauldron in which this potion boiled. He stirred for a year and a day, until there were only three drops left. The drops splattered onto his finger; he thrust his burned finger into his mouth and instantly realized the terrible power of Cerridwen. He fled the lake in terror.

Furious, Cerridwen went after Gwion Bach. In an attempt to escape the goddess, he changed himself into a series of shapes. Cerridwen changed along with him. He finally changed into a grain of wheat, and she turned into a hen and ate him.

Nine months later Cerridwen gave birth to a baby boy, whom she cast into the sea in a little boat. The boat washed up against a fishing weir, where Elphin, son of a wealthy landowner, rescued him. Elphin named the boy Taliesin (radiant brow). The child remembered all the knowledge he had gained from the potion and grew up to be a talented, important bard.

There is always at least one initiation on any spiritual path; more often than not, there are several that we must pass before we can advance to a higher state. We do not pass these initiations by running away from the God and Goddess, but by merging with Them. The merger creates a rebirth of and change in our talents, our lives, our goals and desires, and ourselves. Then, like Taliesin and the Bards, we can say we are truly Sons/Daughters of the God and Goddess.

The Dagda of Ireland, with his never-empty cauldron, was called the first magician; this cauldron, the Undry, restored the dead and produced poetic inspiration. Gwydion of Wales was the brother of Govannon and Arianrhod, and the son of the goddess Don. The greatest of enchanters and a warrior-magician, Gwydion was a multi-talented wizard, bard, and shapeshifter. Manannan mac Lir of Ireland was known in Wales as Manawydden ap Llyr. He was a shapeshifter and wise in magick.

Among the later Celtic Arthurian tales, one finds the great magician Merlin or Myrrdin. Old Welsh legends called him a "wild man of the woods," one who had prophetic and shamanic skills. Merlin was associated with the Faery religion or tradition. As an artisan and smith, Merlin was said to have forged Arthur's magick armor and the Holy Grail. Tradition also says he built Camelot's palace and made the Round Table for Arthur's knights.[3]

Merlin was an adept in the use of the cosmic powers of magick. He had advanced in his spiritual pursuits to the point that he had no trouble manifesting physical things through magick. However, his manifestations were for a specific purpose: to provide a consecrated safe place for Arthur to consolidate his kingdom and create peace for his people. At the end of his career, however, Merlin was defeated through not seeing the truth in another's purposes and actions.

Like Merlin, when we have advanced along the spiritual path far enough that we have complete trust in the God and Goddess, we will be capable of manifesting without delays or problems. To keep that ability, and not be bound as Merlin was, we must always see the reality of all things. There is really no conflict between the use of magick and advancement in spiritual growth if we keep a close watch on our true motives in both.

In one of his aspects, the Greek god Hermes was a deity of magick and occult knowledge, similar to the Egyptian Thoth, the Roman Mercury, and the Norse Odhinn. All these deities had great knowledge of occult powers, magick, and the secret of rebirth; this knowledge was granted to their initiates. Hermes was thought to be a hermaphrodite, a combination of male and female; his priests wore artificial breasts and women's clothing.[4]

Hermes had great power over life and death, as shown in the story of how he transferred the unborn Dionysus from the womb of his dead mother into the thigh of his father Zeus. His caduceus wand was said to have healing power to raise the dead. He invented astronomy and astrology, music, and divination by knucklebones. He was even said to aid the Fates in inventing the alphabet. He had control over the Elements, and his caduceus transformed whatever it touched.[5] The original "sign of the cross" was the number four, Hermes' sacred number; he was called the Fourfold God because he controlled the four Elements.

The belief that Hermes' staff could change things into gold made him the patron of alchemists during the Middle Ages. His name during this period changed to Hermes Trismegistus, or Hermes the Thrice-Blessed One. He was believed to have founded the Hermetic magickal system, which was used extensively by the Arabs.

Although Hephaestus was connected with underground fire and volcanoes, he was also associated with the magick needed to create things of metal and gems. His Roman counterpart, Vulcan, was called the Divine Smith and was the consort of Maia, an Earth goddess. Shunned by his mother, Hera, Hephaestus set up his forge under the earth. Soon the gods were aware of his skills in making jewelry and other useful objects, and often called on Hephaestus to make them something special. But Hera remained cool toward this son until he sent her a beautiful throne. However, when she sat down on it, she was stuck fast and couldn't be freed until Hephaestus was brought to Olympus.

The Norse god Heimdall (the White God) was born from nine waves through Odhinn's magick. He was connected with magickal defense against evil, and beginnings and endings. When Loki stole Freyja's Brisingamen necklace, Heimdall went after the Trickster; after shapeshifting through several forms, he finally fought Loki as a seal and retrieved the magickal necklace.

Bragi was the son of Odhinn and Frigg and the god of poetry and eloquence; the Norse skalds said that inspiration, poetry, and music were gained through magickal knowledge. The Norse god most proficient in magick was Odhinn himself. Associated with wolves, horses, and ravens, Odhinn was a shapeshifter. The raven, a black bird of death, has long been associated with initiation into mystical knowledge.[6] The skalds called upon him for the gifts of prophecy, music, poetry, magick, and divination.

Odhinn was a master shapeshifter, often going into the world of humans in disguise. He would then test the hearts of those about him for truth of purpose to see if they deserved his help and knowledge.

The God, in the aspect of Magician, often presents Himself in disguise when dealing with humans. Because we are unaware of His true identity, we will act as we naturally would. Thus we reveal our true character and natural inclinations, so that we, when He reveals Himself, can offer no excuses.

Odhinn was the only Norse god to practice the *seidr* of Freyja. Freyja taught Odhinn this magick herself.[7] *Seidr*[8] was the feminine form of shamanism, probably a remnant of a matriarchal society and religion. The practice of *seidr* by males was discouraged; in the Lokasenna, Odhinn himself was rebuked for doing this type of magick.

The Egyptian Moon god Thoth, under his title of the Elder, was considered the greatest of magicians, the Supreme Magus. His powers were greater than even those of Osiris or Ra. He was the patron of priests and god of all magick, the inventor of the Four Laws of Magick.

The first and greatest of magicians, the Elder of the Egyptian deities, Thoth held the secret to words of great magickal power. In other words, the God in the aspect of Magician can share with us His wisdom of the power of the voice and the spoken word. If we truly believe in the magick we use, our words can be spoken with such conviction that they must manifest. In the spiritual sense, our use of voice and words describes the true self and the beliefs of the subconscious mind.

Thoth's temple and center in Upper Egypt was one of the greatest learning centers in the world. His priests taught that Thoth created by the sound of his voice alone. This god's sacred books of magick were kept in a crypt under his temple, which was open only to his disciples. The Greeks and later races translated these books into the works of Hermes Trismegistus and the Kybalion.

Through his wisdom and magick, Thoth performed the first embalming with Isis on Osiris. Later, during the terrible battle between Horus and Set, Thoth used his magick to heal their dreadful wounds. His wives were Sheshat and Nehmauit, but he was also associated with the goddess Maat.

All occult mysteries speak of a key that is needed to unlock mystical secrets of enlightenment. Without the "key," no one could hope to gain knowledge of magick and the afterlife. The Egyptians believed in *hekau,* or "magickal words of power," which could be learned by initiates to do great magick; the ankh was a tangible symbol of this "key." Even Sophocles spoke of a "golden key" on the tongue of the hierophant who led the Eleusinian Mysteries.

The Egyptian god Khensu/Khons (the Traveler; the Navigator; he who crosses the sky in a boat; god of the New Moon) was the son of Amen-Ra and Mut. He was called upon for exorcisms. Set (god of the unclean, the murderer, the terrible desert, and the Underworld) was also associated with dark magick and cursing.

The Finnish-Ugrian god Ilmarinen was a magickal smith of great power. He was capable of using his magick to create wondrous talismans out of such things as the point of a swan's feather, the milk of a sterile cow, a small grain of barley, and the fine wool of a ewe. Ilmarinen knew how to create through the four Elements.

When we learn the proper use of the Elements (Earth, Air, Fire, and Water), we can manifest what is needed or desired in our lives. When we move beyond the purely physical attraction of manifestation and work magick in the spiritual sense, we can manifest much more important changes. We can advance our spirituality as well as pave the way for others to more easily find and explore their own spiritual paths.

In the Hindu pantheon, Mara was said to be a master magician; however, he dealt in illusion and dark magick. In Buddhism, Mara was called a demon and was said to have attacked the Buddha. In Tibet, Mara was known as the Evil One and the master magician of illusion.

The Chinese deity Erh-Lang (Second Lord) was the god who chased away evil spirits or gave the power to do exorcisms. Hsuan-T'ien-Shang-Ti was the Supreme Lord of Heaven and Regent of

Water in China. He was a great magician and exorcist. In Japan, O-Kuni-Nushi was a god of sorcery and cunning.

Ea/Enki of Mesopotamia, Babylon, and Sumeria was believed to be the source of all secret magickal knowledge. The Phoenician god Latpon was called upon as the god of wisdom and magick, as was Kusor, god of magickal formulae, incantation, and divination.

The Aztec god Xolotl was a magician and shapeshifter who could assume the forms of various animals.[9] Aztec magicians invoked this god. Xolotl was the twin brother of Quetzalcoatl.

The Yoruba of Nigeria, Africa, believed that their god Shango was a magician, although he also carried a double-headed axe like the hammer of Thorr. Similarly, the god Eshu was considered to be a magician, a kind of combination of the gods Hermes, Thoth, and Mercury. In Polynesia, Tawhaki was called the god of cunning and magick.

UNDERSTANDING THE MAGICIAN

The Magician aspect of the God is behind humankind's civilization and inventions. He holds secret and hidden knowledge, which He can help us find. This knowledge may affect the material world, but it can also affect our spiritual growth.

The Magician is the master initiate of hidden occult knowledge of all kinds; one of His tasks is to initiate humans who seek this aspect of the God. Any human who taps into this aspect must be prepared to see things as they really are—the evil that masquerades as good, the good that seems to be hidden in evil. In order to learn the very deepest knowledge under the teaching of the Magician, we must discern our own subconscious motives and plumb the depths of our own psyches before we can reach the Divine Center within. Without touching this Center, we have no true magickal power. We must reach the point where we realize that things are not always what they seem; what we call reality is only the tip of the iceberg. The energy of this aspect can teach us to detach from the inner and outer distractions of life and to connect with deep, inner, Divine resources.

XI

LORD OF THE WATERS

In His aspect as Lord of the Waters, the Pagan God has an effect on not only the Element of Water and physical water, but also the emotional state of humans and other creatures. Without emotion of some kind, there can be no creation on any level. How we respond to His influence in this area is determined by our spiritual progression.

Gods of water usually controlled, in secondary ways, the land masses (with earthquakes, floods, and erosion), the sky (with storms), and the waters of the world (with tidal waves). So too do emotions often affect other areas of our personal lives.

On July 23, Neptune was honored in the Neptunalia. He carried a trident and whip and was the god of earthquakes as well as oceans. As lord of the seas, Neptune worked with the Goddess, whose womb brought forth life through cosmic forces.

Neptune/Poseidon[1] was the son of the Titan Cronus and his sister, the goddess Rhea; he was also brother to Zeus/Jupiter. After Zeus liberated his swallowed siblings from Cronus, there was an argument over who would rule where. Zeus took the heavens and Olympus; Hades/Pluto chose the Underworld; Neptune/Poseidon made his realm in the Earth's oceans and seas. However, Neptune/Poseidon always desired to expand his kingdom and was often in contention with Zeus over land. He never completely won and had to settle for only part of what he wanted.

His immortal wife was the nereid Amphitrite, daughter of the Titan Oceanus; his mortal wife was Cleito. He drove a chariot pulled by Tritons blowing conch horns; tridents, bulls, and horses were his symbols. He had the power to summon monsters from the depths of the ocean to avenge himself on humans, and did so on several occasions.

One of Poseidon's earlier myths tells how the women of the Xanthian plain ended the god's watery battle on their land by hoisting their skirts and exposing their genitals, thus reminding him that he was subject to the will of the Goddess.[2]

In later times, Poseidon was called the Supreme Lord of the Inner and Outer Seas, the god of everything that swam in or on water.

Like the God, we are reminded of the all-pervading power and will of the Goddess through every creative event or possible manifestation. Without the central core of Divine Energy, we would be sterile. Without seeking to find and understand the energies of the true Pagan God, we cannot hope to use Goddess-energy, nor can we understand the true nature of spiritual growth.

Poseidon/Neptune was also called Earth-Shaker, a title more frequently used by the Greeks than the Romans. This deity's power over earth tremors was known by the earliest Mediterranean cultures. Since earthquakes were a common part of Mediterranean life, this aspect of the god was honored with special festivals.

Neptune, besides his role as lord of the seas and waters, also represented the emotions and emotional state of humans. The storms he raised are the turbulent tides of emotions. In his aspect as destroyer, through ferocious tempests and earthquakes, Neptune symbolizes the emotional extremes and loss of control that can bring about our own destruction.

The Greek god Oceanus was the primary deity of the seas and water long before Poseidon. He was called "he who belongs to the swift queen." Oceanus was an ancient sea god who took part in the creation of the Cosmos from Chaos, and whose powers were later given to Poseidon. An even older sea god was Nereus/Phorcys (old one of the sea), who was a shapeshifter and prophet.

The net is often depicted as a tool of gods connected with waters. The Hindu Varuna carried a net, as did the Middle Eastern god Ea/Enki. In battle against the primordial monsters, Ea caught them in his net, rather than fight them in other ways. Later, Marduk trapped the goddess Tiamat in a net.

Divine energies are not something one can take or trap by direct force. We need to weave a net of our desires and spiritual goals, thus enticing these energies into our hearts and souls. Once there, we can experience them fully before we take our first steps in using them.

The trident is also a tool of gods who ruled over water and/or the emotions. Shiva the Terrible carried a trident, symbol of his ability to fertilize the Triple Goddess. His strength was multiplied three times, yet he willingly lay beneath the dancing feet of Kali the Crone.

Long before the Christians decided to appropriate the fish symbol for their savior-god, the fish was a symbol of Ichthys, a son/consort of the ancient sea goddess Atargatis. This goddess had many other names, and all of her images showed her in mermaid form.[3] One of her aspects was called Mari, who wore a blue robe and a pearl necklace.

In Egypt, the god Hapi was known as the deity of the Nile, crops, fertility, water, and prosperity. Although he was a god, he was shown with heavy breasts, a symbol of fecundity.

The Philistine sea god Dagon was portrayed as half-fish, half-man. His consort was the whale goddess Atargatis. The Babylonians knew this fish-tailed god as Ea or Oannes;[4] as king of the sea, he symbolized the Sun going down into the sea at night and being reborn the next day.[5] In Canaan, he became the grain god Dagon, father of the god Ba'al and consort of Anath.

The Celts of Ireland and Wales had two important gods who ruled over water. Llyr/Lir was called god of the sea and water, the mysterious deep, and possibly the waters of the Underworld.

Lud/Llud/Nuada/Silver Hand was similar to Neptune and called the cloud-maker and he who bestows wealth. He was associated with healing, arts and crafts, and sorcerers.

Aegir (Alebrewer) was a Norse god of the sea. Consort of the unpredictable goddess Ran, he could be either good or evil, depending on the circumstances. Like many of the Underworld gods, he ruled over prosperity and treasure as well as control of the wind and waves.

Njord, the father of Freyr and Freyja, was the primary sea god of the Norse. His second wife was Skadi, goddess of the mountains; Skadi chose Njord because of his beautiful feet. They later parted because there were few points of agreement between them. Njord was also associated with success, oaths, and wisdom. The Finnish-Ugrian god Ahto was the god of waters and seas. He was the consort of the goddess Vellamo.

In Japan, O-Wata-Tsumi was called the old man of the tide. He was the most important of the Japanese sea gods.

In the Polynesian cultures of the Pacific Ocean one of the primary sea deities was Aluluei (Micronesia), a god with two faces who knew all the secrets of navigation. Ta'aroa of the Maori of New Zealand personified the destructive power of the ocean. One creation myth says that the seas were formed from the sweat of Ta'aroa as he labored to form the world.

UNDERSTANDING
THE LORD OF WATERS

By exploring our emotions, we can sensitize ourselves to our natural instinctive senses. We can also open ourselves to the spirits who inhabit the Elements. With their help, we learn to see their mirror image within our subconscious minds. Knowing the truth buried within your subconscious enables you to enhance the positive parts and transform the negative ones.

XII

THE SACRIFICED
SAVIOR

The savior deity or hero who gave his life for his people is a common theme in world mythology. These sacrificed saviors died, went to the Underworld, and then ascended into the heavens. They were also believed to have the power to remove sins and grant eternal life to those who believed in them.

Many of these saviors had Mystery Religions attached to them. However, the aim of these savior-gods was not atonement so much as illumination. Their Mysteries taught that initiates should seek spiritual knowledge and enlightenment to enter the process of death and rebirth with knowledge, as opposed to the uninitiated, who floated through the life and death process like a leaf in a stream.

The Mystery Religions instructed their followers in esoteric spiritual knowledge through various levels of initiation. However, the primary ritual was open to all initiates and was a re-enactment of the suffering, death, and resurrection of the savior deity.

The Greek word *soter*, which we translate as Savior, was frequently attached to god names, such as Dionysus Soter. The literal meaning of *soter* is "one who sows the seed"; thus, the Savior is the consort of the Earth goddess. After sowing the seed, the Savior was sacrificed, only to be reborn from the Earth goddess. This is a metaphor for the continual recycling of all life and energy by the Goddess. In all Mysteries and rituals honoring this Savior, his birth was acknowledged by the words "He is risen."[1] The Savior is the one who shows the way.

It was common for the Savior deity to have three names, such as in the Eleusinian Mysteries: Iacchus the child, Triptolemus the sower, and Dionysus the sacrificed god. All these particular names and aspects refer to one god: Dionysus. This pattern is seen in the human use of nicknames for close friends, given names for the public, and the secret name of the initiate.

Myths of the Greek god Dionysus show his development from the Divine Child to the Lover to the Sacrificed Savior. Dionysus was called the Horned God, the Roaring One, and Dithyrambos (double-birth). Centaurs and satyrs were his companions. His female followers were the Maenads or Bacchantes. They celebrated with naked orgies, drinking, and wild behavior; if any man spied on their rituals, they tore him to pieces.

Dionysus had a cult center in nearly every major city in the Middle East, including Jerusalem.[2] Zeus was the father of Dionysus. When Dionysus sat on the Olympian throne holding the lightning-scepter, he was called King of Kings.[3]

As an Anointed One (Christos) and under the title of Dendrites (Young Man of the Tree),[4] legends hint at his crucifixion.[5] Another of his names, Dionysus Melanaigis (Dionysus of the Black Goatskin),[6] refers to the aspect of scapegoat-martyr, which the sacrificed savior often took. The same savior symbolism is found in the story of the Titans tearing Dionysus to pieces and devouring his flesh.

Dionysus was known as the god of wine, among his many titles. Wine was often associated with the savior deities. Red wine in particular symbolized blood and sacrifice during rituals. Bacchus, a Roman version of Dionysus, was sometimes called the Son of God.

The Dionysian Mystery was one of the rare opportunities for women to release repressed physical and sexual energy, and quite probably the rage they felt at their enforced, reduced place in society. By immersing themselves in the divine energy of the God, they reached a state of ecstasy unknown in any other phase of their lives. Unfortunately, when a person has not resolved life issues in a positive way but manages to tap into divine ecstasy, violent behavior can often result. These people exhibit no self-control or self-discipline in other areas, and therefore have none in spiritual areas.

In Greek myths of the Lapiths, Ixion (their sacred king) married the sky goddess Dia. He was sacrificed by being tied, spread-eagle, on a burning wheel.

The Greek hero Hercules, born of the virgin Alcmene and Zeus, was called the Savior[7] and Good Shepherd; his other titles included Only Begotten Son and Prince of Peace. When he died, he went first to the Underworld, then to Olympus (heaven). A solar eclipse was said to mark his death, just as with Krishna, Buddha, and Osiris.[8]

The Savior in Thrace was Zalmoxis, who was often identified with the god Orpheus. Zalmoxis was said to have held a Last Supper where he promised eternal life to his followers; then he descended to the Underworld, only to rise again in three days. He established a Mystery Religion where secrets of the afterlife were taught to initiates.[9]

The death of Mithras was said to have occurred during an eclipse of the Sun. After rising from the grave and before ascending to heaven, Mithras met with his twelve disciples (who represented the twelve zodiac signs) for a Last Supper; he was said to have ascended to heaven on the Spring Equinox. During the ceremonies of later followers of Mithraism, one of their rituals was to share a sacred meal of bread which was marked with a cross.[10] These rituals were always held in a cave, either natural or carved by the followers. These caves were symbols of the cave-womb that gives birth and the cave-cauldron that remolds the body after death.

Mithras was said to carry the keys of heaven; in his later years, he raised the dead, cast out demons, healed the sick, and cured the blind and the lame. He was called Light of the World, Sun of Righteousness, and the Savior. His teachings said that the world would end in a great battle of fire between the forces of Light and Darkness. The non-believers would be cast into hell, but the followers of Mithras would go to heaven. Symbols of Mithras, used in his Mysteries, were the boar Verethraghna and the rayed Sun disk. Only males were allowed to worship this deity.

The Mithraic followers also believed that they had to be baptized in the blood of a sacrificed bull or ram for the removal of their sins. They were marked on the forehead with a secret symbol during their rituals.

A number of Mithraic words and practices were adopted by Christianity. The Rock where Mithras was born was called Petra, which the Christians turned into Peter. A crowing cock was their symbol for the Sun god. They believed in purgatory. Their sacred ritual cake was called *myazd* or *mizd;* this became the Latin word "mass." Their chief priest was called the Papa or Father. Another of their priest-grades was the Patres Sacrorum (Fathers of the Mysteries) and the Pater Patrum (Father of the Fathers), whose authority was in Rome.[11]

The sacred bread or cakes are symbols of the self-sacrifice each person must make, in small ways or large, in order to attain a greater reward. We do this each day, usually without consciously thinking about it; we can call this action either compromise or goal-planning. On the spiritual path, these "sacrifices" should be consciously considered, then accepted or rejected. If we are drawn to a Pagan path of worship, for instance, we must decide to continue study in that area, thus rejecting orthodox religions, or give up the idea and stay where we are. The sacrifice may come in the form of disapproval from family and old friends.

Another god of the Persian mythology is Saishyant or Saoshyant, the Savior. This deity, however, has not yet made his appearance. He is the one who will come at the end of the world to remove all evil and renew all life. He will also throw all the wicked into hell. Saishyant was virgin-born, one of a trinity, grouped with a divine Mother and associated with the Holy Spirit.[12]

The Persian title Messiah (Son of Man) corresponds to the Greek Christos (Anointed One). The Persian Messiah is to return to Earth just before the end of the world. This story may be based on the Kalki Avatara, or final incarnation of Buddha. Some of the Persians thought that Zoroaster,[13] who was born to a virgin, was the Messiah, and that he would return as his own "son" just before the battle between Ahura Mazdah (God of Light) and Ahriman (God of Darkness).[14]

Osiris of Egypt was a savior god with over two hundred divine names,[15] some of which were Lord of Lords, King of Kings, God of Gods, the Resurrection and the Life, the Good Shepherd,[16] Eternity, and Everlasting.[17] As Savior of the World, Osiris was symbolized by the ankh, or Cross of Life.

In the Osirian Mysteries, the flesh of Osiris was believed to enter into the wheat cakes[18] offered to his followers. These cakes were made of wheat flour, honey, and milk; on top of each was cut a cross, probably the original hot cross buns. Since Osiris was said to be Truth, all those who ate the cakes could become Truth as well. As Un-nefer ("the Good One"), Osiris was believed to be the only god who could give eternal life.[19]

The "eternal life" spoken of by initiates in ancient Mystery Schools did not mean the current orthodox "heaven," but meant conscious participation in the endless cycle of rebirth into other lives. "Heavenly food" or the sacred cakes was a metaphor for spiritual knowledge. Eating these cakes or bread was symbolic of taking in the cosmic energy of the God and using it to further spiritual growth.

The old myths speak of the Shepherd as caretaker of the stars (souls). The gods Tammuz and Adonis were both called Shepherds, as were many other savior gods. The ancient mystical initiates knew that the Shepherd really was the psychopomp who guided souls to the Land of the Dead.

The crook or crozier (also known as the Shepherd's Cross) was originally a symbol of Osiris in his role of the Good Shepherd of souls. Osiris is often shown holding both the crook and the flail, symbols of his being both the harvest and the harvester. In Assyria and Babylon, the god-kings, known as "Shepherds of the People," are pictured holding such an emblem. The Greek Hermes also carried such a crook under his title of the Shepherd of Souls or Kriophoros (sheep-bearer). Christian bishops later stole this emblem to use as proof of their divine right.

The Egyptian god Set was crucified[20] on the *furka*[21] or "fork." His blood and death were said to make the yearly rebirth of the world possible. Set was said to carry a reed scepter, a symbol of castration and sacrifice, which was broken before his crucifixion; he was also wounded in the side.[22]

The ass-headed Egyptian god Set was one of the earliest sacrificed gods, the alter ego of Horus. Palestine was named after another ass-headed god, Pales, an androgynous deity who protected flocks and herds; the Romans later brought Pales into their pantheon.

During his fight with Horus, Set was castrated, another sign of the sacrificed savior. He was the rival and opposite of the god Horus; Set tried to supplant the Good Shepherd Osiris by defeating Horus, the Divine Child and Only Begotten One.

There are both positive and negative energies for every deity form in the universe. This does not mean there is a great, all-powerful, good deity who is opposed by an evil, destructive, human-hating deity. It means that everything in the spiritual is balanced by currents of both in-flowing and out-flowing energies. Set represents the out-flowing energy, the times when we have to stand our ground and fight for what we want. Horus is the in-flowing energy, the times when everything goes right and we only have to ride with the tide of events.

The Syrian god Adonis (the Greek version of the Semitic word Adonai, "The Lord"; in Jerusalem he was known as Tammuz) was a sacrificed deity. Another of his titles was Christos (Anointed One),[23] a title also applied to Attis, Tammuz, and Osiris. He was said to have died at the Spring Equinox, close to what is now known as Easter. His spilled blood created the blood-red anemone. He was buried in a cave, the same one which had been his birthplace; this cave is now called the Milk Grotto and is in Bethlehem.[24]

The Syrian god Attis was born to the virgin Nana, who conceived by eating a pomegranate. He was the sacrificed victim who was crucified on a pine tree to redeem humans, and whose body his worshippers symbolically ate in special bread.[25] His death occurred about March 25, near or on the Spring Equinox, a day which was called Black Friday or the Day of Blood. When Attis was buried, he first descended to the Underworld before rising from the dead three days later on Sun-day. After his resurrection, Attis was called the Most High God.[26]

The Mysteries of Attis and Cybele eventually became popular with the Romans. The Roman processions for Attis were always proceeded by "reed-bearers."[27] Those chosen to impersonate the god at the annual sacrifice rode to their fate on an ass.

The number three has long been a number sacred to the Goddess, particularly in Her aspect as the Triple Goddess. It is the number of creativity and inspiration. Many of the ancient Mystery Traditions required initiates to undergo three days of fasting and meditation before they were accepted. The savior-god was knowledgeable on all three planes of existence: the Underworld, Earth, and the Upperworld (heaven). Unless we strive to understand all levels of spiritual knowledge, we cannot hope to "rise," or transcend the endless cycle of karma.

The crucifixion, cross, and tree are common symbols in savior-god stories. The Norse god Odhinn hung on Yggdrasil, the World Tree, for nine days and nights, symbolic of death and resurrection, before he attained full magickal power. The Hindu god Krishna died on a tree, as did Attis. Osiris, in his dead phase, was entombed in a tree. Even the Mayas of the Yucatan Peninsula had a First Tree of the World, which was represented in the shape of a cross; their savior-god was crucified on it and called Our Lord of the Tree. When a savior god was crucified on a World Tree, the tree was shaped like a cross; he was crowned with greenery, usually leaves, and his arms sometimes ended in branches.[28]

A circle containing an equal-armed cross represented male and female in cosmic union. Among the Germanic peoples, this was called Wotan's (Odhinn's) Cross. The Germanic god Teutatis also used this symbol.[29] This equal-armed cross represented the four Elements, the four divisions of the year, the four winds, and the Solstices and Equinoxes.[30]

Ashes have long been associated with sacrificed savior gods, the scapegoats who carried away the sins of the people. In India, the Vedic sages believed that Agni gave his seed in the form of ashes, thereby making it possible to remove transgressions by bathing in ashes. The Romans also had a New Year atonement ritual in March when they bathed in ashes.[31]

The Roman god Mars is rarely thought of as a savior deity, yet there are clues in mythology that he may have originally been such. The predecessors of the Romans were the Etruscans, who had a fertility-savior god called Maris.[32] The early Phrygians also had a similar sacrificed deity, the flayed satyr Marsyas, who was hung on pine trees "between heaven and Earth." Mars was also called the "red god," a title borne by the Indo-European Rudra. Sacrifices to Mars were made in March; this month began the Roman year and was the month of atonement in Babylon.[33]

Even those who are the most warrior-like in spirit cannot continue their aggressive stance forever. The universal law of balance will not allow it. We must experience the highs and lows of physical life, as well as the peaks and valleys of spiritual progression. There must be a time of reflection, of atonement, of taking our own measure and determining to do better.

The pre-Vedic god Rudra of India was a flayed god; thus his name the Howler,[34] Wild, Chaotic. He was the father of the Maruts (sacrificial victims), who were made red with their own blood. Like the Roman Mars, Rudra was called the "red one." He also had the title of Tryambaka, "He Who Belongs to Three Mother Goddesses." He was a wild, unpredictable god, much like the Greek satyrs,[35] who also ruled over the woodlands and wild animals. The name Rudra was incorporated into Latin as "rude."

In India, the boar was identified with Vishnu and his three boar sons, who were sacrificed.[36] In Scandinavia, one of Freyr's emblems was the boar; Swedish priest-kings wore boar masks, symbolizing their role as husbands of the goddess Freyja. In the Middle East, Attis, Adonis, and Tammuz were sacrificed in boar form. Greeks swore oaths by the holy blood of boars.

The original title of Son of Man was applied to the Hindu god Vishnu under the name Narayana.[37] Although later patriarchal myths said that Vishnu had no need of a mother, a hymn of Vishnu's to Mother Kali is recorded; in this hymn Vishnu calls Kali the mother of all. The Persians adopted the title of Son of Man for Yima the Splendid, who became the Lord of Death and the Good Shepherd. Son of Man came to mean a man born of flesh, water, and spirit; one who could defeat death.

Stories of the Hindu deity Krishna follow the traditional Divine Child-Savior theme. Krishna's birth featured a star, angelic voices, adoration by shepherds, and gifts from wise men. He also survived a Slaughter of the Innocents. He was called Redeemer, Firstborn, Sin-Bearer, Liberator, and Universal Word. Krishna met the usual sacrificial death, that of hanging between heaven and Earth, with his blood spilling on the ground.

The stories of Krishna are marvelous tales of a deity who enjoyed life to the fullest, accepted his responsibilities, and in the end was willing to pour out his blood (energy) to gain great spiritual wisdom. Although he began his life surrounded by angels (spiritual guides), he also had to endure hardships. He was not afraid to savor love, thus finding the beautiful Radha who satisfied his need for affection and companionship. His message to us is to enjoy every moment of physical life, yet also to seek, giving what we must, for spiritual wisdom. Spiritual knowledge, like everything else, is not without cost.

The Buddha is known throughout the Middle and Far East. In India, the Buddha is considered to be a divine teacher, the Enlightened One, and guardian of the world. He was not sacrificed by others, but sacrificed himself by austerities. In Japan, one Buddha is known as Sakyamuni, while another is called Amida-Nyorai.

In Tibet, there are several deities called Buddhas, besides the Buddha who was Gautama Siddhartha.[38] Amitabha is the meditating Buddha; Amitayus is the Buddha of longevity; Amoghasiddhi, the Cosmic Buddha; Maitreiya, the Buddha yet to come and the Benevolent One. Yamantaka, the opponent of Yama the Lord of Death, is the Buddha who brought civilization and will eventually destroy death.

The Celtic god Lugh or Lug was honored at Lughnassadh or Lunasa,[39] a harvest festival. Harvest gods were often savior deities in that they allowed themselves to be sacrificed for the good of the people. Joseph Campbell writes that Lugh's name may be connected with ancient Mesopotamia, where the title of the sacred king (the Goddess' consort) was *lugal*.[40]

In Welsh legend we find Gwyn ("White God"), who was born to the goddess Arianrhod and became her consort. Gwyn was a savior-god slain by his rival Gwythur ap Greidawl. Sometimes he is identified with King Arthur.

King Arthur of Britain was also known to the Welsh as Arth Vawr, the Heavenly Bear. The Welsh Triads say that he was the consort of three Guineveres,[41] symbolic of the Triple Goddess. At his death, three Ladies took him on a boat to an island while they sang his death song. This island was later called the Western Isle of Paradise or Avalon.

In this tale, which has unfortunately been heavily overlaid with later Christian symbolism, the three Guineveres and the three Ladies are simply forms of the Triple Goddess. Arthur (an aspect of the God) did the Goddess' work in reuniting and rebalancing the land. Singing the dying into death was a common practice of early Celtic priestesses. I have known several people who talked of hearing celestial music at the death of a loved one or close friend. There is no reason to believe we are all not sung out of life and sung back into rebirth. Avalon, or Apple Island, is the symbol of the cosmic cauldron of the Goddess, where we all go to rest before we are ushered into a new life.

The Norse god Odhinn was also a sacrificial deity, although he sacrificed himself. Odhinn All-Father was known as the God of the Hanged because of his own ordeal and the fact that human sacrifices were hung on his sacred trees.[42] For nine days and nights, Odhinn hung on the World Tree to learn the magick of the runes, which were invented by Freyja.[43] He was wounded in the side by a spear during this time, and had previously sacrificed one eye to drink from the Fountain of Wisdom. The skalds called the rune power, words of power, and poetry "the sea of Odhinn's breast," a kenning which meant that Odhinn shed his blood upon the Earth.[44]

Developing psychic senses, learning magick, gaining inspiration, or studying the spiritual all require payment of one kind or another. As Odhinn hung on the tree and shed his blood to get what he desired, so all seekers must endure various degrees of hardship and spend energy to reach their goals.

The Norse god Balder falls into the category of the sacrificed savior, like Hercules, Siegfried, and other solar gods and heroes. Balder may be a Scandinavian name for the Celtic Bel or the Middle Eastern Ba'al. The son of Father Odhinn, Balder was slain by his blind brother Hodr, whose hand was guided by the trickster Loki. The lowly mistletoe was the death weapon used by Hodr or Hod.[45] The Norse word for mistletoe was *guidhel* ("guide to hel").[46]

Balder went down into the Underworld (Hel's kingdom or womb) where he will stay until the Second Coming, or the final battle

between the gods and the evil forces. At this Doomsday, the god Hei-
dall will blow his Gjallarhorn (the last trumpet).[47] When Balder arises,
he will establish a new heaven and Earth. His cremation on a ship
symbolizes regeneration through fire and water.

The God, like the Goddess, knows the occult secrets of working
with the Elements. The death of Balder involved all four Elements:
the wood (Earth) of which the ship was made; the cremation (Fire)
that purified and destroyed his old body; the sea (Water) on which
the ship floated; the smoke (Air) that arose from the cremation.
When an old cycle of this life, or even this life itself (Doomsday) is
finished, we can rebuild a new life or world for ourselves if we are
knowledgeable in the use of the Elements, either through magick or
spiritual application.

In rural Scandinavia, May fires (Balder's balefires) were lit on
Beltane; a man chosen to represent the god leaped through the fires
as a symbol of sacrifice.[48] In Scotland and Ireland, Balder (under the
name of Bel) was burned in effigy, symbolic of Balder's sacrificial
death and cremation. The traditional man-shaped Beltane cake was
made in Balder's, or Bel's, image and used in much the same manner
as the dough "victims" of the Far East.[49]

In Mexico, the festival for the god Xiuhtzilopochtli included a
dough image of the god raised on a cross. This image was eaten by
the people, and the festival was called "Eating the God." The
Mayan god of maize or corn was Yum Caax, who was sacrificed
each harvest.

Xipe Totec was the Aztec god of agriculture. His festival on
February 22 was to help the corn grow. The Aztecs called this god
"Our Lord the Flayed One," and celebrated his festival by skinning
humans alive. The Aztec sacred cycle was fifty-two years long. At the
end of this cycle, a man was chosen to represent Xipe Totec. This
victim was taken to the Hill of Stars,[50] where he was castrated and
flayed; the priest dressed in the victim's bloody skin to symbolize the
god's rebirth.[51] Then the people took fire from the temple of Xipe
Totec to start their hearth fires. The Aztecs believed that this sacrifice
and re-enactment would put off the coming of the end of the
world.[52] The original myth of this deity says that Xipe Totec skinned
himself to help the corn break through the ground.

During April, the Aztecs held a festival for another god of corn, the deity Cinteotl. Reeds smeared with blood were fastened to the house doors as an offering.

The Aztecs also had a savior-god, Quetzalcoatl. He was born to the virgin Chimalman, who was one of three divine sisters. Chimalman was also known as Sochequetzal; a heavenly messenger announced to her that she would bear a son.

Quetzalcoatl's death and resurrection symbolized the planting, growth, and harvest. Like many Mesopotamian deities, he had both avian and reptilian features; he was commonly called the Feathered Serpent. He used blood from his penis to create the human race after the great flood; this made him one of the "castrated Fathers."[53] He was sacrificed, went to hell, then rose from the dead. It was believed that he will return at the Second Coming. Sometimes Quetzalcoatl was shown back-to-back with his brother Death, making him a dual deity of creation and destruction. In comparison to the other Aztec deities, Quetzalcoatl was not a blood-thirsty god.

Here again, as with the Egyptian Set, we are dealing with the balance of opposite energies. However much we would like to get away from the rise and fall of cycles in our lives, it is merely part of being human and learning. Sometimes the valleys are extremely deep, causing us great heartache and despair. But if we reach for a spiritual connection with the God, we will find the inner strength and guidance to work our way through difficulties and once more emerge on the mountaintop. Connection with the God can give us the knowledge to avoid the extremes in either direction.

Viracocha of the Incas is similar to Quetzalcoatl in many ways. He went about performing miracles, preaching to the people, and promoting good. He disappeared; legend says he will return in the future.

Viracocha was treated harshly in some villages, even though everything he did was for the benefit of the people. This is a valuable symbolic lesson. The God will not stay where He is not acknowledged and greeted with love. If you desire His guidance and aid in all things, you cannot half-believe in Him.

The Russian Kupila and the Slavic Yarilo were gods of abundance and harvest, and considered to be sacrificed gods. Hou-Chi (Prince Millet) was an ancient Chinese harvest god.

UNDERSTANDING THE SACRIFICED SAVIOR

As the Savior, the God has reached His ultimate goal, that of spiritual self-sacrifice for the children and creations He formed with the Goddess. He has experienced everything humans will experience; therefore, He, as well as the Goddess, has the answers to our physical and spiritual dilemmas.

Connecting with this aspect of the God is the one most likely to fill us with divine ecstasy. This indescribable experience may be one massive, overwhelming event, or it may creep up on us little by little. Understanding this aspect of the God will make us look at ourselves, our fellow humans, and the Earth itself with new eyes. It is also the phase that will enable us to face our final initiation in this life without fear—that of physical death and the awakening into a spiritual plane of existence.

XIII

LORD OF DEATH &
THE UNDERWORLD

The most damaging false image of the God created by the orthodox religions is the Lord of Death. They seem to have lumped a great many of the God's attributes into this one aspect. What was originally the Lord of Comfort for the dying has become the Lord of Punishment. He has become the orthodox "I'll strike you dead if you don't follow my laws" god. There is no compassion left in this deity; he and his earthly priests rule by fear of annihilation and everlasting torture.

The original, and centuries-old, Lord of Death was totally different in nature. Although He fulfilled the decrees of the Fate Goddess, He did this with compassion, for He understood, through personal experience, the act of dying and being reborn. He had no desire to lower Himself through unwarranted revenge or petty torture just to see humans suffer. He was the Gatherer who took souls at the proper time, the Guide for souls seeking their place in the afterlife, the Comforter of those in pain and suffering. Although His methods may seem harsh to those who remain behind, the Lord of Death is filled with love and understanding.

Hermes as the Ram-Bearer and Good Shepherd was the God's aspect of caretaker of the Goddess' creations. He was responsible for protecting and guiding humans in their physical lives, then guiding their souls back to the Goddess when they died. He does not interfere in human free will unless directly instructed to do so by the Goddess. If we need help from the God, we can call on the Goddess with our requests. But we had better be certain that we have done all we can before asking Her, or the Good Shepherd can become the Trickster who will jolt us out of our self-pity through drastic and unforeseen methods.

The Greeks often called Hermes both the Good Shepherd (Shepherd of Men, Poimandres) and the psychopomp or conductor of souls. The psychopomp was the sacred guide who led souls to their proper place in the Underworld or afterlife.

Hades is perhaps the best-known Greek Underworld deity. One of his earliest names was Eita or Ade; his consort was Persipnei. The Romans called him Pluto or Pluton, god of riches;[1] the Etruscans knew him as Februus. The Greeks also called him Aidoneus ("blind one"), which Robert Graves says was a title of a phallic god, hidden in the Earth's womb.[2]

His consort was usually listed as Persephone (Roman, Proserpina), daughter of Demeter the Earth goddess, although he was sometimes paired with Hecate. The Greek Underworld consisted of more than one place, and the god Hades ruled them all.

The Roman Vulcan (similar to the Greek Hephaestus) was placated on August 23 during the festival of Vulcanalia. This festival, to ward off accidental fires, was held outside the city boundaries. He was a smith god who had his forge inside a volcanic mountain, either (or both) Mount Etna or Mount Vesuvius. Although Vulcan did not rule the Underworld, he still lived in part of it. He was petitioned for protection from fire, something a smith must be able to control. Vulcan was the consort of the Earth goddess Maia, mother of springs. He was also a magician of metal, gems, and mechanical inventions. The name Vulcan came from the Cretan god Velchanos, who was identical to Hephaestus.

The Greek Hephaestus[3] was an Underworld god, although he did not rule the Underworld. He was honored in Greece during

October in a festival called Chalkeia. Hephaestus was a pre-Hellenic smith deity cast in the role of the crippled son of Zeus. Zeus himself threw him out of Olympus for trying to protect his mother Hera. Although Hephaestus was the consort of Aphrodite, he shared a temple with the goddess Athene. A highly skilled god, Hephaestus made intricate jewelry and mechanical devices as well as weapons and armor for the Olympians.

The god Dis Pater was known to more than one ancient culture. To the Etruscans, he was the wolf-headed god of the dead; the Romans accepted him in this aspect also. The Gallic Celts called him simply Dis and said he became the "father" of their race by shedding his blood and dying. To both the Etruscans and Romans, Dis Pater was more than just the Lord of Death; he was also the ruler over mines, gems, and buried treasure.

In the Orphic Mystery Religions, the Underworld was called Erebos, "the Abysmal Womb,"[4] the Land of Death. The initiates believed Erebos was a place of regeneration, which is what the Underworld was in all ancient religions. Followers of the Orphic Mysteries, which were based on the teachings of the demi-god Orpheus, believed that an incarnation of this deity was torn apart by dogs.

The God of the Wild Hunt is the most misunderstood of all the God's aspects. He is the Celtic equivalent of the Greek goddesses the Erinyes. The Lord of the Hunt carries out the will of the Fate Goddess; he makes certain that souls that are ready for the transition from life to physical death are in the right places at the right times to meet their destinies.

Unfortunately, the Christians have turned the Lord of the Hunt into their devil, who kidnaps unsuspecting souls. Although on one hand they say their devil does not have the powers of their god, they also say that their devil can chase, torment, and take away those who call upon their god.

The story of the Wild Hunt or the Ride of Death is known all over Europe. The Nordic and Germanic cultures say this Ride is led by Odhinn/Wodan or the Erl King. Others also were said to lead a Wild Hunt: Dietrich of Berne (Teutonic), the French Grand Huntsman of Fontainebleau, the Celtic deity Arawn, the Norse Lusse (an evil spirit in the form of a great bird of prey), and King Arthur.

Even the folk hero Robin Hood (whose story goes back much further than medieval times) was a type of Lord of the Hunt. He used his arrows (like the killing weapons of the other Lords) to bring down and punish offenders.

The Hounds of the Hunt are known by a variety of names. In England, they are called the Gabriel Hounds, Yeth Hounds, the Dartmoor Hounds, and the Wisht Hounds. The Irish called them the Hounds of Hell, while the Welsh knew them as the Annwn.

Although the Annwn Hounds and others were in existence long before the beginning of the Christian religion, the Christians have changed the true meaning of the Hounds, along with their Master. The Hounds who hunt for lost souls and guide them to their proper afterlife places have become the Hounds of Hell, who snatch souls from the living under the direction of their devil, and the Hounds of Heaven, whom their god sent to harry those who were falling away from their religion.

The Hunt, which occurs in stormy weather, was thought to be a search for lost souls, especially those unbaptized by the Church. To see or hear the dreaded Hounds and the riders on horseback on their night ride through the air was considered to be an evil omen, as they brought destruction and death.

Arawn of Wales was the god of Annwn, the underground kingdom of the dead. Gwynn ap Nudd of Wales was the King of the Faeries and also ruled a section of the Underworld. The Dagda of Ireland was known as the god of death and rebirth.

Goidniu/Gofannon was known in both Ireland and Wales as the Great Smith, a deity similar to Vulcan. He was associated with blacksmiths, weapon-makers, brewing, and fire.

Odhinn had a Lord of Death aspect.[5] He was God of the Hanged, and collected his share of warrior-souls from the battlefields. His wolves, Geri (Greedy) and Freki (Voracious), ran with Odhinn and the Valkyries when he led the Hunt. A shapeshifter, Odhinn produced the battle panic called "battle-fetter," a psychological state that caused men to be unable to act. He also produced the berserker battle frenzy. The Danes called this aspect of Odhinn the *ellerkonge* (Erl King) or king of elves. The Erl King was associated with the elder tree and Hel in her aspect as Old Lady of the Elder.[6]

The Norse god Hod or Hodr slew Balder. Hod was sometimes shown as a malicious god, wearing a death mask and a hood, similar to the father of Robin Hood.[7] Loki helped the blind Hod thrust a mistletoe spear through Balder.

The Egyptian god Osiris was married to his sister Isis while still in the womb of their mother Nut. Isis and Osiris taught humans all the arts of civilization. While Osiris wandered the world, teaching other cultures beyond Egypt, Isis ruled in his place. When Osiris finally returned home, his jealous brother Set gave a feast for him. At the feast was a beautifully decorated box that Set said would belong to whomever fit inside it. Osiris climbed in, and Set and his followers sealed the box with lead. Then they threw it into the Nile. The box washed out to sea, then ashore in a foreign land where a tree grew around it.

Isis was heartbroken when Osiris disappeared. She searched a long time, and finally found the box by following a sweet odor to a pillar inside a king's palace. She recovered the body and took it back to Egypt, where she reanimated the body long enough to conceive her son Horus. Isis and her sister Nephthys hid the body deep in the swamps of the Nile Delta, but Set found it while hunting. He cut the body into many pieces, which he scattered throughout Egypt. The sisters found all the pieces, except the phallus, and fastened them back together. With the help of the god Thoth, they embalmed Osiris. This embalming enabled Osiris to live in the afterlife, where he chose to stay and rule.

The Egyptians said that Osiris alone was Un-nefer, the "Good One" or Savior, and that only he could give eternal life and cause humans to be reborn. Prayers to him began with "O Amen, O Amen, who art in heaven."[8] An ancient Egyptian text which calls Osiris the Good Shepherd says he will lead the souls of the dead into green pastures and still waters of nefer-nefer land and restore the soul to the body. An Osirian text says that there are many Arits (Mansions) in the blessed land of Osiris.[9]

Osiris, in his role as Lord of Death, was sometimes portrayed in a serpent-like form with his toes touching his head. The Underworld was known as the House of Osiris.[10] Initiates of the Osirian Mysteries were taught secret words of power that, after death, they could use to enter the presence of this god. These words were called "keys to heaven."[11] The all-important ceremony called "Opening the Mouth" was performed so that the deceased could speak these words.

Anubis of Egypt was a jackal-headed deity of the Underworld, a psychopomp who helped judge the souls of the dead. He aided Isis in the first mummification, that of Osiris. Plutarch wrote that Anubis, connected with the goddess Maat, was similar in power to the Greek goddess Hecate. The cult of Anubis was an ancient one, perhaps even older than that of Osiris.

Jackals, wolves, and dogs were considered to be the guardians of the Underworld gates. This depiction of the Underworld guardian as a jackal went far beyond Egypt; in India, Shiva was also called a jackal in his death aspect. The sacrificial Underworld priests of Anubis were thought to have jackal-heads, as Anubis did.[12] This god's sacred city was Canopis (Eye of the Dog). As a servant of Nephthys the dark goddess, Anubis was sometimes a messenger between heaven and hell.[13] When the Osirian Mysteries were practiced in Rome, a priest wearing a jackal-mask always led the sacred processions.

The Great Serpent of the Egyptian Underworld was Apep, who tried to swallow the Sun god every night as the Sun boat passed through Tuat, or the Underworld of Darkness. Budge[14] wrote that the chambers of Tuat were actually the inside of Apep's serpentine body. Sebek (the Hidden One; Lord of Death; he who is shut in) was the Egyptian crocodile god, who was believed to live at the bottom of the Underworld in a secret pyramid filled with total darkness.

Ptah (the Opener; the Divine Artificer) in many ways was similar to the Greek Hephaestus, an Underworld deity. Ptah was associated with regeneration and the goddess Sekhmet.

Another Egyptian Lord of Death was Seker, who was the Black Sun that lay hidden inside a lightless pyramid in the Underworld.[15] The necropolis at Sakkar was named after him.[16] In Babylon, he was known as Zagar, the messenger from the Moon or the Land of the Dead.

The idea of the Moon being linked with the Underworld was a widespread idea in the Middle East and the Mediterranean area. The Phrygians god Sabazius was similar to the gods Attis and Dionysus;

Robert Graves even links this deity with the Hebrew Jehovah.[17] The Greek god Zeus also had the name Zeus Sabazius. This Phrygian god Sabazius was a serpent-deity of the Underworld or the Dead, and was worshipped at night. It is possible that the words Sabbath and Sabbat came from the name Sabazius. The Babylonians and Assyrians believed that every seventh day was holy and that it was bad luck to do anything mundane at that time. The Jews and Christians adopted this idea, calling this seventh day the Sabbath. Both sects believed that their god rested on the seventh day; however, long before these religions evolved, the gods Ba'al, Ptah, Ahura Mazdah, and Marduk were said to have rested on the seventh day.

The Hindu god Shiva is one of the oldest of the Vedic pantheon. He was known as the Lord of Yoga, the Corpse, Lord of Cattle, Great Lord, Lord of the Dance, Beneficent One, Lord Who is Half Woman, God with the Moon in His Hair (Shakala Shiva),[18] He Who Belongs to the Triple Goddess, He Who Gives and Takes Away, the Condemned One, the Destroyer, and the Howler.[19] He has several God aspects, among them the Lover, Sacrificed Savior, Lord of Creation, and Lord of Death.

As Shiva the Corpse, he lay under the feet of Kali. One of the most dramatic images of Kali Ma shows her squatting over the dead Shiva, devouring his penis with her vagina, while physically eating his intestines.[20] This image is not meant to be taken literally. In a spiritual sense, Kali takes the seed into her eternal womb to be recreated. She also devours and destroys all life in order for it to be reformed.

As the corpse, Shiva is symbolic of the necessity of everything to die or disintegrate at the end of a given cycle of life. He also shows us that death is not the end, but merely the beginning of another existence.

As Lord of the Dance, Shiva copied Kali's Dance of Life, which brings all things into being. Shiva is said to perform this dance in the Center of the Universe, which is really within the human heart.[21] However, as Kali gives life and takes it away, so does Shiva. Thus, his Dance is also the Dance of Death. He is rarely shown alone, for he cannot act without his union with Kali. As the Dancer, Shiva symbolizes the power of the Pagan God when He acts with the Goddess within the framework of Her universal laws.

In the Hindu pantheon, the god Yama, Lord of Death, was said to have a twin sister, Yami. He wanted to keep himself pure, so he refused to mate with her. Because Yami represented his feminine side and the life-giving aspects, Yama died and went into the Underworld where he became king.[22] His worshippers know Yama as a psychopomp.[23] Another of Yama's titles is Samana ("the Leveller"). Sometimes he is portrayed as having a bull-head and blue skin.[24] Connected with owls, pigeons, and brindled watchdogs, Yama judged humans for fulfillment of their dharma.

Two gods in Tibet were associated with the Underworld and death: Mara and Yama. Mara was called the Lord of Death and the Evil One, while Yama (the Restrainer) was hailed as King of the Underworld and the judge of human souls. Yama's rival and opponent was Yamantaka (Destroyer of the Lord of Death).

It is possible that he was known in Persia as Yima the Splendid, who was called the Good Shepherd; this Persian deity was said to give immortality to humans. In ancient Canaan, there was a similar god, Yamm, Lord of the Abyss; according to legend, Yamm was defeated annually by Ba'al in an unending conflict for the favors of the goddess Astarte.

The Hindu Agni, a Vedic god of fire, was in many ways similar to the Greek Hephaestus.[25] Since the sages said that everything in the universe is composed of blood and fire, Agni was believed to consume the sacrifices burned on the altars. His consort was Ambika ("Little Mother"), an aspect of Kali. The Hindu dwarf-god Kubera was ruler of the Earth and all treasures within the Earth. He is similar to Hephaestus.

Rudra was an ancient Vedic god of the dead and prince of demons. He was associated with death, disease, and wild animals. Puchan (the Nourisher) was the god who conducted the souls of the dead to the afterworld.

In Persian mythology, Ahriman was known as the Great Serpent and the Lord of Darkness, the rival of Ahura Mazdah. The prophet Zoroaster called this god the leader of the daevas or devils, although the word *daevas* originally meant "gods" in the Indo-Iranian language.

Ahriman and Ahura Mazdah were twins, born to the androgynous deity called Zurvan, who was actually the Crone of Time.

These twin brothers were rivals over heaven and Earth and the Earth's inhabitants. The Persians called Ahura Mazdah the Heavenly Father. Ahriman created the material world, however, and his influence was actually greater.

Ahriman of Persia was the spirit of Darkness and deception. He introduced physical death into the world and was considered to be the leader of the evil daevas (demons). He was called Prince of Demons and the Great Serpent.

Ahriman and his daevas fought a war in heaven against Ahura Mazdah. When Ahriman was defeated, he and his army were thrown into the Underworld; this is the origin of the Christian story of the fall of Lucifer and the eternal struggle between good and evil. Ahriman is also said to have tempted the first humans on Earth. Persian legends say that at the end of the world there will be a last great battle between Ahriman and his brother, with Ahriman and his daevas being defeated.

Although Ahriman was called the Lord of Darkness, the Persian Magi sacrificed to him as the source of their magickal power. Mithraic shrines have been found as far north as Yorkshire, England; one such shrine was dedicated to Arimanius, an Underworld god who was the source of magickal arts.[26]

The Canaanite god Mot was the rival and twin of the god Aleyin or Ba'al. A deity of vegetation in the winter season, Mot represented death or sterility. Legend says Mot was forsaken by his father El and castrated. He was cut with a sickle, beaten with flails, and his pieces scattered over the fields by the goddess Anat or Anatha. In Babylon and Jerusalem Mot was known under the names of Tammuz and Dumuzi.

The Babylonian god Nergal was the god of the Underworld and the Black Underworld Sun. At one time, he may have been a deity of the desert, like the Egyptian god Set, for he was said to rule over desert storms; however, when he was exiled by the gods to the Underworld, he conquered the goddess Ereshkigal and made her his wife.

The god Nergal was an Akkadian Underworld deity also accepted by the Babylonians. As consort of Ereshkigal, queen of the dead, Nergal was the Black Sun,[27] or God of Darkness, much like Saturn and Hades.

Many cultures in the Middle East believed that a Black Sun ruled in the Underworld as the Bright Sun did in the heavens. Aciel, of Chaldea, was the Black Sun of the Underworld and god of the darkness at the bottom of the seventh pit there.

Chernobog, the Black God of the Slavs, was the rival of their White God, Byelobog. Chernobog was an Underworld deity, a Lord of Death, the negative half of the spiritual. The Finnish-Ugrian god Tuoni was called the Lord of Manala (the Underworld) and death.

In China, Chu-Jung was known as the god of fire, executions, revenge, and death, while Yeng-Wang-Yeh was one of the ten Lords of Death and the ruler of hell.[28] Emma-O/Emma-Hoo of Japan was associated with death, revenge, and destruction; he was honored as the ruler of the Underworld.

In Africa, the tribes of the Volta regions had a god called Kaka-Guia; he was a funerary deity who brought dead souls before the Supreme God to be judged.

The Aztecs had several gods of death and destruction. Huitzilopochtli (Hummingbird on the Left or South) was associated with war and death. Itzcoliuhqui (Twisted Obsidian One) was a god of darkness, terrible cold, volcanic eruptions, and disaster. Tezcatlipoca (Mirror that Smokes; the Shadow) was the dark aspect of Quetzalcoatl; he was connected with evil, dark magick, and disaster. Mictlantecuhtli (Lord of the land of the dead) was called the god of the Underworld, as was Xolotl (the Animal). Tezcatlipoca, sometimes called the Soul of the World, represented the Winter Sun. Among the Incas, Supai was known as the god of the Underworld and death.

On the Pacific Island of Fiji, the people said that the Lord from Hades came in December to push the yam shoots through the soil.

UNDERSTANDING THE LORD
OF THE UNDERWORLD

The true Pagan God, in His aspect as the Lord of Death, is not a fearsome entity. Rather, He is one of great compassion. His appearance takes away pain and suffering; He guides the departing soul to a place of peace, where it can be healed and then move on to greater learning opportunities. Through Him, we learn to know and understand the darker aspects of the Goddess in Her role as the Elder One, the Crone of Wisdom, and the Lady of Death.

XIV

RECOVERING THE FORGOTTEN TRUE GOD

There is a vital need in the world today to return to, recognize, and understand the God in His true form. This is the only way both women and men can gain completeness in their physical, mental, emotional, and spiritual lives. If we continue to ignore the damage done by the false god-image created by patriarchal religions, humankind will only sink deeper into the mire of disconnection, self-condemnation, and carefully bred fear of all who do not belong to a specific "chosen" religion.

Many women and men have turned away from any aspect of the God because of the manipulation of the orthodox deity. They are no longer comfortable relating to any aspect of the God, nor, ironically enough, do they feel complete without Him. Perhaps this book will aid them in discovering their way back to the original, and still viable, God.

Women probably have the most difficulty, since they have been alienated by the patriarchal view of God. After all, when the patriarchies remade the God in their image, they created a deity who saw females as slaves, child-bearers, and sexual satisfiers, not as people.

Men are finally getting wise to this god who has been held up as their impossible role model and deity. This god is a deity of subtle destruction: destruction of the world, and most importantly, of individual belief in the self and abilities to make choices.

The soul-barrenness caused by this needs to be filled. Reconnection is needed for humans to be complete. We cannot reach our birthright of spiritual heights without this reconnection with the true nature of the God.

Neither the Goddess nor the God is complete alone. As with the shaktis of the Hindu deities, they must work together. Also, each has within His/Herself a small portion of the other, just as humans have both female and male aspects. Their partnership has stood from the beginning of the universe and continues, even though we may not acknowledge it. Humans can learn a lot from this cosmic example of how to cooperate for the mutual good of the Earth and its inhabitants.

A side benefit, which should be of interest to us all, is the knowledge of how to further personal spiritual growth. The God and Goddess work with sincere individuals who seek esoteric knowledge; they do not hand out ideas to religions, churches, or large groups. The ancient Mystery Religions were well aware that enlightenment came one person at a time, not from large memberships.

Joseph Campbell says that there are three stages of spiritual growth: separation, initiation, and return. Separation occurs when individuals pull away from religious organizations because they are unfulfilled. This is exactly what is happening today. Thousands of members are leaving orthodox religions because of the problems they find there. The crumbs of spirituality dispensed are few and far between, if any.

The initiation phase begins when the seeking person discovers a path that feels right and pursues study of that path. The word "initiation" used by Campbell does not refer to acceptance into a group, baptism, or even initiation into a Pagan or esoteric belief. All true initiations come privately, individually, in the heart and soul of each person.

Return is perhaps the hardest phase of spiritual growth. The initiated seeker must eventually come down out of the spiritual clouds and face reality. It means that each person must apply what he or she has learned in everyday life. This is not done by preaching at others, proselytizing, or feeling smug that you "have found the way." Being spiritual does not give anyone the right to walk away from responsibility, to break national laws, or to annoy others. That kind of attitude places you in the same camp as the orthodox religions. Return means that you quietly live your life according to the spiritual beliefs that satisfy your inner longing.

We experience these phases in our everyday physical life, in nearly everything we do. We become disenchanted with a job, relationship, or project and disconnect ourselves. We seek until we discover something better, losing ourselves in it for a period of time. Then we return to a balance in our way of living and our outlook on life itself.

Humanity has taken centuries to get to the point of dissatisfaction with orthodox spiritual ideas and claims. The tiny crack in the orthodox dam (which conceals the truth) is just beginning to show. A trickle of people are searching for the spiritual truth about the true God and Goddess. According to cosmic law, each seeker will return to her/his everyday place, setting an example for others. Slowly but surely, these examples will lead others to search for the truth about the God and the Goddess.

A return of both the true Goddess and true God will help heal many world problems. True, perfect, and complete enlightenment comes only through recognition of the place, purpose, and necessity of both the Goddess and the God in their true Pagan forms.

I hope this book has given you food for thought and the incentive to search for the truth. May you have a pleasant and rewarding journey.

APPENDIX I

MEDITATIONS

One of the most viable and valuable ways to make a connection with the true God is through meditation. The process is relaxing to the physical body, but stimulating and enlightening to the mind and spirit. If you have not tried meditation or have experienced poor results before, it is easier than you expect. Complete, easy instructions for meditation follow. Just be patient, and don't expect too much of yourself in the beginning.

There is nothing to fear about meditation. You will be completely safe and protected at all times. If you encounter anything within a meditation that frightens you, you are able to leave the meditation at once without any problems. After each meditation, you will feel healthier, happier, and better about yourself.

Each time you enter meditation, there are certain things you should think about doing. You need a room or place where you will not be disturbed; sudden noises or interruptions can be a shock to the body. Soft, non-vocal music helps by covering small background noises, but this is not absolutely necessary. Candles and incense are not necessary, either; however, if you do wish to use them, be certain you set the candle where it will not be accidentally overturned and the incense where you won't choke on the smoke. Choose a comfortable chair where the light will not shine in your face, but the room need not be dark. Lying down usually leads to sleep, so I don't suggest this position.

As you close your eyes and begin each meditation, visualize yourself surrounded by brilliant white light. Mentally wrap it around you and breathe it in; this gives you protection while you meditate. Relax your body, beginning with your feet and ending with your head. Your neck, shoulders, and jaw will probably take more time as tension builds up there. Don't try too hard to relax, as that will defeat the purpose.

Next, visualize standing beside a well or pool of water. Take all the negative people, events, and situations in your life and drop them into the water. Then turn and walk away. This tells your subconscious mind, which communicates only in symbols, that you want to be rid of these problems. It also keeps you from carrying negatives along with you during the meditation.

Each person will experience a God aspect in a different way. In fact, you may well experience a God aspect differently each time you explore it. This is natural. The God may look different; He can appear as any racial type, not necessarily your own or the one you prefer to visualize.

The following meditations are not difficult and will gradually lead you into greater communication with the true God. In fact, each time you do a meditation, you may experience many things in a slightly different manner. Details within the scenery may change from time to time, such as different flowers, figures, and other scenery. Just remember, if at any time you feel uncomfortable, you can always leave safely. If you become frightened or merely are ready to leave, simply return to the door or other portal where you entered.

Toward the end of each meditation, you are provided with a space where you can explore on your own without guided directions.

SEEKING THE GOD ASPECTS

You can repeat this meditation to explore further any aspect of the God you wish. Each time you return, you will feel better about yourself and your spiritual goals.

Prepare yourself for meditation according to the above instructions. As you walk away from the well or pool where you left your negative problems, you see before you a path leading to gates in a high wall. As you approach the gates, they swing open to reveal a beautiful garden. You enter, and the gates shut behind you.

It is very peaceful in this garden. The flowers and trees are brilliant with color. Little paths lead in many directions. As you walk along one of the paths, you see benches and fountains, little pools with fish, alcoves with seats, and statues. Birds and little animals are everywhere. They are friendly and curious.

As you wander through this peaceful setting, you realize you can smell the flower scents on the warm air. You drink from one of the fountains and find the water cool and sweet in your mouth. The sun is warm on your skin as you walk along.

Then, off through the trees, you see several marble buildings. Each one is built in a different architectural style. Some have the columns and porches of Greece, while others look like Egyptian temples. Every ancient culture is represented by a building somewhere in this garden.

You follow the path onward until you come to a great circular building of white and black marble. The door is slightly open, and the sound of beautiful, enticing music is coming from inside. You climb the shallow steps and walk inside.

The building is cool and pleasant. Filtered light shines down through stained glass windows set into the domed roof. All around the curved walls are a series of doors, and beside each one is a small bench. In the center of the room is a round altar, decorated with gold and silver symbols; on it is a vase of flowers and greenery.

You walk around the room and find that each door has the name of a God aspect written on it: child, lover, sky, forest, healer, trickster, judge and prophet, hero/warrior, magician, waters, savior, and underworld.

Take all the time you need to decide which God aspect you want to experience. When you have decided, open that door and step through.

If you want to end the experience at any time, think of the door and it will appear. Go back through it into the circular room. Then, you can wander back through the garden or choose to end the meditation. To return to your physical body, simply think of it and you will be there. Sit still for a few minutes, readjusting and remembering your experiences.

PURIFICATION OF OLD, OBSTRUCTING IDEAS

This meditation can be repeated as many times as you like, until you can dissolve the beliefs that cause you to be separated from the truth about the God.

Before you begin this meditation, take time to consider all the false ideas you have about each aspect of the God. It doesn't matter why or how you got the ideas, just that you recognize them for what they are—false. It helps if you write these down.

Prepare yourself for meditation according to the above instructions. As you walk away from the well or pool where you left your negative problems, you see before you a path leading to gates in a high wall. As you approach the gates, they swing open to reveal a beautiful garden. You enter, and the gates shut behind you.

You may want to wander through the garden before you seek out the circular temple. You can enjoy the birds and animals, the beautiful flowers and trees, or the peacefulness of the sheltered alcoves with benches.

When you are ready, follow any path, for they all lead to the round building. Climb the shallow steps and go inside. The stained glass windows in the high dome reflect their brilliant colors onto the marble floor and the round altar in the center of the room. This time, beside the altar is a large incense burner, its smoke gently lifting toward the ceiling.

Walk to the altar and stand beside it. There you will see your list of false ideas about the God written on parchment in a beautiful ancient style of writing. Read over the parchment, and consider which false ideas you can now replace with the truth. Reach out with one finger and touch the old idea on the parchment. That idea will come loose like a strip of ribbon. Drop it onto the burning coals in the burner. It will immediately curl into ashes and disappear.

If the idea refuses to burn, it will float up from the coals and return to the parchment. This means that you have not truly removed the false idea and are holding on to some part of it. You will need to try again during another meditation.

As you successfully rid yourself of each falsehood, you will hear what sounds like wind chimes or tiny bells. When you are finished, a white bird flies in through the door and lands on the altar. In its beak is a piece of greenery. It drops the green twig and looks at you. You can feel the message of love it brings. You feel at peace with yourself. The bird flies out of the temple, leaving you alone.

You can now wander about the garden, or you can choose to return at once to your physical body. Whenever you are ready to end the meditation, simply think of your body and you will be back inside it.

INITIATION IN THE UPPERWORLD

Prepare yourself for meditation according to the above instructions. As you walk away from the well or pool where you left your negative problems, you see before you a path leading to gates in a high wall. As you approach the gates, they swing open to reveal a beautiful garden. You enter, and the gates shut behind you.

You may wish to wander about the garden for a time before you get further into the meditation. Take what time you need. When you are ready to experience your initiation into the Upperworld, you see a white stag with regal antlers coming through a grove of trees toward you. Unafraid, the stag comes to your side and looks at you with its dark eyes. In your mind you hear its words, "Follow me."

You follow the stag as it steps back among the trees. Within a few steps, you see a path before you that leads through the grove. In the distance stands a tall tower, silhouetted against the blue sky. The stag leads you until you stand at the foot of the tower. Then it turns and disappears back into the grove of trees.

The door into the tower is tall and narrow. You push it open and step inside. Candles light the way to a staircase which goes around and around the inside of the tower until it disappears through an opening in the top. You climb the stone steps quickly and step out onto a fluffy white cloud that feels like a thick carpet beneath your feet. Other clouds swirl about you like fog. This is the Upperworld, the area where the God, in His aspect of creator of the present life and future possibilities, can be found.

Suddenly, the clouds before you move apart and you see an ethereal-looking great hall. You walk through the clouds and step out onto a floor paved with silver and gold. You are met by a glowing figure, who gently guides you to a comfortable chair. You realize that this is part of the energy of the true God, come down to speak with you on your level of understanding.

The Upperworld God speaks with you about necessary changes in your present life. He may even tell you of possible outcomes. You may ask any questions about your present life and problems you might be having. Listen closely to what is said to you.

Whenever you are ready, the God gives you a beautiful red rose as a spiritual reminder of your visit. He holds up His hands, and the air about you begins to swirl and thicken. You feel the impurities blocking your spiritual path begin to dissolve. Your heart and soul open wide to the truth of the God. The swirling slows to a stop, and you are alone in the great hall.

You can either go back to the garden for a time, or you can choose to end the meditation. Whenever you want to end the meditation, just think of your physical body and immediately you are back within it. Relax for a few moments before writing down any details you want to remember about the meditation.

INITIATION IN THE UNDERWORLD

Prepare yourself for meditation according to the above instructions. As you walk away from the well or pool where you left your problems, you see before you a path leading to gates in a high wall. As you approach the gates, they swing open to reveal a beautiful garden. You enter, and the gates shut behind you.

You wander through the garden for a time. Suddenly, you find yourself in a thick grove of trees. Great boulders lie scattered among the trees, some alone, others grouped together. They are covered with green moss and surrounded by fragile woodland flowers. As you walk among them, you see a dark opening in a cluster of boulders and step forward to look at it closely.

You feel something brush against your leg and look down. A huge gray wolf stands there, his yellow eyes looking up into yours, his tongue hanging from his mouth as if he were smiling.

You feel no danger from the wolf, but hear his words, "Follow me," within your mind. He trots into the opening, and you go with him.

There is a faint glow inside the cave, as if a dim light comes from the walls themselves. The way leads quickly and easily downward, until the hidden path breaks into a gigantic underground cavern. The cavern is filled with spectacular rock formations and glittering crystals set in the walls. It is lit by numerous torches. You continue to follow the wolf as he leads you to the center of the cavern where a glowing figure awaits you.

There are stone benches and chairs covered with thick furs, all facing a central seat. On this seat is the bright form of the God in His aspect of lord of death, rebirth, and past lives. The wolf lies down at the God's feet. You are not afraid; a feeling of compassion and understanding sweeps over you as you sit beside the God.

The God speaks with you about your fears of death and rebirth. We have small "deaths" within each life, such as the end of relationships, goals, or even a way of life. He may even tell you of past lives that are still affecting your present one. You may ask any questions about your past lives and what talents or interests might be brought forward to help you in the present life. Listen closely to what is said to you.

Whenever you are ready, the God shows you a beautiful blue rose as a spiritual reminder of your visit. He holds up your red rose from the Upperworld and presses it against the blue rose of the Underworld. The two roses melt together, leaving a unique purple rose in His hands. He gives this to you.

The God touches your forehead, and you feel a swirling deep inside your body. The impurities blocking your spiritual path begin to dissolve. Your heart and soul open wide to the truth of the God. The swirling slows to a stop, and you are alone in the great cavern.

You may wish to return to the garden for a time, or you may choose to wander about the cavern. Take what time you need.

Whenever you want to end the meditation, just think of your physical body and immediately you are back within it. Relax for a few moments before writing down any details you want to remember about the meditation.

APPENDIX II

GODS & THEIR ATTRIBUTES

The following list by no means covers all the gods of the world's cultures. These descriptions will aid you in learning more about the various male deities and the powers associated with them.

Aciel (Chaldean): Black Sun of the Underworld; god of Darkness at the bottom of the seventh pit.

Addad/Haddad (Canaanite, Babylonian, Assyrian, Syrian, Mesopotamian): Lord of Foresight; the Crasher; Master of storms. His symbol was forked lightning, his animal the bull. Storms, foreseeing, destruction, the future, divination.

Adonis (Semitic, Greek, Roman): "Lord"; the Anointed One. Associated with the goddesses Aphrodite and Persephone. Celebration of his death and resurrection was at the Spring Equinox. Harvest, death, love and beauty, resurrection.

Adroa (African): "God in the sky"; "God on Earth"; Creator God; both good and evil. Social order, law, death.

Aegir (Norse): "Alebrewer"; Vanir god of the sea. He could be good or evil. Associated with the goddess Ran. Prosperity, sailing, brewing, control of wind and waves.

Agni/Pramati (Indian): "Thrice-born"; demon-slayer; god of fire; mediator between the gods and humans. His symbol, the sacrificial flames, represents the element of life in humans and animals. He purifies offerings and solemn ceremonies. Associated with the goddess Agnayi, another fire deity. Protector of the home, wealth, power, new beginnings, rebirth, immortality, justice, forgiveness, virility.

Ahriman/Angra Mainyu (Persian): Spirit of Darkness and deception; prince of demons; Great Serpent; twin spirit of Ahura Mazdah. Evil, destruction, rumor, lies, doubt, death, trickery.

Ahura Mazdah (Persian): The Lord; Great God; Master of Heaven; twin of Ahriman. Universal law, light, goodness, purification, prophetic revelation.

Amen/Amon (Egyptian): "Hidden God"; "Great Father"; similar to Zeus and Jupiter. A phallic deity, he was sometimes pictured with the head of a ram. Part of a trinity with Khensu and the goddess Mut. God of reproduction, fertility, generation, wind, air, prophecy, agriculture.

An/Anu (Mesopotamian, Babylonian, Assyrian, Sumerian): Father God; King of the Gods; Protector; God of Heaven. Associated with the goddess Antu. Power, justice, judgment, fate.

Anansi (African): Mr. Spider; the great Trickster; Creator God. The original source of the tar baby story.

Angus mac Og/Angus of the Brugh/Oengus of the Bruig (Irish): "Young Son." Youth, love, beauty.

Anubis (Egyptian): Pictured with the head of a dark-colored jackal. The messenger from the gods to humans, his cult was very ancient, probably older than that of Osiris. As god of embalming and tombs, protector of the dead, judge of the dead, and lord of the Underworld, he, along with the goddess Maat, weighed each human soul for truth. Wisdom, death, endings, truth, justice, spiritual journeys, protection, astral traveling.

Apollo (Greek, Roman): "Shining"; god of solar light; greatest of the gods after Zeus. His arrows brought illness or death. He demanded tolerance by his followers. Prophecy, poetry, music, medicine, reason, inspiration, magick, the arts, spiritual goals, woodlands, springs, justified revenge.

Apsu (Mesopotamian, Babylonian, Assyrian): First god; primordial ocean; the watery abyss.

Arawn (Welsh): King of Hell; God of Annwn, the underground kingdom of the dead. Revenge, terror, confusion.

Ares (Greek): God of war, uncontrolled anger, brute strength, untamed passions. Was considered bloodthirsty, a liar, and insensitive. The rival of the goddess Athene. Revenge, raw energy.

Asa (African): "The strong Lord"; Father God. Mercy, help, surviving the impossible or insurmountable.

Asagaya Gigaei (Cherokee): Thunder god.

Asclepius/Asklepios (Greek): God of healing and medicine. His college of medicine was the Asklepiades, where sleep and dream therapy were used; vast libraries were also found there. Associated with the goddesses Hygeia and Panacea. Rebirth, healing.

Asshur (Assyrian, Babylonian): King of gods; warrior and Sun god; supreme god; maker of the sky and Underworld. His symbol was a winged disk. Associated with the goddess Ninlil. Fertility, time, protection, victory, bravery, success.

Atea/Atea Rangi (Polynesian): Creator God; god of the sky, stars, and the regenerative life-force.

Atius Tirawa (Pawnee): Creator God; god of the Sun, Moon, and stars.

Ba'al/Baal (Canaanite, Phoenician): Supreme God; Master; Lord of the North. Associated with the goddess Asherat-of-the-Sea. Thunder, storms, fertility, death and resurrection, rebirth.

Bacchus/Liber/Liber Pater (Roman): The Liberator; similar to Dionysus. Associated with the goddess Libera. The ever-young god of wine, good times, ecstasy, fertility, wild Nature.

Balder/Baldr/Baldur (Norse): "The Bright One"; Shining God; the Bleeding God; Sun god. Associated with the goddesses Frigg and Nanna. Light, advice, reconciliation, beauty, gentleness, reincarnation, wisdom.

Bel/Belenus/Beli Mawr (Irish): "Shining"; Sun and fire god; Great God; similar to Apollo. Connected with the May festival of Beltane. Purification, fertility, agriculture, animals, fire, success, prosperity, healing, science.

Bes (Egyptian): "Lord of the land of Punt." Pictured as a leopard-skin-clad dwarf with a huge head, prominent eyes, and protruding tongue. Protection, luck, marriage, childbirth, music, dance.

Bragi (Norse): God of poetry and the skalds. Associated with the goddess Idunn. Eloquence, music, writing, the arts.

Brahma (Indian): Father of the gods and humans; creator of the universe; guardian of the world. Guardian of the sacred Vedas. Associated with the goddess Sarasvati. Magick, wisdom, knowledge.

Bran the Blessed/Benedigeidfran (Welsh): "The Blessed"; "Raven." His animal was the raven. Associated with the goddess Branwen. Prophecy, the arts, music, writing, leadership.

Buddha (Indian, others): "The Enlightened One"; Divine Teacher. In Tibet there were a number of Cosmic Buddhas. Associated with his deified mother Maya. Spiritual illumination, wisdom, self-realization.

Byelobog (Slavic): The White God; the positive half of the spiritual. Light, good, creation.

Cernunnos/Cernowain/Cernenus (all Celtic areas): The Horned God; god of Nature; god of the Underworld and the astral plane; Great Father. The Druids called him Hu Gadarn. He wore antlers; his animals were the stag, ram, bull, and horned serpent. Fertility, physical love, Nature, woodlands, reincarnation, crossroads, wealth.

Chac (Mayan): "Long-nose"; a rain and vegetation god.

Chernobog (Slavic): The Black God; the negative half of the spiritual. Dark, evil, destruction.

Chimati No Kami (Japanese): God of crossroads and footpaths; the positive creative force of life; a phallic deity. Fertility.

Chuku/Chineke (African): "The first great cause"; "Creator." Associated with the goddess Ale. Help, goodness.

Cinteotl (Aztec): God of corn who took the original place of the goddess Cihuacoatl.

Coyote (many Native American tribes): Similar to the Norse Loki. A Trickster who represented the breaking free of negative power from the universal order of things.

Cronus/Kronos (Greek): Father Time; the Old King; the Great Lesson-Giver; Ruler of the Golden Age. Associated with the goddesses Gaea and Rhea. Agriculture, prosperity, the arts, magick, the Earth's riches.

Dagda, The (Irish): "The Good God"; "All-father"; Lord of the Heavens; Lord of Life and Death; god of magick; Earth God. Associated with the goddesses Brigit and the Morrigan. Protection, magick, the arts, prophecy, weather, reincarnation, initiation, healing, regeneration, prosperity, music, knowledge.

Dagon/Dagan (Philistine): Sea god shown as a merman or serpent-man. Associated with the goddess Atargatis. Fishing, agriculture.

Danh (African): Snake god; the origin of the Haitian god Don Petro. Wholeness, unity.

Daramulun (Australian): Sky god with a stone axe, a mouth full of crystal, and an exaggerated phallus. The bull-roarer was his symbol. Fertility, creation, initiation.

Diancecht/Dian Cecht (Irish): Physician-magician of the Tuatha. Associated with the goddess Airmid. Healing, medicine, regeneration, magick.

Dionysus (Greek): "Horned God"; "Savior"; "the Roaring One"; "the Initiated"; "the bull-headed god"; also called Dithyrambos ("double-birth" or "twice-born"). Connected with the Eleusinian Mysteries as the Divine Child Iacchus. Associated with the goddesses

Demeter and Persephone. Pleasure, ecstasy, total abandon, woodlands and all Nature, initiation, rituals, rebirth.

Dumuzi/Tammuz (Mesopotamian, Sumerian): Only-begotten Son; Son of the Blood; Anointed One. Associated with the goddess Ishtar. A sacrificed god. Harvest, fertility, the Underworld, resurrection.

Ea/Enki (Mesopotamian, Babylonian, Sumerian): House of the Water; Lord of Earth; Lord of the Sacred Eye; Lord of the Underworld or primordial ocean. Represented as a goat with the tail of a fish. Considered a friend of humans and the source of all secret magickal knowledge. Purification, initiation, crafts, wisdom, prophecy, judgment, justice, weather, knowledge.

El (Canaanite, Phoenician, Akkadian, Babylonian): Master of Time; Supreme God; Father of Years; creator and war god. Wore bull horns. Strength, victory, fertility, power.

Emma-Hoo/Emma-O (Japanese): Male Ruler of the Underworld. Death, destruction.

Enlil/Bel (Sumerian, Babylonian, Assyrian): Lord of the world; dispenser of good and evil. He held the Tablets of Destiny by which the fates of humans and gods were decreed. Associated with the goddesses Ninhursag and Belit. Storms, destruction, destiny, order, the laws, influence, wisdom.

Erh-Lang (Chinese): "Second Lord"; the great restorer; the sustainer; god who chases away evil spirits; a shapeshifter. Protection from evil.

Eros (Greek): God of bringing together; God of erotic love. Associated with the goddess Aphrodite. Useless self-sacrifice.

Faunus/Lupercus (Roman): "Little God"; Horned God; very ancient and similar to Pan. Honored in February. Gardens, orchards, flocks, agriculture, fertility, Nature, woodlands, music, dance, medicine, prophecy. He also had Pan's dark side.

Freyr (Norse): "Lord"; Vanir Sun god; "the Lover"; god of Yule. His animals were boars and horses. Associated with the goddesses Freyja and Gerda. Sensual love, fertility, growth, abundance, joy, happiness, weather.

Fugen Bosatsu (Japanese): God of enlightening wisdom, intelligence, understanding, intuition, long life.

Ganesha/Ganesa/Ganapati/Gajani (Indian): "Elephant-face"; Lord of obstacles. His festival was in August. It is said that if Ganesha is worshipped at this time, wishes will come true. Associated with the goddess Parvati. Wisdom, good luck, literature, writing, worldly success, prosperity, peace, beginnings, journeys, overcoming obstacles, taming dangerous forces.

Gauna/Gawa/Gawama (African): Leader of the spirits of the dead. Disruption, harassment, death.

Ge (African): Moon god. Associated with the goddess Mawu.

Gidja (Australian): Moon god and totemic ancestor of the Dreamtime. Dreams, physical sex.

Gluskap (Algonquin): Similar to King Arthur. Strength, wisdom, rescue.

Goidniu/Gofannon/Govannon (Irish, Welsh): "Great Smith"; similar to Vulcan. One of a triad with Luchtaine the wright and Creidne the brazier. Metal-working, magick, jewelry, brewing, fire.

Green Man (Irish, British): Opener of the Gates of Life and Death. In Old Welsh his name was Arddhu (The Dark One), Atho, or the Horned God. God of the woodlands. See **Cernunnos**.

Gucumatz (Mayan): "Feathered Snake." God of agriculture and civilization; a shapeshifter. He lived in both heaven and hell.

Gwydion (Welsh): Prince of the Powers of Air; a shapeshifter. Wizard and bard of north Wales. A many-skilled deity like Lugh, he was the greatest of enchanters and a warrior-magician. His animal was the white horse. Illusion, changes, healing.

Gwynn ap Nudd (Welsh): King of the Faeries and the Underworld. Later he became the king of the Plant Annwn, or subterranean faeries. Leader of the Wild Hunt.

Gwythyr (Welsh): King of the Upper World. Opposite of Gwynn ap Nudd.

Hades (Greek): "The invisible one"; Ruler of the Underworld. Also called Pluto or Pluton, Lord of Riches. Associated with the goddess Kore/Persephone. Springs, gems, minerals, material gain, elimination of fear of death, astral projection.

Hay-Tau (Phoenician): Similar to Adonis; his symbol was the bull. Forests, Nature.

Heimdall (Norse): "The White God"; Vanir god of Light and the rainbow. Associated with the goddess Freyja. Protection, beginnings and endings, defense against evil.

Helios (Greek): God of the actual Sun. Riches, enlightenment, victory.

Hephaestus (Greek): God of volcanoes, fire, and metal-working. Manual dexterity, hard work, inventiveness, all creative crafts.

Hermes (Greek): "The ram-bearer"; the Good Shepherd; "Leader of Souls"; messenger of the gods. A Trickster deity, but also a highly skilled Magician. Travel, medicine, occult wisdom, success, profits, crossroads.

Herne the Hunter (British): Similar to Cernunnos and the Green Man. He has come to be associated with Windsor Forest and has taken on attributes of Gwynn ap Nudd with his Wild Hunt. The forest, wild animals, alertness, annihilation, panic.

Hodur/Hoth/Hothr/Bjorno-Hoder (Norse): "The blind god"; Aesir god of winter. Associated with the goddess Frigg. Passiveness.

Horus (Egyptian): Falcon-headed Sun and sky deity; Divine Child or reborn Sun; identified with Apollo. He was pictured as very fair with blue eyes, and was associated with cats. As the Divine Falcon, his eyes were the Sun and the Moon. Mainly connected with Isis, although he is associated with many goddesses. Prophecy, revenge, justice, success, problem solving, the arts.

Hou-Chi (Chinese): "Prince Millet"; ancient harvest deity. Harvest, crops.

Hsuan-T'ien-Shang-Ti (Chinese): "Supreme Lord of the Dark Heaven"; regent of water. Deity who removes evil spirits and demons. Exorcism.

Huehuecoyotl/Ueuecoyotl (Aztec): "Old, old coyote"; an uncontrollable Trickster. Physical sex, gaiety.

Huehueteotl/Xiuhtecuhtli (Aztec): "Turquoise Lord"; "Old God"; fire god. His festival was August 1.

Huitzilopochtli (Aztec): "Hummingbird on the Left (South)"; "Left-Handed Hummingbird." The Sun, death, storms, journeys.

Hurukan (Mayan): "Triple Heart of the Universe"; a very ancient god. Hurricanes, destructive winds, spiritual enlightenment.

Ilma (Finnish): God of the air. Associated with the goddess Luonnotar/Ilmatar.

Imhotep/I-Em-Hetep (Egyptian): "He who comes in peace." Similar to the Greek Aesculapius. Study and knowledge, medicine, magick, compassion, herbs.

Indra/Parjanya/Svargapati (father of the shining palace)/**Meghavahana** (cloud-rider)/**Vajri** (thunderer)/**Sashra** (Indian): King of the gods; Lord of Storm; Great God. His symbol is the thunderbolt, his animals are the white elephant and horses. Associated with the goddesses Indrani and Lakshmi. Fertility, storms, bravery, strength, reincarnation, love, personal intervention, law, magick, creativity.

Inti (Incan): Sun god pictured as a great golden disk with a face. Associated with Mama Quilla, the Moon goddess. Festival celebrated at the harvest of the maize. Fertility, crops.

Ioskeha (Iroquois): Good creator deity, the twin brother of Tawiscara, who personified complete evil.

Itzamna (Mayan): Sky god; father of the gods and creator of humans; Lord of Day and Night; considered omnipotent. Associated with the goddess Ixchel. His animal was the jaguar. Healing, knowledge, fertility, regeneration.

Itzcoliuhqui (Aztec): "Twisted obsidian one"; "curved obsidian knife." Darkness, volcanic eruptions, disaster.

Izanagi (Japanese): Creator God; Earth god; Great Father; the male principle. Associated with the goddess Izanami.

Janus (Roman): Called Janus Pater (god of gods), he came before even Jupiter. He had two faces or heads, each looking in opposite directions. Past wisdom and future knowledge, beginnings and endings, journeys, success.

Jizo Bosatsu (Japanese): Protector of humans; rescuer of souls from hell; protector of women in childbirth. Death, comfort, counsel for the dead, protection from evil.

Julunggul/Great Rainbow Snake (Australian): Totemic deity of the Dreamtime; bisexual life-giver; Great God. Rain, procreation, magick, life.

Jumala/Mader-Atcha (Finnish): Supreme God; Creator God. The oak was sacred to him. Associated with the goddess Rauni. Thunder, weather.

Jupiter (Roman): "The smiter"; "best and greatest"; "stayer"; Supreme God; Lord of the heavens. Protector of the laws, justice, and the weak. The Elements, agriculture, storms, health, luck, protection, friendships.

Kaka-Guia/Nyami (African): A funerary god, he brought dead souls to the Supreme God.

Kama/Kamadevi/Dipaka (the inflamer)**/Gritsa** (the sharp)**/Mayi** (the deluder)**/Mara** (the destroyer)**/Ragavrinta** (the stalk of passion)**/ Titha** (fire) (India): Great God; god of desire. An ever-young deity, he is associated with the goddesses Rati and the Apsaras.

Kannon Bosatsu/Kannon/Kwannon (Japanese): A male form of the Chinese Kuan Yin. Mercy, compassion.

Katonda (African): Creator God; Savior; First King; Father God. Help, judgment, aid against all odds, control over spirits, divination.

Khensu/Khons/Khonsu (Egyptian): "Traveler"; "the Navigator"; "He who crosses the sky in a boat." As god of the New Moon and son of Amen-Ra and Mut, his head was shaved except for the scalp-lock tress of a royal child.

Khepera/Khepra/Khepri (Egyptian): "He who becomes"; the scarab beetle; symbol of creative energy and eternal life. Transformation, resurrection, reincarnation, new beginnings, miracles, exorcism, healing.

Khnemu/Khnum (Egyptian): "The Molder"; "the Divine Potter." Pictured as a man with a ram's head and long, wavy horns. Associated with the goddess Anqet. Arts and crafts, fertility, creation.

Kitcki Manitou/Kici Manitu/Manitou (many Native American tribes): "Great Spirit"; "the Father"; Master of Light; Supreme Creator; the spirit in everything.

Krishna (Indian): The Dark One; "Black"; "Stealer of Hearts"; the Savior God. The Hindus called him Redeemer, Firstborn, Sin Bearer, Liberator, the Universal Word. Associated with the goddess Radha. Erotic delights, love, music, savior from sins.

Kubera/Kuvera/Khanapati/Dhanapati (lord of riches)**/Jambhalla** (Indian): A dwarf god of the Earth and treasures from the Earth. Fertility, wealth, gems, metals.

Kuan Ti (Chinese): God of war and fortunetelling. Protection, valor, justice, divination, revenge, death.

Kukulcan (Mayan): "Feathered Serpent"; a form of Quetzalcoatl. Light, learning, culture, organization and order, laws, the calendar.

Lao-Tien-Yeh (Chinese): "Father Heaven"; the Jade Emperor; Great God.

Leshy (Slavic): God of the forests. He was dangerous, especially in the spring after a long winter's sleep.

Llyr/Lear/Lir (Irish, Welsh). God of the sea and water, possibly of the Underworld. Associated with the goddess Branwen.

Loki (Norse): "Father of lies"; the Trickster; Sky-Traveler; a shapeshifter. Blood-brother of Odhinn. Associated with the goddess Sigyn. Earthquakes, fire, storms, cunning, wit, deceit, trickery, revenge, destruction, death, lies.

Lud/Llud/Llud Llaw Ereint/Llud of the Silver Hand/Nuada/Nudd/ Nodons/Nodens (Irish, Welsh): "Silver Hand"; "he who bestows wealth"; "the Cloud-Maker"; similar to Neptune. Healing, the seas, childbirth, youth, crafts, writing, magick, incantations.

Lugh/Lugh Lamhfada (of the Long Arm)**/Llew/Lug/Lug Samildananch** (many-skilled)**/Lleu Llaw Gyffes** ("bright one of the skillful hand")/**Lleu/Lugos** (Ireland, Wales): The Shining One; "Fair-haired one"; "white or shining"; Sun god. He was honored at Lunasa on August 1. His animals were the raven, hound, and white stag. Crafts, music, poetry, healing, magick, commerce, reincarnation, journeys, initiation, prophecy.

Maitreiya/Metteyya (Tibetan): Name of the Buddha to come; "the Benevolent One"; Buddha of the future.

Manannan mac Lir/Manawydan ap Llyr/Manawydden (Irish, Welsh): A shapeshifter; sea god. His animal was the pig. Boat journeys, fertility, weather, magick, the arts, rebirth.

Mara (Tibetan): Lord of Death; the Evil One; demon of desire. Master magician of illusion and magick.

Marduk (Mesopotamian, Canaanite, Sumerian, Babylonian, Assyrian): Bull calf of the Sun; Great God; Lord of Life. Governor of the four quarters of the Earth. Associated with the goddesses Tiamat and Sarpanitu. Fate, courage, healing, magick, agriculture, resurrection, justice, law, rebirth, victory, purification, initiation.

Marruni (Melanesian): Creator God; deity of earthquakes.

Mars (Roman): God of Spring, war, agriculture. Originally he was the Etruscan fertility-savior, Maris. His animals were the woodpecker, horse, and wolf. Terror, anger, revenge, courage.

Math Mathonwy (Welsh): God of sorcery, magick, enchantment.

Maui (Polynesian): "Maui of the thousand tricks"; greatest of Tricksters and a shapeshifter; helper of humans. Magick, the sea, death, sorcery.

Menthu/Mont (Egyptian): "Lord of Thebes." A Sun god, often with a bull head, wearing a solar disk. Associated with the goddess Rat-Taui. Protection, war, vengeance.

Mercury/Mercurius (Roman): Messenger of the gods; similar to Hermes. He carried the caduceus and wore winged sandals. Cunning, commerce, success, magick, travel, profits, crossroads, eloquence, messages.

Merlin/Merddin/Myrddin (Welsh, British): Great sorcerer associated with the faery religion of the Goddess. Old Welsh traditions called him a wild man of the woods with prophetic skills. Associated with Morgan and Nimue. Illusion, shapeshifting, magick, prophecy, crystals, spells.

Michabo (Algonquin): "Great Hare"; creator of humans, Earth, and animals. A shapeshifting magician.

Mictlantecuhtli (Aztec): "Lord of the land of the dead"; god of the Underworld; "Dead Land Lord." Associated with the goddess Mictlancihuatl.

Mimir/Mimr/Mimi (Norse): Very wise Aesir god whose head was kept at the Fountain of Mimir after his death. Wisdom, knowledge, springs, the arts.

Min/Menu (Egyptian): "Lord of Foreign Lands"; god of the eastern desert. Always portrayed with an erect phallus; the Greeks identified him with Pan. His symbols were the white bull and the thunderbolt. Sex, fertility, crops, harvest, roads, journeys.

Mithra/Mitra/Mithras (Persian): All-wise and knowing son of Ahura Mazdah. His symbol was the rayed Sun disk, his animals the boar and bull. His birthday was December 25. Moral purity, courage, predictions, wisdom, protection, spiritual illumination.

Mot (Canaanite, Phoenician): Lord of the Underworld. Twin and rival of the god Aleyin or Ba'al. Worshipped in Babylon and Jerusalem as Tammuz. Associated with the goddess Anat or Anatha. Harvest, regeneration, resurrection.

Nabu (Mesopotamian, Sumerian): Son of Marduk and deity of writing and destiny. His animal was a serpent-headed dragon. He was able to increase or decrease the length of a person's life. Associated with the goddess Tashmetum. Wisdom, accounting, literature, intercession.

Neptune (Roman): A sea god, he carried a trident and whip. His animals were horses and bulls. Earthquakes, storms, the seas.

Nereus/Proteus/Phorcys (Greek): "The old one of the sea"; a shapeshifter. A just and kind god, he knew the future.

Nergal/Meshlamthea (Babylonian): Lord of the great dwelling; Lord of attack; God of the Underworld; judge of the dead. A form of the black Underworld Sun, his symbol was a lion's head. Associated with the goddess Ereshkigal. Desert storms, battle, evil, death, wisdom, revenge, destruction.

Ninurta/Ningirsu (Sumerian, Akkadian, Assyrian, Babylonian, Mesopotamian): The Throne Carrier; God of war; messenger from the gods to humans. Son of Enlil, he was associated with the goddess Bau. Water and wells, destroyer of evil and enemies, agriculture, fertility, hunting.

Njord (Norse): Vanir god of the sea. Associated with the goddess Skadi. Winds, sailing, prosperity, success, journey, wisdom.

Oceanus/Okeanos (Greek): "He who belongs to the swift queen." An ancient serpent-sea god who took part in the creation of Cosmos out of Chaos, and whose power was later given to Poseidon. The arts, magick.

Odhinn/Odin/Wodin/Woden/Wotan/Othinn (Norse): Aesir king of the gods; "All-father"; Sky God; Great Father; All-Seeing; "Frenzied, mad"; God of the hanged and the Wild Hunt; a shapeshifter. He can inspire humans or possess them with a blind, raging fury; he can also produce a paralyzing panic. He was unpredictable when invoked. His animals were wolves, ravens, and horses. Associated with the goddess Freyja, Frigg, and the Valkyries. Poetry, words of power, magick, divination, storms, death, rebirth, knowledge, justice.

Ogma/Oghma/Ogmios/Grianainech (sun face)/**Cermaid** (honey-mouthed) (Irish): Similar to Hercules, he invented the Ogham script alphabet. Associated with Etan. Eloquence, poetry, writing, physical strength, inspiration, magick, the arts, music, reincarnation.

Ogun/Ogoun (African): God of iron and warfare. Removal of difficulties, justice, metal-working.

O-Kuni-Nushi/Okuninushi (Japanese): "Great Land Master"; Earth God. Medicine, sorcery, cunning, self-realization.

Olorun/Olofin-Orun (African): "Lord of heaven"; "Almighty"; "Supreme"; "Owner." Truth, control over the Elements, foreseeing, victory against odds, destiny.

Osiris (Egyptian): Lord of life after death; Sun god; Universal Lord; Nature god; Lord of Lords; King of Kings; Good Shepherd, Eternity and Everlasting. His annual birth was celebrated at the rising of the Nile. His flesh was symbolically eaten in the form of a communion cake of wheat in the Osirian Mysteries. Fertility, harvest, success, initiation, death and reincarnation, judgment, justice, crafts, codes of law, discipline, growth, stability.

O-Wata-Tsumi/Shio-Zuchi (Japanese): "Old man of the tide"; most important of several sea deities.

Pachacamac (Incan): "Lord of the Earth"; Supreme God; son of the Sun; god of fire and earthquakes. Pictured as a white man who worked miracles. The arts, oracles.

Padmasambhava/Rin-Po-Che (Tibetan): "Lotus-Born"; the Great Magician; Destroyer of Demons. He had extraordinary magickal powers.

Pan (Greek): "Little god"; Horned God; goat-foot god; the Horned One of Nature. A very ancient horned and hoofed woodland deity who was associated with Dionysus and called the positive life force of the world. He also had a dark side. Male sexuality, animals, fertility, medicine, agriculture, divination.

Perun/Pyerun/Piorun/Peron/Perkaunas/Perunu (Slavic): "Thunder"; "Lord of the universe"; Supreme God; Creator God; similar to Jupiter and Thorr. He had a magick hammer or axe. His animals were the cock, goat, bear, and bull. Storms, fertility, crops, purification, victory, forests, rain.

Pluto/Dis Pater (Roman): The Etruscans called him Februus; god of death and the Underworld; god of riches.

Poseidon (Greek): "Earthshaker"; Supreme Lord of the Inner and Outer Seas; Overlord of Lakes and Rivers; god of the seas and earthquakes. His symbol was the trident, his animals horses, bulls, and all sea creatures. Associated with the goddesses Amphitrite, Demeter, and Medusa. Intuition, human emotions, storms, revenge.

Priapus (Greek): God of fertility and animals. Shown with an enormous phallus. Fertility, healing.

Ptah (Egyptian): "The Opener"; "the Divine Artificer"; "the Father of beginnings"; "the Master Builder." Connected with the four Elements and the sacred Apis bull. Associated with the goddess Sekhmet. Arts and crafts, regeneration, science, miracles, gentleness.

Puchan/Pushan (Indian): "The Nourisher." He conducted souls to the afterworld and protected travelers from bandits and wild animals. Marriage, journeys, prosperity.

Quetzalcoatl (Aztec): "Most precious twin"; "Feathered Serpent"; "Plumed Serpent"; "Morning Star"; Master of Life. Civilization, the arts, fate.

Ra/Re (Egyptian): "The Creator"; "the Supreme Power"; "the only one"; Great Father; father of the gods; Sun god; eternal god without end. Agriculture, magick, prosperity, rituals, destiny, truth.

Rashnu (Persian): Just judge. He judged the souls of humans with his spiritual scales.

Raven (Native American): A Trickster god, similar to Coyote.

Rimmon/Rammon (Syrian): God of weather, storms, thunder. The pomegranate, symbol of life and death, was sacred to him.

Rudra/Pasupati (Indian): "The Howler"; Lord of Beasts; Dark God; the Red God; He who belongs to three Mother Goddesses. An ancient Vedic god of the dead and prince of demons. His animal was the bull. Protection, death, healing, wild animals, woodlands, intelligence, judgment.

Saishyant/Sraosha (Persian): Savior; one who will come at the end of the world to remove all evil and renew all life. The wicked followers of Ahriman will be purged in a type of hell called Druj. Regeneration.

Sakyamuni/Shaka-Nyorai (Japanese): Japanese name for the Buddha. Virtue, enlightenment, self-realization.

Saturn (Roman): Father Time; the Old King; Father of the Gods; the Great Lesson-Giver; Ruler of the Golden Age; similar to Cronus. Honored in December. Associated with the goddess Ops. Abundance, agriculture, prosperity, karmic lessons.

Seb/Geb/Keb (Egyptian): An Earth god similar to Cronus. Always shown with an erect phallus. Associated with the goddess Nut. Fertility, new beginnings, creation, crops.

Sebek/Suchos (Egyptian): "The hidden one"; "he who is shut in"; Lord of Death and the powers of darkness; a crocodile god. He was said to live at the bottom of the Underworld in a secret pyramid filled with total blackness. Endings, death.

Set (Egyptian): "He who is below"; god of the unclean, the terrible desert, the murderer, cruelty, evil, war, and the Underworld. Known to the Greeks as Typhon. Hunger, thirst, storms, suffering, revenge, death, evil, destruction, chaos.

Shamash/Chemosh (Mesopotamian, Sumerian, Babylonian, Assyrian): Protector of the Poor; Judge of the Heavens and Earth; Sublime Judge of the Anunnaki; Lord of Judgment. Son of the Moon god, he was a Sun deity. Associated with the goddess Aya. Divination, retribution, courage, triumph, justice, the future, fertility, judgment, lawgiving.

Shango/Schango (African): God of thunder, storm, and war. He carried a double axe like the hammer of Thorr. Magick, defense.

Shiva/Siva/Mahakala (Indian): Lord of the Cosmic Dance; Lord of the World; Lord of Stillness and of Motion; Lord of Yoga; Great Lord; Beneficent One; he who gives and takes away; demon slayer. God of contrasting characteristics representing the principle of unification. Associated with the goddesses Kali, Parvati, and Uma. His animals are white bulls and elephants. Fertility, physical love, destruction, medicine, storms, long life, healing, magick, rhythm, meditation, righteousness, judgment.

Shou-Hsing/Shou/Lao (Chinese): God of longevity and old people; keeper of the book of the life-span of humans. His animal was the stag. Life plan, date of death, reincarnation.

Sinn/Nanna/Nannar (Mesopotamian, Assyrian, Babylonian, Sumerian): Lord of the Calendar; Lord of the diadem. A Moon deity, he held the chief place in the triad with Shamash and Ishtar, who were both his children. His sky-boat was the crescent Moon, his diadem the Full Moon. He was associated with the goddesses Ishtar and Ningal. Enemy of evil doers; destiny, predictions, wisdom, secrets, destruction of all evil, decisions.

Susanoo/Susanowo (Japanese): God of storm and thunder; mischief-maker. Agriculture, earthquakes, storms, bravery.

Svantovit/Svantevit/Svyatovit (Slavic, Georgian, Armenian): God of the gods. Four-headed god with faces turned toward all directions. His animal was the white horse. Divination, prosperity, victory, weapons.

Ta'aroa (Maori): Creator God; personified primal darkness. Destructive power, moisture, oceans.

Taliesin (Welsh): Prince of Song; Chief of the Bards; a poet and shapeshifter. Writing, wisdom, music, magick, knowledge.

Tangaroa (Polynesian): Great God; Creator God. Fish, snakes, crafts.

Tapio (Finnish): "Dark Beard"; god of water and woods. Associated with the goddess Mielikki. Forests, wild animals.

Tawhaki (Polynesian): God of thunder and lightning. Cunning, magick.

Tekkeitsertok (Inuit): Most powerful Earth god of deer and hunting.

Teshub (Hittite): A weather god who carried a thunder hammer and a fistful of thunderbolts. Destruction, damage.

Tezcatlipoca (Aztec): "Mirror that smokes"; "the Shadow"; "He who is at the shoulder"; "it causes the black mirror (night) to shine." Rival and opposite of Quetzalcoatl. His animal was the jaguar. Divination, harvest, music, magick.

Thorr/Thor/Thunar/Thunor/Donar (Norse): "The High Thunderer"; protector of the common person; champion of the gods and enemy of the Giants and Trolls. His symbol was his magick hammer Mjollnir (Destroyer), his animal was the goat. Associated with the goddess Sif. Strength, law and order, defense, thunder, lightning, courage, protection.

Thoth/Tehuti/Thout (Egyptian): "Lord of Books and Learning"; "Lord of Holy Words"; "the Elder"; judge and scribe of the gods; identified with Hermes. An ibis-headed deity, he was the inventor of the four laws of magick. Associated with the goddess Seshat. Magick, writing, inventions, the arts, learning, prophecy, healing, initiation, success, wisdom, peace, truth, the Akashic records.

Ti-Tsang-Wang-Pu-Sa (Chinese): God of mercy, he visited those in hell and tried to arrange for a good incarnation. Knowledge for reincarnation.

Tlaloc (Aztec): "The one who makes things sprout"; "Lord of the sources of water"; an ancient Nature and fertility deity. Associated with the goddess Chalchihuitlicue. Thunder, fertility, mountains.

Tsai Shen/Ts'ai-Shen (Chinese): God of wealth. His animals are the cock and carp. Abundance, success.

Tuoni (Finnish): Lord of Tuonela or Manala (the Underworld). Associated with the goddesses Kalma, Kivutar, and Vammatar. Death.

Tyr/Tiu/Tiwaz/Tiw/Ziu (Norse): "The One-handed"; the bravest of the gods; patron of the Thing or Assembly. Giver of victory in battle against odds, he was never deceitful. Law, legal contracts, judicial matters, victory in combat, justice, meaningful self-sacrifice, honor.

Ukko (Finnish): "Ancient father who reigns in the heavens"; Supreme God. Help with the impossible.

Unkulunkulu/Nkulnkulu (African): Great God; Earth God. Fertility, organization, order.

Uranus/Ouranos (Greek): Original Great God; father of the Olympians. Associated with the goddess Gaea.

Varuna (Indian): God of the Sun and cosmic law and order; linked with Mitra. "The coverer"; creator of the Cosmos; Lord of creative power and life-force; judge of human deeds. By using his *maya*, or creative will, he created the heavens, earth, and the air between them. Truth, justice, punishment, law, magick, death, prophecy, rewards.

Vertumnus (Roman): "Changer"; god of the returning seasons and Earth fertility; a shapeshifter. Fertility, changes.

Viracocha/Huiracocha (Incan): The Creator; "Foam of the Lake"; Great God; being without beginning or end. The arts, storms, oracles, moral codes, fertility.

Vishnu (Indian): "The Preserver"; Lord of the principle of Light that permeates the entire Universe; conqueror of darkness. With three steps he measured the seven worlds. Intermediary between the gods and humans. His animals are the Garuda bird, white horses, and cobras or serpents. Associated with the goddess Lakshmi. Judgment, peace, power, compassion, abundance, success.

Volos/Vyelyes/Veles/Vlas/Vlaho (Slavic): "God of cattle"; "god of beasts"; Lord of horned animals. Peace, tame animals.

Vulcan/Volcanus (Roman): The Divine Smith; a tough, practical craftsman. His symbols were the hammer, anvil, and thunderbolts. Associated with the goddess Maia. Metal-working, storms, fire, volcanoes.

Wakonda (Lakota): "The power above." Source of all wisdom and power, enlightenment.

Wele (African): "The high one"; "one to whom sacred rites are paid"; Creator God; sky god. Storms, lightning, creating, prosperity, harvest.

Wepwawet (Egyptian): "Opener of Roads"; god of the Underworld. Pictured as wolf-headed, his symbol was always carried at the head of the processions in the Osirian Mysteries. Protection, defense, journeys.

Xipe Totec (Aztec): "The flayed one"; god of agriculture. His festival was in February. Associated with the goddess Xochiquetzal, who was his mother. Harvest, corn.

Xochipilli (Aztec): "Flower Prince"; Sun god. Music, dance, flowers, pleasure.

Xolotl (Aztec): "The Animal"; Lord of the Evening Star; Lord of the Underworld. Rival of the Sun deities.

Yama/Dharmaraja (Indian, Tibetan): Judge of the dead; god of death, truth, and righteousness. Also called Samana (the Leveller), he judges dharma. His animals are the owl, pigeon, and dogs. In Tibet he was called "The Restrainer," King of the Underworld and judge of humans. Judgment, destiny, death, punishment.

Yamantaka (Tibetan): "Destroyer of the Lord of Death"; "the Annihilator." A protective Buddha-type deity, he brought enlightenment, protection, and rescue to sinners.

Yanauluha (Zuni): The Great Medicine Man. Agriculture, civilization, healing, knowledge.

Yarilo (Slavic, Georgian, Armenian): "Passionate"; "uncontrolled"; similar to Eros. Carnal love, fertility, harvest, agriculture.

Yeng-Wang-Yeh (Chinese): "Lord Yama King"; foremost of the ten Yama Kings or Lords of Death; ruler of hell. He screened all the new arrivals and decided if they went to a special court for trial, were punished, or sent straight back onto the Wheel of Life. Judgment, punishment, karmic justice.

Yum Caax (Mayan): "Forest Lord"; "Lord of the harvest fields"; god of maize or corn. Fertility, growth, life, good crops.

Zeus (Greek): Supreme God; Great God; Lord of the heavens. His animal was the eagle, his symbols the oak and lightning bolt. Associated with the goddesses Hera, Metis, Themis, Demeter, and Athene. Protector of the laws, justice, and the weak. The sky, storms, wisdom, justice, the law, honor, friendships, health, luck, punishment.

APPENDIX III

GOD SYMBOLS

Ankh, cross, furka, World Tree, Tree of Life: All these symbols were connected with the sacrificed savior-god. The Egyptian god Set was crucified on the *furka,* or "fork." His blood and death were said to make the yearly rebirth of the world possible.

The crook or crozier (also known as the Shepherd's Cross) was originally a symbol of Osiris in his role as the Good Shepherd of souls. Osiris was shown holding both the crook and the flail, as symbols of his being both the harvest and the harvester. In Assyria and Babylon, the god-kings, known as "Shepherds of the People," were pictured holding such emblems. The Greek Hermes carried a crook under his title of the Shepherd of Souls. Christian bishops later stole this emblem to use as proof of their divine right.

A circle containing an equal-armed cross represented male and female in cosmic union. Among the Germanic peoples this was called Wotan's Cross.

The Norse god Odhinn hung on the World Tree for nine days and nights before he attained full magickal power, symbolic of death and resurrection. The Hindu god Krishna died on a tree, as did Attis.

Osiris, in his dead phase, was entombed in a tree. The Mayas of the Yucatan Peninsula had a First Tree of the World, which was represented in the shape of a cross; their savior-god was crucified on it and called Our Lord of the Tree.

Arrow: Both a phallic symbol and the weapon of a war deity. As with the Balkan storm god Perkun, the arrow also denotes lightning. The arrow was a symbol of such gods as Mars, Tyr, and Mithras.[1]

Ashes: Ashes have long been associated with the sacrificed savior gods, the scapegoats who carried away the sins of the people. In India, the Vedic sages believed that Agni gave his seed in the form of ashes, thereby making it possible to remove transgressions by bathing in ashes. The Romans also had a New Year atonement ritual in March during which they bathed in ashes.

Ass, donkey: Ass-headed gods were connected with guardianship of fields and flocks and were usually sacrificed deities. The ass-headed Egyptian god Set was one of the earliest such deities; he was a sacrificed god, the alter ego of Horus.[2] Palestine was named after Pales, an androgynous god who protected flocks and herds; the Romans later brought Pales into their pantheon.

Boar: One of the earliest substitutes for the sacrificed god in Indo-European cultures. In India, the boar was identified with Vishnu and his three boar sons, who were sacrificed. In Scandinavia, one of Freyr's emblems was the boar; Swedish priest-kings wore boar masks, symbolizing their role as husbands of the goddess Freyja.[3] In the Middle East, Attis, Adonis, and Tammuz were sacrificed in boar form.[4] Greeks swore oaths by the holy blood of boars.

Bull: Bulls have been connected with sacrifices to the Great Mother since the beginning of religious worship. In Phoenicia, the god El ("the Bull") was the supreme Semitic deity. In the Minoan culture on the isle of Crete, the bull (symbol of Poseidon and the god-kings) was worshipped through the Bull Dances. Among the Hindus, sacrificed bulls were said to embody Shiva, consort of Kali. Osiris was considered to be incarnate in the Apis bull during its sacrifice. During the Mystery rites of both Attis and Mithras, a bull was sacrificed and the initiates baptized in the blood to ensure being "born again for eternity."[5]

Caduceus: A staff with two serpents twined around it. In Mesopotamia, a double-sexed, two-headed snake (Sachan) was the symbol of Ningishzide, a healing god and one of Ishtar's lovers.[6] An early version of the Greek caduceus was a staff topped by a solar disk with two snake heads as horns.[7] Later this became two snakes twined around the staff of Hermes, particularly in his role as Psychopomp, or Conductor of Souls. The son of Hermes was Asclepius, a healing and medicinal god who was said to be able to raise the dead with this emblem.[8] This symbol is also found in ancient India, among the Aztecs, and in some of the Native American tribes.[9]

Calf: In Egypt, certain calves were considered to be sacred, as they represented Horus, child of Isis in her role of the Golden Cow.

Chariot: These vehicles have long been connected with gods, particularly solar deities. The Greek gods Helios and Apollo, both solar gods, drove chariots through the sky. During a yearly festival on the Isle of Rhodes, a chariot was thrown into the sea just as the Sun set.[10] An Indian temple of Vishnu was built to resemble a gigantic chariot. During the annual Puri festival, images of Vishnu (in his role of Jagganath, "Lord of the World") and his consort were drawn through the streets in a huge chariot. We get our word *juggernaut* from this title of Vishnu.

Circle: Originally a Goddess symbol, but later used to denote a Sun god. Sometimes this disk had wings, such as represented the Sun god Ra in Egypt. This winged disk in Egypt had the hawk wings of Horus, the ram horns of Amen, and two hooded cobras.

   The Sun was considered to be paired with the Moon; in the cultures where the Sun was masculine, the Moon was feminine, such as the Greek god Apollo and his twin sister Artemis. This circular symbol of the Sun represented not only the shape of the heavenly body, but also the "wheel" of the circling year.

Circle, Black: Several cultures used a blackened circle as a symbol for the Sun god during his nightly passage through the Underworld. This Black Sun deity was thought to be the dark twin brother of the daily Sun god, the opposing force of darkness against light, the Lord of Death and Darkness.

However, this idea was originally not of an evil, dark deity, but a secret, extremely wise one who knew both the Underworld and the heavens of day. The Black Sun was the Sun god who died each night, returned to the womb of the Great Mother, and was reborn each morning. The Egyptian god Seker was said to be hidden in a secret pyramid of intense darkness at the Earth's core.[11]

Crown: From India to northern Europe, the crown originally was used to denote a sacred marriage between the God and the Goddess, or the Goddess and Her chosen human consort. The Egyptian pharaohs wore the double diadem; the god-kings of the Middle East had tiaras; the Greeks used holy wreaths of flowers or leaves.

Deer, stag: These animals have always been considered extremely magickal creatures, and horned deer have always been symbols of the Horned God. The stag has been a substitute sacrifice for the Horned God for millennia. Later myths speak of this sacrifice in a mysterious manner. In a myth of Artemis/Diana, the man Actaeon was torn apart by dogs after he saw the goddess undressed. Since the stag represented the male spirit of the forests and woodlands,[12] this may refer to the sacred marriage and its sacrificial outcome after a specified length of time.

Dog: Dogs have long accompanied the Dark or Underworld Goddess in many cultures. They symbolized the God, who took this form on His missions to carry out the Goddess' wishes and enforce Her laws. Nodens, a Celtic god of healing, was said to be able to shapeshift into a dog.[13] When Hel rode out on the Wild Hunt, she was accompanied by Odhinn and a pack of dogs; the Celtic Cwn Annwn, or Hounds of the Underworld, are similar to the hounds of the Wild Hunt.

Dorje: A type of scepter-dagger in Tibet and India; double-ended and six-pronged. Also called "the diamond-holder lingam," referring to the divine spirit sensed through sex as taught by Tantra. A symbol of lightning and the phallus; the lightning phallus that the God used to fertilize the Earth Mother. The city of Darjeeling takes its name from this item.

Fly: A common soul-symbol in ancient cultures. Connected with the Philistine god Beelzebub (Ba'al-zebub, "Lord of the Flies" or "Lord of Souls").

Fox: In ancient Lydia, Dionysus was said to take on the shape of a fox; in this aspect the god was known as Bassareus, and his fox-skin wearing priestesses were called Bassarids. Orpheus was also connected with foxes. This fox-deity survived in the form of the Trickster Renaud or Reynard the Fox.

Halo: A halo is merely a circle drawn around or behind the head of a figure. Originally, it denoted divinity. The word *halo* comes from the Greek *halos,* which means "threshing floor." This threshing floor was circular in form and was important in the Haloa[14] festival of the Eleusinian Mysteries, when harvest dances were performed there in honor of Triptolemus, who was an aspect of Dionysus.

Hat, pointed: Pointed caps or miters have long been associated with gods and the priests who represented them. Images of Freyr show him wearing a conical cap, as do those of the Middle Eastern/Roman Mithras. Rome's highest priest, the Pontifex Maximus, also wore a pointed miter, later copied by the Christians. This type of hat symbolized spiritual power coming down from heaven.[15] The "fool's cap" of the medieval jesters, later placed on children in school, was a subconscious remnant of an attempt to draw down sacred power and knowledge.

Hawk: Hawks were emblems of psychopomp gods. Horus was often pictured as a man with a human body and a hawk's head. However, there was also a little-known Egyptian hawk-god named Khu-en-ua, who ferried souls across the underground river in the afterlife. Later, in Greece, he became Charon of the river Styx. The hawk was sacred to Apollo.

Horns: Horns were frequently used on the heads of gods to symbolize their virility. Horns also represented deities whose blood would fertilize and renew the Earth. Sacrificed gods, such as Cronus, and fertility deities, such as Cernunnos and Apollo Karnaios, are examples.

Some scholars say that the name Cronus means "horned," and may come from the Assyro-Babylonian *garnu,* the Hebrew and

Phoenician words *geren, qarnuim,* or *kerenos.* The horned Apollo Karnaios resembles Cronus,[16] just as the Celtic Cernunnos is very similar.

Jackal: A revered companion of the Goddess in her aspect as Receiver of the Dead. Along with wolves and other canines, the jackal was a guardian of the Underworld gates, a psychopomp who took care of souls after death. As consort of Kali, Shiva was called a jackal.[17]

The Egyptian god Anubis, who had a jackal-head, was connected with both Isis and Nephthys. He was the god of mummification, keeper of souls, and said to be the father of sacrificial priests.[18] During processions of the Osirian Mysteries, a priest wearing an Anubis mask always proceeded the image of Isis.

Jar: Although the image of a jar is an ancient Goddess symbol, it was also used as an emblem of resurrection gods. From the beginning of civilization in the Middle East and Egypt, a water jar was a fertility symbol. During resurrection rituals of the Osirian Mysteries, according to the ancient writer Apuleius, a chalice was elevated, just as it is in orthodox churches today.[19] A jar-bearer led the Babylonian savior-god Nabu to his sacrifice and resurrection. In Hindu ceremonies, a jar of water was considered the seat of any worshipped deity for the length of the ritual.[20]

The same applied to the ancient Cabirian Mysteries of Phrygia, in which Demeter and her young consort Cabirius were represented by jars of water. The whole Greek festival of Dionysus called Anthesteria revolved around jar ceremonies. The first day was called Jar Opening when new wine was opened and tasted. The second day was the Pitcher Feast when the chief archon's wife presented herself to the god for impregnation. The third day was the Feast of Pots, a time for honoring the dead and asking for their resurrection through new life.[21]

Key: Keys have always been symbols of mystical knowledge, particularly knowledge about the afterlife. The Egyptian ankh was such a key. The Egyptians also considered certain magickal formulae as keys to the Inner Shrine; their word *hekau* meant "words of power." Initiates of the Osirian Mysteries were taught holy words that were said to be keys to heaven and could not be divulged to noninitiates.[22] The hierophant of the Greek Eleusinian Mysteries spoke of a golden key on his tongue, which had the same mystical meaning as to the Egyptian initiates.

Lion: An animal identified with solar deities, such as Apollo Chrysocomes ("He of the Golden Locks"), Heracles, and the Arabic Sun god Shams-On. One of the Mithraic symbols was a lion's head surrounded by a mane of Sun rays.

Maypole: A phallic symbol of the May King in European Pagan Beltane celebrations.

Obelisk, pillar, standing stone: Phallic symbols of the God. Obelisk comes from the Greek *obelischos,* which means a pointed pillar. Egyptian obelisks were originally created to represent the phallus of the god Geb, the Earth god who lay under the sky goddess Nut.[23]

In India, stone pillars symbolized the lingam, or penis, of Shiva. Wherever such a lingam was set up, Shiva's kingdom was believed to extend for 150 feet around it; it was said that miracles could happen and sins would be forgiven within this sacred area.[24]

Pillars and solitary standing stones have long been used to symbolize the God, particularly in His fertility aspect. Shiva had the title of Sthanu ("the Pillar or Great Lingam"). Wooden pillars were symbols of the Saxon god Irmin and the Norse god Freyr. The Romans erected stone pillars to Jupiter throughout their Empire. In Japan, the stone pillar represented the god Nu-boko. Unfortunately, most of these pillars were destroyed by Christians.[25]

The *herms* of ancient Greece were simply phallic pillars with a head on top. They were dedicated to Hermes, the god of magick and crossroads.

Palm: A symbol of virility of the God. The Roman celebrations of Osiris, as the savior and sacrificed and resurrected Lord, displayed palm branches.[26] The Phoenician cult of Ba'al-Peor held sacred palm trees growing between two large stones.

Panther: In Greek, this animal's name meant "all-beast," referring to the god Pan. It was also a symbol of Dionysus, whom Pan accompanied.

Pine: Emblems of such savior gods as Attis, Dionysus, Marsyas, and Osiris. The cones of this tree were symbols of male genitals. In his temple at Denderah, Osiris was shown enclosed in a pine tree. Dionysus carried a pinecone-tipped staff (thyrsus).

Reed, bulrush: The reed was used as a scepter by sacrificial gods and kings. Whenever myth speaks of the king or god's reed scepter being broken, it means that the ruler was sacrificed.

Bulrushes or reeds are also connected with the Divine or Sacred Child. The tale of Moses was taken, almost word for word, from an ancient Egyptian story of a hero named Ra-Harakhti, who was the reborn Sun god of Canopus.[27] Isis placed the child Horus in a basket made of bulrushes and hid him in the swamps.[28]

Scarecrow: An effigy of a man hung on a wooden cross. In later times, a magickal protection for fields and crops; originally an actual sacrifice to encourage the crops.[29] (See **ankh.**)

Spear: Another phallic symbol, similar to the Maypole,[30] lightning, and obelisk. However, as with most, if not all, gods who fertilized the Earth Mother, the spear also represented the sacrificial death of these gods.

Square: Sometimes called an Earth square, this symbol represented the four guardian spirits who held up the sky. In Babylonian ritual and magick, the four corner-gods, as they were called, were Shamash before the priest-magician, Nergal at the right, Sinn behind, and Ninib at the left.[31] The Babylonians also used animal symbols as these guardians: the lion of Ishtar, bull of Marduk, eagle-headed dragon of Nergal, and a male figure for Enlil.[32]

Sword: Although swords were considered the personal property of European males and buried with them, or disposed of in some manner at their death, the sword was also a symbol of ancient sacred kings. The sacred king ruled only for a limited time or until his virility was gone; then he was killed (usually beheaded) and his blood poured out to fertilize the land of his kingdom. This beheading has survived in the symbolic gestures used to bestow knighthood: the sword touching each shoulder.

Thyrsus: A wand with a pinecone tip; the ancient sacred rod of Dionysus. The Romans knew the thyrsus as *baculus,* connecting it with their god Bacchus. The word *thyrsus* is related to the Hittite *tuwarsa* ("grape") and the Ugaritic *tirsu* ("strong drink").[33] The followers of Dionysus believed that a touch of the thyrsus turned water into wine, a standard Dionysian miracle.[34]

Three-leaf clover, trefoil: As far back in history as the Indus Valley civilization (c. 2500–1700 B.C.E.), the trefoil emblem was used to denote triple deity or divinity. The Celts had a god, Trefuilngid Tre-Eochair, who was represented by the shamrock. Both he and Shiva were known as the Triple Bearer of the Triple Key.

Torch: One of the prominent symbols of the Mithraic religion. The Heavenly Twins each held a torch, one pointing upward, the other downward. The upward torch symbolized the Sun god of the Light; the downward torch represented the Black Sun of the underground passage.

Trident, triple arrow: The trident represents a triple phallus used by the God to fertilize the Triple Goddess. As the consort of Kali, Shiva was called the Trident-Bearer"; his trident represented the *vajra*. Among the Chaldeans, the trident symbolized lightning used by the gods to fertilize the Goddess.[35] In later times, the trident became associated with gods of the abyss and oceans, such as Poseidon and Neptune. The triple arrow symbolizes the same concept.

Wolf: A guardian animal of the Goddess in Her dark forms. The wolf, as well as other canines, usually was a symbol of the gods. Odhinn had two wolves as companions; he also rode out on the Wild Hunt with packs of wolves and dogs to gather souls. In Egypt, the wolf-god Wepwawet accompanied Isis and Osiris.

APPENDIX IV

CROSS-REFERENCE

Abundance: Cronus, Saturn, Hades, Freyr, Njord, Hermes, Mercury, Agni, Kubera, Vishnu, Tsai Shen, Lu-hsing, Svantovit, Ilmarinen, Zeus, Jupiter, Pluto, Dis Pater, Bes, Osiris, Puchan.

Agriculture: Gucumatz, Terminus, Amen, Osiris, Cronus, Saturn, Pan, Faunus, Odhinn, Mars, Amen, Hapi, Adonis, Marduk, the Horned God, Yum Caax, Susanoo, Ra, Hades, Jupiter, Bel, Thorr, Perun, Lono, Tirawa, Itzamna, Xipe Totec.

Akashic Records: Anubis, Thoth.

Animals: Hurukan, Pan, Poseidon, the Horned God, Mars, Odhinn, Fryr, Faunus, Cernunnos, Nuada, Rudra, Anubis, Hermes, Tekkeit-sertok, Hurukan, T'ai-Yueh-Ta-Ti, Neptune, Mercury, Bel, Herne the Hunter, Thorr, Volos, Indra, Puchan.

Anointed One: Adonis, Dumuzi, Tammuz, Dionysus, Mithras.

Air: See **Sky.**

Architecture: Osiris, Ptah, Khnemu, Thoth, Lugh, Tangaroa, Ganesha.

Arts and crafts: Khnemu, Ptah, Thoth, Apollo, Bragi, Mimir, Odhinn, the Dagda, Lugh, Manannan mac Lir, Ogma, Lupan, Anubis, Taliesin, Merlin, Hermes, Mercury, Osiris, Hephaestus, Ea, Itzamna, Pachacamac, Ganesha, Vulcan, Ogun, Bran the Blessed, Quetzalcoatl.

Astral travel: Anubis, Taliesin.

Beauty: Adonis, Angus mac Og, Apollo, Balder, Bes, Nuada, Freyr.

Beginnings: Janus, Heimdall, Ptah, Terminus, Svantovit, Agni, Ganesha.

Blacksmiths: See **Metal-working.**

Boats: Tien-hou, Manannan mac Lir, Njord, Janus, Neptune, Aegir, Freyr, Anubis.

Brewing: Aegir, Goibniu.

Calendar: Thoth.

Carpenters: Lu-pan, Ptah, Tangaroa, Khnemu, Ea, Lugh, Nuada.

Cemeteries: Anubis.

Changes: Gwydion, Khepera, Janus. See **Magick.**

Childbirth: Bes, Nuada.

Civilization: Gucumatz, Bes, Osiris, Dionysus, Zeus, Jupiter, Horus, Thoth, Quetzalcoatl, Enlil, Mithras, Odhinn.

Commerce: Osiris, Hermes, Mercury, Lugh, Manannan mac Lir, Ganesha, Thoth, Cernunnos, Herne the Hunter, Thorr.

Compassion: See **Mercy.**

Contracts: Mithras, Zeus, Jupiter, Tyr, Osiris, Njord, Freyr.

Courage: Ares, Mars, Hercules, Thorr, Shamash, Marduk, Hoenir, Kuan Ti, Susanoo.

Creativity: Apollo, Odhinn, Khnemu, Ptah, Thoth, Khepera, Osiris, Ra, Byelobog, Indra, Rudra, Varuna.

Creator God: Ptah, Osiris, Sebek, Khnemu, Rama, Rudra, Buddha, Varuna, Ea, Marduk, Ta'aroa, Tangaroa, Hurukan, Izanagi, Seb, Ra, Cronus, Odhinn.

Crossroads: Hermes, Mercury, Cernunnos, Herne the Hunter.

Crystal reading: Osiris, Merlin. See **Psychic abilities.**

Cunning: Hermes, Mercury, Bragi, Loki, Odhinn, Susanoo, Maui, Pwyll.

Cursing: See **Revenge, Justified revenge.**

Dance: Dionysus, Shiva, Bes, Pan, Faunus, Tezcatlipoca.

Darkness: Hades, Loki, Chernobog, Apep, Set, Ahriman, Ta'aroa, Sebek.

Death: Adonis, Adroa, Anubis, Rudra, Ares, Apollo, Hades, Odhinn, Tyr, Mars, Chernobog, Tuoni, Apep, Set, Ahriman, Nergal, Sebek, Shiva, Amen, Kuan Ti, Shou-hsing, Yen-lo, Emma-O, Pluto, Arawn, Gwynn ap Nudd, the Dagda, Ogma, Osiris, Yama, Pwyll, Bes, Dis Pater, Ba'al, Mithras, Kaka-Guia, Loki, Maui, Agni, Mara, Huitzilopochtli, Xipe Totec.

Destiny: See **Fate.**

Destruction: Addad, Ahriman, Loki, Ares, Mars, Loki, Thorr, Horus, Set, Ahriman, Ta'aroa, Sebek, Enlil, Nergal, Chernobog, Kama, Shiva, Emma-O, Yama.

Diplomacy: Anubis.

Disaster: Enlil, Mars, Ares, Loki, Tezcatlipoca.

Divination: Addad, Tezcatlipoca, Viracocha, Kuan Ti, Shiva, Apollo, Zeus, Faunus, Janus, Mithras, Odhinn, Svantovit, Thoth, Ea, Shamash, Merlin, Osiris, Pan.

Divine Child: Apollo, Arthur, Buddha, Cupid, Eros, Dioysus, Hermes, Horus, Iacchus, Krishna, Maui, Mithras, Modred, Pan, Prajapati, Zeus, Zagreus.

Domestic arts: Ptah, Osiris.

Dreams: Gidja, Osiris, Asclepius, Chandra.

Earth God: Hurukan, Unkulunkulu, Tekkeitsertok, Pachacamac, O-Kuni-Nushi, the Dagda, Seb, Adonis, Enlil, Dumuzi, the Horned God, Pan, Cernunnos, Nuada, Osiris, Faunus, Ea, Adroa, Izanagi.

Earthquakes: Poseidon, Neptune, Loki, Enlil, Susanoo.

Eclipse: Apep.

Ecstasy: See **Passion.**

Elements: Merlin, Taliesin.

Eloquence: Hermes, Mercury, Ogma, Bragi, Osiris.

Enchantment: Marduk, Gwydion, Math Mathonwy, Odhinn, Merlin. See **Magick.**

Endings: Anubis, Janus, Heimdall, Terminus, Svantovit.

Evil: Ahriman, Loki, Legba, Chernobog, Leshy, Set, Nergal, Sebek.

Exorcism: Kupalo, Bes.

Fate: Anu, Janus, the Dagda, Manannan mac Lir, Odhinn, Osiris, Ra, Saturn, Enlil, Marduk, Sinn, Yama, Fu-hsi, Yeng-Wang-Yeh, Quetzalcoatl.

Fertility: Agni, Amen, Pan, Faunus, Cernunnos, the Horned God, Osiris, Freyr, Asshur, Indra, Shiva, Amen, Dionysus, Bacchus, Itzamna, Tlaloc, Legba, Kubera, Poseidon, Khnemu, Ba'al, Dumuzi, Gidja, Viracocha, Vertumnus, Mithras, Bel, Herne the Hunter, Bes, Hapi, Ninurta, Perun.

Finding lost things: Anubis.

Fire: Hurukan, Agni, Hephaestus, Vulcan, Loki, Bel, Goibniu, Merlin, Svantovit, Gibil, Xiuhtecuhtli, Nergal, the Dagda, Perun, Shiva, Tirawa, Ogun.

Fishing: Njord, Tangaroa, Pan, Faunus, Neptune, Nuada, Maui.

Flowers: Xochiquetzal, Pan, Kama.

Forest Lord: Robin Hood, the Green Man, King of May, the Horned God, Jack in the Green, Faunus, Pan, Lupercus, Vertumnus, Cernunnos, Herne the Hunter, Athos, Hu Gadern, Rudra, Vajrapani,

Tapio, Pellervoinen, Krukis, Leshy, Volos, Lono, Tekkeitsertok, Tlaloc. See **Woodlands.**

Foretelling: Apollo, Thoth, Zeus, Jupiter, Janus, Mithras, Ea, Pan, Faunus, Addad, Olorun, Merlin, Odhinn, Kuan Ti.

Forgiveness: Agni.

Gambling: Hermes, Mercury.

Gates, doors, portals, harbors: Janus, Legba, Bes.

Gems and minerals: Hephaestus, Hades, Pluto, Kubera. See **Jewelry.**

Great God: Pachacamac, Amen, Osiris, Ra, Cronus, Uranus, Zeus, Jupiter, Ahura Mazdah, Ba'al, Anu, Ea, Enlil, Marduk, Adroa, the Dagda, Odhinn, Perun, Tangaroa, Indra, Kama, Rudra, Shang-ti, Kitcki Manitou.

Growth: Freyr.

Guardian: Heimdall, Anubis, Bes, Janus.

Happiness: Freyr, Dionysus, Yum Caax, Fu-hsing, T'ien-kuan, Balder.

Harvest: Adonis, Balder, Saturn, Cronus, Ra, Amen, Dumuzi, Osiris, Thorr, Hapi, Vertumnus, Cinteotl, Odhinn, Tezcatlipoca.

Healer, The: Saturn, Apollo, Asclepius, Priapus, Bacchus, Hermes, Mercury, Ningishzida, Thoth, Imhotep, Diancecht, Nodens, the Asvins, Shiva, Shen Nung, Yao-Shih, Fu-hsi, Huang Ti, O-Kuni-Nushi, Yanauluha, the Underwater Panthers.

Healing: Kupalo, Imhotep, Khensu, Apollo, Asclepius, Pan, Faunus, Cernunnos, Bel, Lugh, Yao-Shih, Thoth, Merlin, the Asvins, Itzamna, the Dagda, Diancecht, Gwydion, Nuada, the Underwater Panthers, Pachacamac, Marduk, Rudra, Shiva.

Health: Imhotep, Apollo, Asclepius, Zeus, Jupiter, the Asvins.

Heaven: See **Sky.**

Herbs: Rudra, Marduk, Ioskeha, Pan, Merlin, Tirawa.

Hero/Warrior, The: Vainamoinen, Heimdall, Thorr, Tyr, Cu Chulainn, Mars, Ares, the Dagda, Galahad, Orpheus, Menthu, Fu-hsi, Wepwawet, Ogun.

Hospitals: Anubis.

Hurricanes, typhoons: Hurukan, Enlil, Marduk, Tawiri.

Illusion: Merlin, Gwydion, Pan, Faunus, Loki, Odhinn, Kama, Mara. See **Shapeshifter.**

Initiation: Osiris, Apollo, Odhinn, the Dagda, Lugh, Thoth, Merlin, Dionysus. See **Patron of priests and priestesses.**

Inspiration: Apollo, Merlin, Osiris, Ogma, Odhinn.

Inventions: Khnemu, Ptah, Thoth, Merlin, Pan, Mercury, Hermes, Enlil, Hephaestus.

Jewelry: Hephaestus, Vulcan, Lugh, Diancecht, Goibniu, Bes, Ptah, Kubera.

Journeys: Puchan, Janus, Njord, Thorr, Hercules, Hermes, Mercury, Lugh, Ganesha, Legba, Huitzilopochtli, Anubis.

Judgment, Lord of: Apollo, Dionysus, Zeus, Jupiter, Saturn, Janus, Varuna, Ahura Mazdah, Yama, Thoth, Osiris, Anubis, Odhinn, Forseti, Tyr, Shamash, Zoroaster, Kingu, Enlil, Marduk, Gibil, Kuan Ti, Lei-King, Shou-Hsing, T'ai-Yueh-Ta-Ti, Ti-Tsang-Wang-Pu-Sa, Yeng-Wang-Yeh, Kannon Bosatsu, Kulkulkan, Fa, Mithras, Anu.

Justice: Anubis, Apollo, Agni, Forseti, Tyr, Anu.

Justified revenge: Apollo.

Karma: See **Fate, Retribution.**

Knowledge: Imhotep, Sinn, the Dagda, Taliesin, Mimir, Osiris, Apollo, Janus, Odhinn, Brahma, Rudra.

Law: Adroa, Ahura Mazdah, Odhinn, Lu-hsing, Zeus, Jupiter, Horus, Varuna, Tyr, Osiris, Marduk, Forseti, Thoth, Apollo, Enlil, Adroa, Indra.

Light: Ahura Mazdah, Apollo, Kitcki Manitou, Vishnu, Svarog, Osiris, Balder, Odhinn, Mithras, Thoth, Zeus, Jupiter, Heimdall, Byelobog, Agni.

Lightning: Agni, Indra, Hephaestus, Vulcan, Zeus, Jupiter, Thorr, Perun, Ba'al, Addad, Svarog, Shiva, Vajrapani, the Thunderbirds, Viracocha.

Long life: Shou-hsing, the Asvins, Shamash, Shiva.

Love: Adonis, Angus mac Og, the Asvins, Krishna, Vishnu, Eros, Cupid, Bes, Fu-hsi, Dumuzi, Kama, Agni, Vajrapani.

Lover, The: Adonis, Tammuz, Attis, Aleyin, Ba'al, Ba'al-Hammon, Hay-Tau, Krishna, Indra, Shiva, Kamadeva, Vishnu, Seb, Osiris, Khnemu, Min, Bes, Cupid, Eros, Dionysus, Pan, Angus mac Og, Lancelot, Freyr, Chimati No Kami, Atea, Daramulun, Tlaloc, Xevioso.

Luck: Kupalo, Puchan, Hermes, Mercury, Saturn, Bes, Zeus, Jupiter, Odhinn, Ganesha.

Magician, The: Taliesin, the Dagda, Gwydion, Manannan mac Lir, Manawydden ap Llyr, Merlin, Hermes, Hephaestus, Heimdall, Bragi, Odhinn, Thoth, Khensu, Set, Ilmarinen, Mara, Erh-Lang, O-Kuni-Nushi, Hsuan-T'ien-Shang-Ti, Ea, Enki, Latpon, Xolotl, Shango, Eshu, Tawhaki.

Magick, Dark: Set, Pluto, Hades, Kuan Ti, Nergal, Mara, Tezcatlipoca.

Magick, Light: Kupalo, Thoth, Apollo, Hermes, Mercury, Odhinn, the Dagda, Gwydion, Lugh, Ogma, Marduk, Mithras, Varuna, Merlin, Shango, Tezcatlipoca, Hephaestus, Zeus, Jupiter, Diancecht, Manannan mac Lir, Math Mathonwy, Legba, Osiris, Ra, Vulcan, Nuada, Taliesin, Brahma, Indra, Krishna, Shiva.

Marriage: The Asvins, Puchan, Bes, Agni.

Mechanics: Hephaestus, Ptah, Vulcan.

Medicine: Apollo, Asclepius, Pan, Faunus, Lugh, O-Kuni-Nushi, the Asvins, Bel, the Dagda, Imhotep, Thoth, Shiva.

Memory: Janus, Odhinn.

Messages: Agni, Anubis, Agni, Hermes, Mercury, Khensu.

Metal-working: Hephaestus, Vulcan, Goibniu, Lugh, Diancecht, Ptah, Ilmarinen, Mimir, Lugh, Hades, Ea, Nuada, Quetzalcoatl.

Moon: Sinn, Atius Tirawa, Khensu, Varuna, Horus, Cernunnos, Thoth, Gidja, Chandra, Soma, Shiva, Ptah.

Mountains: Zeus, Jupiter, Pan, Faunus, Tlaloc.

Music: Apollo, Bes, Pan, Faunus, Bragi, Odhinn, Lugh, Ogma, Taliesin, Thoth, the Dagda, Hermes, Krishna, Mercury, Osiris, Bran the Blessed, Nuada, Vainamoinen, Rudra, Tezcatlipoca.

Mysteries: Osiris, Dionysus.

Nature: See **Woodlands.**

Oaths: Perun, Volos. See **Contracts.**

Ocean: See **Water.**

Opportunities: Ogun, Puchan, the Dagda, Jupiter, Zeus, Osiris, Odhinn.

Oracles: Apollo, Pan, Faunus, Merlin, Osiris, Ea, Mithras, Odhinn, Perun, Viracocha, Pachacamac.

Order: Varuna, Osiris.

Overcoming obstacles: Ganesha, Merlin, Osiris, the Dagda, Odhinn, Taliesin.

Passion: Dionysus, Hercules, Pan, Faunus, Cernunnos, Kama, Krishna, Shiva, Vajrapani, Bacchus, Eros, Cupid.

Patron of priests and priestesses: Osiris, Thoth, Odhinn, the Dagda, Merlin, Freyr, Lugh.

Peace: Ganesha, Forseti, Freyr, Imhotep, Osiris, Mimir, Perun, Volos, Vishnu.

Pleasure: See **Passion.**

Poetry: See **Writing.**

Politics: Ogun, Forseti, Odhinn.

Power: Anu, Hercules, Agni, Mithras, Marduk, Ogun, Odhinn, Varuna, Vishnu, Osiris, Zeus, Jupiter, Enlil.

Problem solving: Horus, Ganesha, Merlin, Osiris, the Dagda, Odhinn.

Prophecy: Marduk, Apollo, Dionysus, Prometheus, Zeus, Janus, Ganesha, Chandra, Soma, Thoth, Osiris, Amen, Odhinn, Mimir,

Bran the Blessed, Lugh, Kuan Ti, Gidja, the Thunderbirds, Pachaca-mac, Ahura Mazdah, Amen.

Prosperity: Aegir, Yum Caax, Tsai-Shen, Ganesha, Kubera, Puchan, Hades, Saturn, the Dagda, Njord, Ilmarinen, Bes, Hapi, Ra, Cronus, Hermes, Mercury, Zeus, Jupiter, Pluto, Dis Pater, Enlil, Bel, Cernun-nos, Freyr, Agni, Rudra, Tvashtar, Vishnu, Lu-Hsing.

Protection: Anubis, Kupalo, Thorr, Agni, Merlin, Legba, Mithras, Puchan, Zeus, Jupiter, Odhinn, Volos, Anubis, Bes, Horus, Sinn, Wepwawet, Ashur, Gibil, the Dagda, Freyr, Heimdall, Perun, the Asvins, Indra, Kuan Ti.

Psychic abilities: Merlin, Osiris, Pan, Faunus, Odhinn, Chandra.

Purification: Agni, Ahura Mazdah, Faunus, Bel.

Rain: The Thunderbirds, Susanoo, Agni, Zeus, Jupiter, Addad, Ba'al, Enlil, Xevioso, Freyr, Odhinn, Ukko, Perun, Maui, Indra, Viracocha.

Regeneration/Rebirth: Agni, Adonis, Mithras, the Dagda, Diancecht, Manannan mac Lir, Yarilo, Amen, Horus, Khepera, Osiris, Ptah, Asclepius, Dionysus, Ba'al, Dumuzi, Odhinn, Itzamna.

Reincarnation: Adonis, Osiris, Indra, the Dagda, Manannan mac Lir, Horus, Khnemu, Balder, Odhinn, Cernunnos, Ogma, Shou-hsing, Ptah, Dumuzi, Bragi, Khepera, Dionysus, Ba'al, Marduk, Lugh, Agni.

Remove difficulties: Ogun, Varuna, Vishnu, Horus, Osiris, Odhinn, Ukko, Ganesha, Indra.

Retribution: Lei-king, Loki, Odhinn, Tyr, Horus, Set, Nergal, Shamash, Arawn, Lugh, Thorr, Varuna, Yama, Yeng-Wang-Yeh, Emma-O.

Revenge: Apollo, Horus, Set, Ares, Mars, Thorr, Lugh, Ninurta, Sinn, Kuan Ti, Emma-O, Mara, Odhinn.

Rituals: Mithras, Odhinn, Osiris, Thoth, Ea, Ra, Dionysus, Merlin, Legba, Xiuhtecuhtli.

Roads: Cernunnos, Lugh, Janus.

Sacrificed Savior: Dionysus, Ixion, Hercules, Zalmoxis, Mithras, Saishyant, Osiris, Tammuz, Adonis, Set, Attis, Odhinn, Agni, Mars,

Rudra, Vishnu, Krishna, Buddha, Lugh, Gwyn, Arthur, Balder, Xipe Totec, Cinteotl, Xiuhtzilopochtli, Yum Caax, Quetalcoatl, Viracocha, Kupila, Yarilo, Hou-Chi.

Sailing: Aegir, Poseidon, Neptune.

Science: Bel, Thoth, Mithras.

Sea: Khnemu, Poseidon, Neptune, Njord, Thorr, Llyr, Enlil, Manannan mac Lir, Bel, Janus, Aegir, Ahto, Tangaroa, Quetzalcoatl, O-wata-tsumi, Ea, Yam, Ta'aroa, Varuna, Susanoo.

Shapeshifter: Gucumatz, Vertumnus, Loki, Manannan mac Lir, Maui, Gwydion, Merlin, Taliesin.

Shepherd of Souls: Hermes, Osiris.

Sky: Uranus, Cronus, Zeus, Jupiter, Brahma, Ilma, El, Beylobog, Kupalo, Shu, Leo-Tien-Yeh, Adroa, Kitcki Manitou, Atius Tirawa, Hahbwehdiyu, Gucumatz, Itzamna, Mixcoatl, Inti, Viracocha, Ukko.

Snake: Kulkulcan, Susanoo, Apep, Asclepius, Varuna, Quetzalcoatl.

Sorcery: O-kuni-nushi, Vertumnus, Gwydion, Manannan mac Lir, Math Mathonwy, Loki, Maui, Tawhaki, Lugh, Merlin, Nuada, Taliesin, Odhinn, Tezcatlipoca.

Spells: See **Magick, Psychic abilities, Divination.**

Spiritual enlightenment: Hurukan, Buddha, Shiva, Odhinn, Osiris, Thoth, Mithras, Chandra, O-kuni-nushi, Anubis.

Storms: Illapa, Addad, Shango, Tlaloc, the Thunderbirds, Viracocha, Susanoo, Zeus, Jupiter, Thorr, Perun, Apep, Set, Enlil, Poseidon, Neptune, Ba'al, Nergal, Manannan mac Lir, Odhinn, Agni, Indra, Shiva, Hurukan.

Strength: Hercules, Shamash, Cernunnos, Ogma, Odhinn, Thorr, Indra, Shiva, Varuna.

Success: Horus, Osiris, Thoth, Hermes, Mercury, Tyr, Bel, Vishnu, Fu-hsi, Lu-hsing, Tsai Shen, Ganesha, Puchan, Saturn, the Dagda, Balder, Njord, Odhinn, Janus.

Sun: Belenus, Lugh, Lleu Llaw Gyffes, Ogma, Apollo, Helios, Vishnu, Balder, Asshur, Ahura Mazdah, Kupalo, Khors, Svarog, Ra, Khepra, Inti.

Supreme Magus: Thoth, Gwydion, Lugh, Varuna, Merlin, the Dagda, Odhinn, Vainamoinen, Mara, Quetzalcoatl.

Surgery: Anubis.

Tarot: Mithras, Thoth, Merlin, Odhinn. See **Psychic abilites.**

Teacher: Anubis, Thoth, Merlin, Taliesin.

Terror: Pan, Leshy, the Horned God, Mars, Arawn, Cernunnos, Herne the Hunter.

Thunder: Thorr, Jupiter, Zeus, Shiva, Indra, Ukko, Jumala, Addad, Rimmon, Teshub, Ba'al, Perun, Akshobhya, Asagaya Gigaei, Addad, the Thunderbirds.

Travel: Hermes, Mercury, Janus, Lugh, Thorr, Njord, Hercules, Puchan, Xevioso, Tlaloc.

Trickster, The: Loki, Enki, Hermes, Rabbit, Mantis, Fox, Badger, Reynard the Fox, Eleggua, Legba, Exu, Pan, Krishna, Susanoo, Maui, Coyote, Raven, Huehuecoyotl, Anansi.

Truth: Anubis, Apollo.

Twins: Apollo, Ahura Mazdah, Ahriman, Ioskeha, Tawiscara.

Underworld: Gucumatz, Hades, Pluto, Vulcan, Velchanos, Hephaestus, Dis Pater, Arawn, Gwynn ap Nudd, the Dagda, Odhinn, Hodr, Osiris, Anubis, Shiva, Apep, Sebek, Ptah, Seker, Sabazius, Yama, Mara, Yamm, Agni, Kubera, Puchan, Ahriman, Mot, Nergal, Chernobog, Chu-Jung, Yeng-Wang-Yeh, Emma-O, Kaka-Guia, Huitzilopochtli, Itzcoliuhqui, Tezcatlipoca, Mictlantecuhtli, Xolotl, Supai, Tuoni, Aciel.

Vegetation: The Thunderbirds, Adonis, Dumuzi, Dionysus, Faunus, Mars, Mithras, Vertumnus, Thorr, Hapi, Osiris, Hades, Bel, Freyr, Ba'al.

Victory: Janus, Marduk, Shamash, Tyr, Odhinn, Perun, Svantovit, Vishnu. See **Success.**

Volcanoes: Hephaestus, Vulcan, Enlil, O-yama-tsu-mi.

War: Mars, Ares, Horus, Menthu, Tyr, Thorr, Gwydion, Lugh, Asshur, Nergal, Indra, Kuan Ti, Ogun, Shango, Tezcatlipoca, Ogun, Zeus, Jupiter, Odhinn, Svantovit, Arawn, Bran the Blessed, the Dagda, Nuada, Volos, Shiva.

Water: Neptune, Poseidon, Oceanus, Varuna, Ea, Enki, Apsu, Nereus, Phorcys, Shiva, Ichthys, Hapi, Dagon, Oannes, Llyr, Lir, Nuada, Aegir, Njord, Ahto, O-Wata-Tsumi, Aluluei, Ta'aroa.

Weather: Aegir, Odhinn, Thorr, the Dagda, Manannan mac Lir, Ba'al, Addad, Agni, Indra, Vajrapani, Enlil, Marduk, Amen, Zeus, Jupiter, Hephaestus, Freyr, Susanoo.

Wild Hunt, Lord of: Odhinn, Wodan, the Erl King, Arthur, Robin Hood, Herne the Hunter.

Winds: Aegir, Amen, Quetzalcoatl, Zeus, Jupiter, Njord, Enlil, Ninurta, Marduk, Kitcki Manitou, Hurukan, Addad, Nergal, Odhinn, Maui.

Wine: Dionysus, Bacchus, Saturn, Hercules, Svantovit.

Wisdom: Anubis, Thoth, Ganesha, Balder, Mimir, Odhinn, Heimdall, Ea, Shamash, Sinn, Apollo, Enlil, Merlin, Taliesin, Janus, Mithras, Nergal, Brahma, Buddha, the Underwater Panthers.

Woodlands: Pan, Cernunnos, Robin Hood, the Green Man, Apollo, Faunus, the Horned God, Leshy, Marduk, Rudra, Dumuzi, Vajrapani, Merlin, Bacchus, Herne the Hunter, Thorr, Tapio, Perun, Susanoo, the Thunderbirds.

Writing: Apollo, Itzamna, Ganesha, Ogma, Bragi, Odhinn, Imhotep, Thoth, Ea, Lugh, Taliesin, Bran the Blessed, Nuada.

Youth: Angus mac Og, Dionysus, Zeus, Jupiter, Nuada.

ENDNOTES

CHAPTER I

1. Moore, Robert and Douglas Gillette. *King, Warrior, Magician, Lover.*
2. The word *deity* traces its roots back to the Indo-European *deiwos,* which means "shining god." The Sanskrit *daevas* or *devas* ("god") is closely related.

CHAPTER II

1. The word *archetype* comes from the Greek *arkhetupon* or *arkhetupos,* which means "first-molded," "chief being or ruler."
2. The word *sacred* ("holy") is related to several Latin words, among them *sancire* ("consecrate") and *sacerdos* ("priest"). The word *sacrum* ("bottom section of the spine," "holy bone") comes from the Greek *hieron osteon,* which alludes to the use of this section of bone in sacrificial ceremonies.
3. The Slavonic-Russian cultures had a Winter Solstice celebration that honored their god Kolyada. This festival also celebrated the end of the reign of Chernobog the Black God.

4. Most Asiatic gods bear the title of firstborn, which in Sanskrit is Hiranyagarbha.

5. *The Egyptian Book of the Dead* spoke of an ancient tradition of sacrificing firstborn children. They considered such children to be extremely sacred.

6. Budge, E. A. Wallis, *Gods of the Egyptians.* Robert Graves, in *The White Goddess,* writes that the Hebrew tale of Moses probably originated from this story and the similar legend of the reborn Sun god (Ra-Harakhti) of Canopus.

7. Budge, ibid.

8. Although another Moon deity is listed in early Egyptian mythology, Osiris is often called god of the Moon.

9. The ancient Greeks did not use the word *mystery* in the same sense as we do today. The word comes from the Greek *muein,* meaning "to close one's eyes and/or mouth." Their Mystery meant to keep something secret; this term was applied only to secret initiation ceremonies. *Muein* ("initiate"), *mustes* ("initiated person"), and *musterion* ("secret ceremony") are all related to *muein.* Therefore, a Mystery was a secret religious ceremony whose contents were not revealed to non-initiates. The same meaning applied to the sacred Mysteries of any culture.

10. Legge, Francis, *Forerunners and Rivals of Christianity.* Angus, S., *The Mystery-Religions.*

11. de Riencourt, Amaury, *Sex and Power in History.*

12. Hooke, S. H., *Middle Eastern Mythology.* Cumont, Franz, *The Mysteries of Mithra.* Smith, Homer, *Man and His Gods.*

13. *Magi* means "magicians"; the Persians said that they were the only ones capable of correctly reading the Messiah star and knowing when the Divine Child would arrive. This astrological wisdom came originally from Egypt, where the three stars in the Belt of Orion were called the Three Wise Men. These three stars were still called Magi in the Middle Ages. Jobes, Gertrude, *Dictionary of Mythology, Folklore and Symbols.*

14. Brewster, H. Pomeroy, *Saints and Festivals of the Christian Church.*

15. December 25 was also the birthday of other gods, such as Freyr, Attis, Helios, Dionysus, Osiris, and Baal. Yule (the birthday of Freyr) was known to the Norse as Modranect, or Night of the Mothers.

16. Angus, S., *The Mysteries of Mithra.*

Notes for pages 15–25

17. Graham, Lloyd M., *Deceptions and Myths of the Bible.*

18. Many early religions used baptism by water (usually sprinkling or pouring) to bless and sanctify babies and holy objects, while the Mysteries used baptism to mark the advancement of spiritual growth. Mithraism required its followers to be rebaptized at specific intervals as a sign of commitment to the religion.

19. Dionysus in this aspect was called the "Horned God," "the bull-horned god," and "Savior."

20. Other myths list Zeus' birthplace as a cave on Mount Lykaion in Arcadia on the mainland and Mount Ithome in Messenia. The Greek writer Pausanias said that on Mount Ithome was a sacred spring of Zeus Ithomatas where the god was first bathed.

21. This is another version of the Slaughter of the Innocents.

22. Harrison, J. E., *Epilegomena to the Study of Greek Religion and Themis.*

23. Pausanias.

24. Jung, Carl and Carl Kerenyi, *The Myth of the Divine Child.*

25. Ovid, *Metamorphoses.*

26. Graves, Robert, *The Greek Myths.*

27. Godwin, J., *Mystery Religions in the Ancient World.*

28. The annual sacred festival of the Greater Eleusinia was celebrated September 23–October 1 in honor of Demeter of Eleusis, Kore, Persephone, and the Holy Child Iacchus (Dionysus).

29. O'Flaherty, Wendy, *Hindu Myths.*

30. Barbara Walker says that this elephant was the god Ganesha, also called Lord of Hosts.

31. Guerber, H. A., *Legends of the Middle Ages.*

32. Malory, Sir Thomas, *Le Morte de'Arthur.*

33. Even Zoroaster was said to have had a Divine Childbirth. The Earth was said to have rejoiced when he was born. Demons came to crush him, but the baby chanted holy prayers and repelled them.

34. Zurvan Akarana was called the First Cause (principle of creation) and was associated with Time, Destiny, and Fate: all powers under control of the Goddess.

CHAPTER III

1. Doane, T. W., *Bible Myths and Their Parallels in Other Religions.* Briffault, Robert, *The Mothers.*

2. This flower was said to have arisen from his blood upon the Earth. His title, Naaman ("darling"), was the source for the flower's name.

3. Graves, Robert, *The White Goddess.*

4. Puhvel, Jaan, *Comparative Mythology.*

5. The shakti is a feminine, complimentary power without which none of the Hindu gods can function.

6. O'Flaherty, Wendy D., *Hindu Myths.*

7. Rawson, Philip, *Erotic Art of the East.*

8. The name Kamadeva means "love god." It is very possible that the ancient Indian sex manual *The Kamasutra* ("love chapters") came from his name; Bierlein, J. F., *Parallel Myths.*

9. Campbell, Joseph, *The Mythic Image.* O'Flaherty, ibid.

10. Baring-Gould, Sabine, *Curious Myths of the Middle Ages.*

11. Budge, E. A. Wallis, *The Egyptian Book of the Dead.*

12. Lindsay, Jack, *The Ancient World.*

13. J. E. Cirlot says that Pan is equated with Satan and represents the base aspects of humanity as well as involutive life. I disagree with this, as nothing about life is base unless humans deliberately twist and pervert it.

14. Freyr's story is in the Elder Edda; Kevin Crossley-Holland in *The Norse Myths* gives a very good rendition.

CHAPTER IV

1. Waddell, L. Austine, *Tibetan Buddhism.*

2. Dyaus piter was a god of India known as Father Heaven; he was wed to an Earth goddess and carried the phallic lightning bolts.

3. Cirlot, J. E., *A Dictionary of Symbols.*

4. The *dorje* is double-ended and has six prongs. It was often called "diamond-holder," meaning it is possible to sense divine spirit through orgasm. The name Darjeeling, an Indian city, comes from dorje-lingam.

Notes for pages 46–59

5. Frawley, David, *Gods, Sages and Kings.*

6. Elisofon, Eliot and Alan Watts, *Erotic Spirituality.* This title has been corrupted into the word *juggernaut.*

7. Lee M. Hollander, in *The Skalds,* says that Thorr bellowed like a bull when he swung his hammer, causing thunder and lightning.

8. Hollander, Lee M., ibid.

9. Branston, Brian, *Gods of the North.*

10. The oldest son of the god Ea, Marduk was called the Bull Calf of the Sun and the Lord of Life. He was the consort of Sarpanitu.

11. Briffault, Robert, *The Mothers.*

12. Beltz, Walter, *God and the Gods: Myths of the Bible.*

13. Joyce, P. W., *A Social History of Ancient Ireland.*

14. O'Flaherty, Wendy, *Hindu Myths.*

15. Turville-Petre, E. O. G., *Myth and Religion of the North.*

16. Budge, E. A. Wallis, *The Egyptian Book of the Dead.*

17. Budge, E. A. Wallis, *Gods of the Egyptians.*

18. Budge, E. A. Wallis, ibid.

19. Budge, E. A. Wallis, *The Egyptian Book of the Dead.* d'Alviella, Count Goblet, *Migration of Symbols.*

20. All seasons are reversed in the Southern Hemisphere.

CHAPTER V

1. Experiments have shown that rats will begin to exhibit aggressive and murderous tendencies when they become overcrowded. As soon as the population thins out and the rats once again have their "space," they no longer attack each other or kill their own young.

2. Walker, Barbara, *The Woman's Encyclopedia of Myths and Secrets.*

3. Graves, Robert, *The Greek Myths.*

4. Funk, Wilfred, *Word Origins and Their Romantic Stories.*

5. Guirand, Felix, ed., *Larousse Encyclopedia of Mythology.*

6. Frazer, James, *The Golden Bough.*

7. Herne the Hunter is still said to haunt the woodlands near Windsor Castle. As recently as 1964 several people saw this apparition riding his fire-breathing horse through the woods.

8. In parts of Britain, the Great Horn Fair is still celebrated in the fall of the year. Men parade through the streets with antlers fastened on their heads. One English town that celebrates the Horn Dance in September is Abbots Bromley, Staffordshire.

9. Campbell, Joseph, *Occidental Mythology*. Other writers have pointed out the similarity of the Assyro-Babylonian *garnu,* the Hebrew and Phoenician *geren,* and Apollos Karnaios (a horned god) to the word Cernunnos; Brown, Robert, *Semitic Influence in Hellenic Mythology.*

10. The hand gesture with raised forefinger and little finger was an appeal by many ancient cultures to the Horned God. The Hindus still use this mudra. (To bring good luck, Italian card players today will make the horned gesture, pointing downward, over the cards.) Deer in general, and the stag in particular, were considered to be magickal animals. Thus, the stag was sacrificed to the Goddess, taking the place of the God or a human male representing the God. One human stag-god was the Greek Actaeon, who was torn to pieces by the dogs of the Goddess.

11. At one time, infertile couples slept on the giant's phallus in order to conceive.

12. Campbell, Joseph, *Oriental Mythology.*

CHAPTER VI

1. Waddell, L. Austine, *Tibetan Buddhism.*

2. La Barre, *They Shall Take Up Serpents.* According to Campbell in *The Mythic Image,* this same symbol was found among the Aztecs and Native Americans.

3. Maspero, Gaston, *Popular Stories of Ancient Egypt.*

4. Green, Miranda, *Gods of the Celts.*

CHAPTER VII

1. Turville-Petrie, E. O. G., *Myth and Religion of the North.*

2. Oxenstierna, Eric, *The Norsemen.*

3. Cavendish, Richard, *The Powers of Evil.*

4. Campbell, Joseph, *Occidental Mythology.*

5. Hays, H. R., *In the Beginnings.*

Notes for pages 80–84

CHAPTER VIII

1. Another of Apollo's names was Phoebus ("the Shining One").

2. Campbell, Joseph, *Hero with a Thousand Faces*.

3. The other sons were Menoetius, who was imprisoned in Erebus; Atlas, who was condemned to stand forever upholding the sky; and Epimetheus ("he who reflects after the event"), who, like Prometheus, was not punished.

4. Loewe, Michael and Blacker, Carmen, *Oracles and Divination*.

5. Saturn with his sickle represented death. Originally, at the Saturnalia a human victim was sacrificed; later, this became the killing of King Carnival in effigy.

6. To Babylonian astrologers, Saturn was the Black Sun. At the city of Harran, Saturn worshippers dressed in black clothes and used black candles.

7. Talbott, David, *The Saturn Myth*.

8. In astrology, the planet Saturn in a chart forces us to learn lessons whether we like it or not. I have found that often Saturn reflects what lessons we have slipped out of in another life, and now hedge us in until we face them.

9. The punishments of Varuna seem to be linked to the Hindu custom of swearing by water; those foresworn were punished by nine years of ostracism. Puhvel, Jaan, *Comparative Mythology*.

10. The stone lapis lazuli was sacred to both Thoth and Maat. Lapis amulets were buried with Egyptian mummies to replace the heart and help with gaining new life in the Underworld; Budge, E. A. Wallis, *Egyptian Magic*.

11. Oracular skulls were part of several ancient cultures. In Greece, the skull of Orpheus was said to be kept in a cave at Lesbos. The Norse drinking toast *skoll* means "skull."

12. Budge, E. A. Wallis, *Gods of the Egyptians*.

13. The Giantess maiden Gunnlod guarded this "wise blood of immortality"; Branston, Brian, *Gods of the North*. The blood came from Kvasir, the "wisest of all men."

14. Branston, ibid.

15. The Germans called this god Ziu or Tiuz; the Scandinavians, Tyr; the Anglo-Saxons, Tiw.

Notes for pages 84–103

16. Graham, Lloyd M., *Deceptions and Myths of the Bible.*
17. The Moon is almost universally connected with dreams and predictions.

CHAPTER IX

1. Rees, Alwyn and Brinley, *Celtic Heritage.*
2. Graves, Robert, *The White Goddess.*
3. O'Flaherty, Wendy, *Hindu Myths.*

CHAPTER X

1. Cirlot, J. E., *A Dictionary of Symbols.*
2. Campbell, Joseph, *Hero with a Thousand Faces.*
3. Guerber, H. A., *Legends of the Rhine.*
4. Graves, Robert, *Greek Myths.*
5. d'Alviella, Count Goblet, *The Migration of Symbols.*
6. The symbol of the first initiation in the Mithraic Mysteries was a raven, which symbolically carried the initiate beyond the lunar sphere. Campbell, Joseph, *Occidental Mythology.*
7. Eliade, Mircea, *The Sacred and the Profane.*
8. Indris Shah writes that the Sufi word for magick was *sihr.* Sabine Baring-Gould says that the Kalmuks (worshippers of Kali) call their magick *siddhi-kur.* H. R. Ellis Davidson, in *Pagan Scandinavia,* wrote that the Lapps called the power of their deities *seidi;* the Celts named their faery ancestor deities the *sidh.*
9. Cooper, J. C., *Symbolic and Mythological Animals.*

CHAPTER XI

1. Guthrie says that originally Poseidon had no specific name and was known only as "spouse of the Earth." Robert Graves says that this god's name may come from *potidan* ("he who gives to drink").
2. Graves, Robert, *Greek Myths.*
3. Cirlot, J. E., *A Dictionary of Symbols.*
4. The legends of this god are the origin of the Hebrew Jonas.
5. Baring-Gould, Sabine, *Curious Myths of the Middle Ages.*

Notes for pages 108–112

CHAPTER XII

1. Briffault, Robert, *The Mothers*.
2. Plutarch believed that the Jews didn't eat pork because the god Diony-sus-Adonai was killed by a boar; Knight, Richard, *The Symbolical Language of Ancient Art and Mythology*.
3. Frazer, James, *The Golden Bough*.
4. Graves, Robert, *Greek Myths*.
5. The cross is a very ancient Pagan symbol. The scarecrow was origi-nally an effigy of the sacred king whose blood fertilized the fields.
6. Guthrie, W. K. C., *The Greeks and Their Gods*.
7. Knight, Richard, *The Symbolical Language of Ancient Art and Mythology*.
8. Lindsay, Jack, *The Ancient World*.
9. Herodotus wrote that human sacrifices were offered to Zalmoxis by impaling.
10. Hooke, S. H., *Middle Eastern Mythology*. Cumont, Franz, *The Mys-teries of Mithra*.
11. Robertson, J. M., *Pagan Christs*.
12. Robertson, J. M., ibid.
13. The name Zoroaster probably comes from the Sanskrit *hari-dyut-astra* ("beautiful light of the star"); Frawley, David, *Gods, Sages and Kings*.
14. Campbell, Joseph, *Occidental Mythology*.
15. Budge, E. A. Wallis, *Gods of the Egyptians*.
16. All savior gods who were called Good Shepherd were said to care for the souls in the "green pastures" of the afterlife.
17. Budge, E. A. Wallis, *The Egyptian Book of the Dead*.
18. Bread and wine (the eucharist) were common symbols for the flesh and blood of savior deities, such as Osiris, Adonis, Dionysus, and oth-ers. In Sanskrit, the holy sacrament was *su-haritas*.
19. Budge, ibid.
20. Campbell, Joseph, *The Mythic Image*.
21. Graves, Robert, *Greek Myths*. Fork comes from the Latin *furca*, "a two-pronged stake."
22. Campbell, Joseph, *The Mythic Image*.

23. Charles Pfeifer, in *The Dead Sea Scrolls and the Bible,* says that the religious sect of the Essenes appointed a priest to be the Sin Bearer, or Christos; he atoned for the sins of the others. The Slavic word *christos* or *krstnik* meant an "accursed sacrifice," or the Sin Bearer who was cursed before his sacrifice; Leland, Charles G., *Gypsy Sorcery and Fortune Telling.*

24. Budge, E. A. Wallis, *Amulets and Talismans.*

25. Guignebert, Charles, *Ancient, Medieval and Modern Christianity.*

26. Graves, Robert, *The White Goddess.*

27. Cumont, Franz, *Astrology and Religion Among the Greeks and Romans.* A sword also symbolized doom for a sacred king and was hung over his head to remind him of his ultimate fate. Later, the beheading evolved into a symbolic gesture of touching each shoulder, such as was used in conferring knighthood.

28. Duerr, Hans, *Dreamtime.*

29. Frank Borchardt, *German Antiquity in Renaissance Myth.*

30. The equal-armed cross was also a symbol of Hermes, god of the crossroads. T. W. Doane, in *Bible Myths and Their Parallels in Other Religions,* says that the Neoplatonists called Hermes the Logos, or God's word made flesh.

31. It is quite probable that this purification with ashes was the origin of the Christian Ash Wednesday ceremonies.

32. Hays, H. R., *In the Beginnings.* The Medes of Persia had a similar god called Immanuel or Imanisi.

33. *Assyrian and Babylonian Literature.*

34. O'Flaherty, Wendy, *Hindu Myths.*

35. Dumzeil, Georges, *Archaic Roman Religion.* Vishnu's followers taught that by sacrifice of the god in boar-form, Vishnu became the Universal Savior.

36. O'Flaherty, ibid.

37. Ibid.

38. Siddhartha means "rich in magick." A master yogi was said to be able to control magick power called *siddhi.*

39. Lunasa became the Saxon Hlaf-mass, or Lammas, the Feast of Bread.

40. Campbell, Joseph, *Oriental Mythology.*

41. Malory, Sir Thomas, *Le Morte de'Arthur.*

Notes for pages 116–125

42. Oxenstierna, Erich, *The Norsemen.*
43. Turville-Petre, E. O. G., *Myths and Religon of the North.*
44. Ibid.
45. Balder and Hodr may be like the Egyptian year-rivals Horus and Set.
46. Hazlitt, W. Carew, *Faiths and Folklore of the British Isles.*
47. Turville-Petre, ibid.
48. Frazer, James, *The Golden Bough.*
49. Waddell, L. Austine, *Tibetan Buddhism.*
50. Reay Tanahil writes that this sacrifice occurred when the Pleiades (a group of seven stars) was at its zenith. In pre-Vedic India, the Pleiades were known as the "cutters"; the god Agni was said to have had sex with the Seven Mothers while they were menstruating, thus producing a solar hero. In Egypt, the Seven Hathors were represented by the seven priestesses of Thebes; in the temple there, a sacred king was either sacrificed or castrated every seventh year.
51. Neumann, Erich, *The Great Mother.*
52. Tannahil, Reay, *Flesh and Blood.*
53. Campbell, Joseph, *The Mythic Image.*

CHAPTER XIII

1. The Roman Dis meant "rich god"; Underworld deities often were said to hold the keys to Earthly treasure. The Christians later assigned this power to their devil. Cavendish, Richard, *The Powers of Evil;* Rose, H. J., *Religion in Greece and Rome.*
2. Graves, Robert, *Greek Myths.*
3. According to J. F. Bierlein in *Parallel Myths,* the name Hephaestus may come from *hemero-phaestos* ("he who shines by day").
4. Lindsay, Jack, *The Ancient World.*
5. The Yew Valley was said to be the home of the Norse god Ullr (an aspect of Odhinn as the death deity); Duerr, Hans, *Dreamtime.* The folktale "Jack and the Beanstalk" probably came from one of Odhinn's names: Jalk the Giant-Killer; MacKenzie, Norman, *Secret Societies.*
6. Keightley, Thomas, *The World Guide to Gnomes, Fairies, Elves and Other Little People.*
7. Wimberly, Lowry Charles, *Folklore in the English and Scottish Ballads.*

Notes for pages 125–168

8. Budge, E. A. Wallis, *Egyptian Magic.*
9. Budge, E. A. Wallis, *The Egyptian Book of the Dead.*
10. Lethaby, W. R., *Architecture, Mysticism and Myth.*
11. Budge, E. A. Wallis, *Egyptian Magic.*
12. Budge, E. A. Wallis, *The Egyptian Book of the Dead.*
13. Budge, E. A. Wallis, *Gods of the Egyptians.*
14. Ibid.
15. Budge, E. A. Wallis, *The Egyptian Book of the Dead.*
16. Budge, E. A. Wallis, *Gods of the Egyptians.*
17. *The White Goddess.* Plutarch wrote that this Hebrew god was also called Sabbi; Knight, Richard, *The Symbolical Language of Ancient Art and Mythology.*
18. Zimmer, Heinrich, *Myths and Symbols in Indian Art and Civilization.*
19. Ibid.
20. Campbell, Joseph, *Oriental Mythology.*
21. Ross, Nancy W., *Three Ways of Asian Wisdom.*
22. Rees, Alwyn and Brinley, *Celtic Heritage.*
23. Ibid.
24. Brandon, S. G. F., *Religion in Ancient History.* Huxley, Francis, *The Way of the Sacred.*
25. O'Flaherty, Wendy, *Hindu Myths.*
26. Legge, Francis, *Forerunners and Rivals of Christianity.*
27. The Black Sun symbolized many Underworld gods, such as Saturn, Hades, Zeus Chthonios, and Yama.
28. No religion except Christianity believed in a hell where sinners were punished forever by hideous tortures. The Egyptians, Persians, Chinese, and others who acknowledged a place called hell believed that punishment was only for a time.

APPENDIX III: GOD SYMBOLS

1. Koch, Rudolf, *The Book of Signs.* Whittick, Arnold, *Symbols: Signs and Their Meaning and Uses in Design.*
2. Campbell, Joseph, *The Mythic Image.*
3. Gelling, Peter and H. R. Ellis Davidson, *The Chariot of the Sun.*

Notes for pages 168–175

4. Graves, Robert, *The Greek Myths.*

5. Angus, S., *The Mystery-Religions.*

6. La Barre, Weston, *They Shall Take Up Serpents.*

7. d'Alviella, Count Goblet, *The Migration of Symbols.*

8. Zimmer, Heinrich, *Myths and Symbols in Indian Art and Civilization.*

9. Campbell, Joseph, *The Mythic Image.*

10. Cirlot, J. E., *A Dictionary of Symbols.*

11. Budge, E. A. Wallis, *The Egyptian Book of the Dead.*

12. Green, Miranda, *The Gods of the Celts.*

13. Ibid.

14. Potter, Stephen and Laurens Sargent, *Pedigree.*

15. Ross, Anne, *Druids, Gods and Heroes from Celtic Mythology.*

16. Brown, Robert, *Semitic Influence in Hellenic Mythology.*

17. *Mahanirvanatantra.*

18. Budge, E. A. Wallis, ibid.

19. Elsworthy, Frederick, *The Evil Eye.* Frankfort, Henri, *Kingship and the Gods.*

20. Zimmer, Heinrich, *Myths and Symbols in Indian Art and Civilization.*

21. Jobes, Gertrude, *Dictionary of Mythology, Folklore and Symbols.*

22. Budge, E. A. Wallis, *Egyptian Magic.*

23. Huxley, Francis, *The Way of the Sacred.*

24. *Mahanirvanatantra.*

25. d'Alviella, Count Goblet, *The Migration of Symbols.*

26. Budge, E. A. Wallis, *Gods of the Egyptians.*

27. Graves, Robert, *The White Goddess.*

28. Budge, E. A. Wallis, ibid.

29. de Lys, Claudia, *The Giant Book of Superstitions.*

30. Gelling, Peter and H. R. Ellis Davidson, *The Chariot of the Sun.*

31. Trachtenberg, Joshua, *Jewish Magic and Superstition.*

32. Beltz, Walter, *God and the Gods.*

33. Duerr, Hans Peter, *Dreamtime.*

34. Smith, Morton, *Jesus the Magician.*

35. d'Alveilla, Count Goblet, ibid.

BIBLIOGRAPHY

Albright, William Powell. *Yahweh and the Gods of Canaan.* NY: Doubleday and Co., 1968.

Anderson, William. *Green Man: The Archetype of Our Oneness with the
Earth.* San Francisco, CA: HarperCollins, 1990.

Angus, S. *The Mystery-Religions.* NY: Dover, 1975.

Arnott, K. *African Myths and Legends Retold.* UK: Oxford University
Press, 1962.

Ashe, Geoffrey. *The Virgin.* UK: Routledge and Kegan Paul, 1976.

Assyrian and Babylonian Literature, Selected Translations. NY: D. Appleton and Co., 1901.

Aswynn, Freya. *Leaves of Yggdrasil.* St. Paul, MN: Llewellyn Publications,
1990.

Avalon, Arthur. *Shakti and Shakta.* NY: Dover, 1978.

Ayto, John. *Arcade Dictionary of Word Origins*. NY: Arcade Publishing, 1990.

Bachofen, J. J. *Myth, Religion and Mother Right*. Princeton, NJ: Princeton University Press, 1967.

Bailey, C. *Phases in the Religion of Ancient Rome*. UK: Oxford University Press, 1932.

Baring-Gould, Sabine. *Curious Myths of the Middle Ages*. NY: University Books, 1967.

Baumgartner, Anne S. *A Comprehensive Dictionary of the Gods*. NY: University Books, 1984.

Bayley, Harold. *The Lost Language of Symbolism*. Vol. I and II. NY: Citadel Press, 1993.

Beckwith, Martha. *Hawaiian Mythology*. Honolulu, HI: University Press of Hawaii, 1971.

Beltz, Walter. *God and the Gods: Myths of the Bible*. UK: Penguin, 1983.

Bierhorst, John, trans. *Cantares Mexicanos: Sons of the Aztecs*. Stanford, CA: Stanford University Press, 1985.

_____, ed. and trans. *The Hungry Woman: Myths and Legends of the Aztecs*. NY: Wm. Morrow, 1984.

_____. *The Mythology of Mexico and Central America*. NY: William Morrow and Co., 1990.

_____. *The Mythology of South America*. NY: Wm. Morrow, 1988.

Bierlein, J. F. *Parallel Myths*. NY: Ballantine Books, 1994.

Birch, Cyril. *Chinese Myths and Fantasies*. UK: Oxford University Press, 1962.

Black, Jeremy and Anthony Green. *Gods, Demons and Symbols of Ancient Mesopotamia*. Austin, TX: University of Texas Press, 1992.

Bolen, Jean Shinoda. *Gods in Everyman*. San Francisco, CA: Harper and Row, 1989.

Bonwick, James. *Irish Druids and Old Irish Religions*. NY: Dorset Press, 1986.

Borchardt, Frank. *German Antiquity in Renaissance Myth*. Baltimore, MD: Johns Hopkins University Press, 1971.

Borgeaud, P. *The Cult of Pan in Ancient Greece*. Chicago, IL: University of Chicago Press, 1988.

Bouquet, A. C. *Comparative Religion*. UK: Penguin, 1942.

Brandon, S. G. F. *Religion in Ancient History*. NY: Charles Scribner's Sons, 1969.

Branston, Brian. *Gods and Heroes From Viking Mythology*. NY: Schocken Books, 1982.

_____. *Gods of the North*. UK: Thames and Hudson, 1955.

_____. *The Lost Gods of England*. UK: Oxford University Press, 1982.

Brasch, R. *How Did It Begin? Customs and Superstitions and Their Romantic Origins*. NY: Simon and Schuster, 1969.

Bratton, Fred Gladstone. *Myths and Legends of the Ancient Near East*. NY: Thomas Y. Crowell Co., 1970.

Breasted, James H. *Development of Religion and Thought in Ancient Egypt*. NY: Charles Scribner's Sons, 1912.

Brewster, H. Pomeroy. *Saints and Festivals of the Christian Church*. NY: Frederick A. Stokes, 1904.

Brier, Bob. *Egyptian Magic*. NY: Quill, 1980.

Briffault, Robert. *The Mothers*. 3 vols. NY: Macmillan, 1927.

Brown, Robert. *Semitic Influence in Hellenic Mythology*. NY: Arno, 1977.

Brundage, Burr Cartwright. *The Phoenix of the Western World: Quetzalcoatl and the Sky Religion*. Norman, OK: University of Oklahoma Press, 1982.

Budge, E. A. Wallis. *Amulets and Talismans*. NY: University Books, 1968.

_____, trans. *The Egyptian Book of the Dead*. NY: Dover, 1967.

_____. *The Gods of the Egyptians*. 2 vols. NY: Dover, 1969.

_____. *Dwellers on the Nile*. NY: Dover, 1977.

_____. *Egyptian Language*. NY: Dover, 1977.

_____. *Egyptian Magic*. NY: Dover, 1971.

_____. *Osiris and the Egyptian Resurrection*. 2 vols. NY: Dover, 1973.

Bulfinch, Thomas. *Bulfinch's Mythology*. NY: Avenel Books, 1978.

Burland, Cottie A. *North American Indian Mythology*. NY: Peter Bedrick Books, 1985.

Burland, Cottie A. and Werner Forman. *The Aztecs: Gods and Fate in Ancient Mexico*. UK: Orbis, 1985.

Campbell, Joseph. *The Hero with a Thousand Faces*. NJ: Princeton University Press, 1968.

_____. *The Inner Reaches of Outer Space*. NY: Harper and Row, 1986.

_____. *The Masks of God: Primitive, Oriental, Occidental and Creative Mythology*. UK: Penguin Books, 1968.

_____. *The Mythic Image*. NJ: Princeton University Press, 1981.

_____, ed. *Myths, Dreams, and Religion*. NY: E. P. Dutton and Co., 1970.

_____. *Myths to Live By*. NY: Viking Press, 1972.

_____, ed. *Pagan and Christian Mysteries: Papers from the Eranos Yearbooks*. NY: Bollingen, 1955.

_____. *The Power of Myth*. NY: Doubleday, 1988.

_____. *Transformation of Myth Through Time*. NY: Harper and Row, 1990.

_____. *The Way of the Animal Powers*. San Francisco, CA: Harper and Row, 1983.

Carlyon, Richard. *A Guide to the Gods*. NY: Wm. Morrow and Co., 1982.

Carter, Jesse Benedict. *The Religious Life of Ancient Rome*. NY: Cooper Square, 1972. (Originally 1911.)

Caso, Alfonso. *The Aztecs: People of the Sun*. Norman, OK: University of Oklahoma Press, 1958.

Cassirer, Ernst. *Language and Myth*. NY: Dover, 1971. Originally 1954.

Catlin, George. *Letters and Notes on the Manners, Customs and Conditions of the North American Indians*. 2 vols. NY: Dover, 1973.

Cavendish, Richard, ed. *Legends of the World*. NY: Barnes and Noble, 1994.

_____, ed. *Mythology: An Illustrated Encyclopedia*. NY: Rizzoli, 1980.

_____. *The Powers of Evil*. NY: G. P. Putnam's Sons, 1975.

Ceram, C.W. *Gods, Graves and Scholars*. NY: Bantam Books, 1972.

Christie, Anthony. *Chinese Mythology*. UK: Paul Hamlyn, 1973.

Cirlot, J. E. *A Dictionary of Symbols*. NY: Philosophical Library, 1978.

Clayton, Peter. *Great Figures of Mythology*. NY: Crescent Books, 1990.

Codrington, R. *The Melanesians: Studies in Their History, Anthropology and Folklore*. UK: Clarendon Press, 1891.

Coe, Michael D. *The Maya*. NY: Penguin, 1966.

Colum, Padraic. *Orpheus: Myths of the World*. NY: Macmillan, 1930.

Conway, D. J. *The Ancient and Shining Ones*. St. Paul, MN: Llewellyn Publications, 1993.

_____. *By Oak, Ash and Thorn: Modern Celtic Shamanism*. St. Paul, MN: Llewellyn Publications, 1995.

_____. *Celtic Magic*. St. Paul, MN: Llewellyn Publications, 1990.

_____. *Norse Magic*. St. Paul, MN: Llewellyn Publications, 1990.

Conze, Edward, ed. and trans. *Buddhist Scriptures*. NY: Penguin, 1960.

Coomaraswamy, Ananda K. *The Dance of Siva*. NY: Farrar, Straus and Co., 1957.

Coomaraswamy, Ananda and Sister Nivedita. *Myths of the Hindus and Buddhists*. NY: Dover, 1967.

Cooper, J. C. *Symbolic and Mythological Animals*. UK: Aquarian, 1992.

Cotterell, Arthur. *A Dictionary of World Mythology*. NY: Perigee Books, 1979.

_____, ed. *Macmillan Illustrated Encyclopedia of Myths and Legends*. NY: Macmillan, 1989.

Crossley-Holland, Kevin. *The Norse Myths*. NY: Pantheon Books, 1980.

Cumont, Franz. *After Life in Roman Paganism*. NY: Dover, 1959.

_____. *Astrology and Religion Among the Greeks and Romans*. NY: Dover, 1960.

_____. *The Mysteries of Mithra*. NY: Dover, 1956.

_____. *Oriental Religions in Roman Paganism*. NY: Dover, 1956.

Curtin, Jeremiah. *Myths and Folk-Tales of the Russians, Western Slavs and Magyars*. Boston, MA: Little, Brown and Co., 1890.

Dalley, Stephanie, trans. *Myths From Mesopotamia: Creation, the Flood, Gilgamesh and Others*. NY: Oxford University Press, 1991.

d'Alviella, Count Goblet. *The Migration of Symbols*. UK: Aquarian Press, 1979.

Daly, Mary. *Beyond God the Father*. Boston, MA: Beacon Press, 1973.

Danielou, Alain. *Gods of Love and Ecstasy: The Traditions of Shiva and Dionysus*. Rochester, VT: Inner Traditions, 1992.

Daraul, Arkon. *A History of Secret Societies*. Secaucus, NJ: Citadel Press, 1961.

Darrah, John. *The Real Camelot: Paganism and the Arthurian Romance*. UK: Thames and Hudson, 1981.

David-Neel, Alexandra. *Magic and Mystery in Tibet*. NY: Dover, 1971.

Davidson, H. R. Ellis. *Gods and Myths of the Viking Age*. NY: Bell Publishing, 1981.

_____. *The Journey to the Other World*. Totowa, NJ: D. S. Brewer Ltd. and Rowman and Littlefield for The Folklore Society.

_____. *Myths and Symbols in Pagan Europe*. Syracuse, NY: University Press, 1988.

_____. *Pagan Scandinavia.* NY: Frederick A. Praeger, 1967.

de Bary, William T., ed. *Sources of Indian Tradition.* NY: Columbia University Press, 1958.

deLanda, Friar Diego. *Yucatan Before and After the Conquest.* NY: Dover, 1978.

de Lys, Claudia. *The Giant Book of Superstitions.* Secaucus, NJ: Citadel Press, 1979.

de Riencourt, Amaury. *Sex and Power in History.* NY: Dell Publishing, 1974.

De Vries, Jan. *The Problem of Loki.* Helsinki: Suomalainen Tiedeakatemia Societas Scientiarum Fennica, 1933.

Doane, T. W. *Bible Myths and Their Parallels in Other Religions.* NY: University Books, 1971.

Dolak, George. *The Religious Beliefs and Practices of the Ancient Slavs.* Springfield, IL: Concordia Theological Seminary, 1949.

Douglas, Mary. *Natural Symbols: Explorations in Cosmology.* NY: Pantheon, 1970.

Dowson, John. *A Classical Dictionary of Hindu Mythology.* UK: Routledge and Kegan Paul, 1950.

Drahomaniv, Mykhailo Petrovych. *Notes on the Slavic Religio-Ethical Legends.* Bloomington, IN: Indiana University Press, 1961.

Driver, G. R. *Canaanite Myths and Legends.* Edinburgh: Clark, 1956.

Duerr, Hans Peter. *Dreamtime: Concerning the Boundary Between Wilderness and Civilization.* Trans. Felicitas Goodman. UK: Basil Blackwell, 1985.

Dumezil, Georges. *Archaic Roman Religion.* 2 vols. Chicago, IL: University of Chicago Press, 1970.

Edwardes, Allen. *The Jewel in the Lotus.* NY: Lancer Books, 1965.

Eliade, Mircea. *A History of Religious Ideas.* 2 vols. Chicago, IL: University of Chicago Press, 1978.

_____. *The Myth of the Eternal Return.* Trans. Willard R. Trask. Princeton, NJ: Princeton University Press, 1954.

_____. *Patterns in Comparative Religion.* Cleveland, OH: The World Publishing Co., 1963.

_____. *Rites and Symbols of Initiation.* Trans. William R. Trask. NY: Harper and Row, 1958.

_____. *The Sacred and the Profane.* NY: Harcourt, Brace and World, 1959.

Eliot, Alexander, ed. *Myths*. NY: McGraw-Hill, 1976.

Eliseev, S. *Asiatic Mythology: The Mythology of Japan*. UK: Harrap, 1932.

Elisofen, Eliot and Watts, Alan. *Erotic Spirituality*. NY: Macmillan, 1971.

Ellis, Hilda Roderick. *The Road to Hel*. NY: Greenwood Press, 1968.

Elsworthy, Frederick. *The Evil Eye*. NY: Julian Press, 1958.

Ensil, Morton Scott. *Christian Beginnings*. NY: Harper and Bros., 1938.

Epic of Gilgamesh. UK: Penguin, 1960.

Erman, Adolf. *Life in Ancient Egypt*. Trans. H. M. Tirard. NY: Dover, 1971.

_____. *The Literature of the Ancient Egyptians*. NY: Benjamin Blom, 1971.

Evans, Arthur. *The God of Ecstasy*. NY: St. Martin's Press, 1988.

Evans-Wentz, W. Y., trans. *The Tibetan Book of the Dead*. UK: Oxford University Press, 1975.

Farrar, Janet and Stewart. *The Witches' God*. Custer, WA: Phoenix Publishing, 1989.

Feuerstein, Georg. *Sacred Sexuality: Living the Vision of the Erotic Spirit*. Los Angeles, CA: Jeremy P. Tarcher, 1992.

Fitzgerald, Robert, trans. *The Iliad*. NY: Doubleday and Co., 1974.

_____, trans. *The Odyssey*. NY: Doubleday and Co., 1961.

Fowler, W. Warde. *Roman Ideas of Deity*. UK: Macmillan, 1914.

Frankfort, Henri. *Kingship and the Gods*. Chicago, IL: University of Chicago Press, 1978.

Frawley, David. *Gods, Sages and Kings: Vedic Secrets of Ancient Civilization*. Salt Lake City, UT: Passage Press, 1991.

Frazer, James G. *Adonis, Attis, Osiris*. NY: University Books, 1961.

_____. *The Golden Bough*. NY: Macmillan, 1963.

Funk, Wilfred. *Word Origins and Their Romantic Stories*. NY: Bell Publishing, 1978.

Gantz, Jeffrey. *The Mabinogion*. NY: Dorset Press, 1976.

Gayley, Charles M. *The Classic Myths in English Literature and in Art*. NY: Ginn and Co., 1939.

Gelling, Peter and Davidson, H. R. Ellis. *The Chariot of the Sun*. NY: Frederick A. Praeger, 1969.

Gimbutas, Marija. *The Goddesses and Gods of Old Europe: Myths and Cult Images*. Berkeley, CA: University of California Press, 1992.

Glover, T. R. *The Conflict of Religions in the Early Roman Empire.* NY: Cooper Square, 1975.

Godwin, Joscelyn. *Mystery Religions in the Ancient World.* NY: Harper and Row, 1981.

Goldenberg, Naomi. *Changing of the Gods.* Boston, MA: Beacon Press, 1979.

Goodrich, Norma Lorre. *Ancient Myths.* NY: New American Library, 1960.

_____. *Myths of the Hero.* NY: Orion Press, 1962.

Graham, Lloyd M. *Deceptions and Myths of the Bible.* NY: Bell Publishing Co., 1979.

Grant, Frederick C. *Ancient Roman Religion.* NY: Liberal Arts Press, 1957.

Grant, Michael. *Roman Myths.* NY: Scribner, 1971.

Graves, Robert. *The Greek Myths.* UK: Penguin, 1981.

_____. *The White Goddess.* NY: Farrar, Straus and Giroux, 1980.

Graves, Robert and Patai, Raphael. *Hebrew Myths.* NY: Anchor Books, 1964.

Gray, John. *Near Eastern Mythology.* UK: Hamlyn, 1963.

Green, Miranda. *The Gods of the Celts.* Totowa, NJ: Barnes and Noble, 1986.

Grey, Sir George. *Polynesian Mythology.* UK: Whitcombe and Tombs, 1965.

Guerber, H. A. *Legends of the Middle Ages.* NY: American Book Co., 1924.

_____. *Legends of the Rhine.* NY: A. S. Barnes and Co., 1895.

_____. *Myths of the Norsemen From the Eddas and Sagas.* NY: Dover, 1992. (Originally published 1909.)

Guignebert, Charles. *Ancient, Medieval and Modern Christianity.* NY: University Books, 1961.

Guirand, Felix, ed. *New Larousse Encyclopedia of Mythology.* Trans. Richard Aldington and Delano Ames. UK: Hamlyn, 1978.

Guthrie, W. K. C. *The Greeks and Their Gods.* Boston, MA: Beacon Press, 1955.

_____. *Orpheus and Greek Religion.* NY: W. W. Norton, 1966.

Hall, James. *Dictionary of Subjects and Symbols in Art.* NY: Harper and Row, 1974.

Hall, Manley P. *The Secret Teachings of All Ages*. Los Angeles, CA: Philosophical Research Society, 1977.

Halliday, W. R. *Greek and Roman Folklore*. NY: Cooper Square, 1963. (Originally 1927.)

Hamilton, Edith. *Mythology*. Boston, MA: Little, Brown and Co., 1942.

Harrison, Jane Ellen. *Epilegomena to the Study of Greek Religion and Themis*. NY: University Books, 1962.

Hays, H. R. *In the Beginnings*. NY: G. P. Putnam's Sons, 1963.

Hazlitt, W. Carew. *Faiths and Folklore of the British Isles*. 2 vols. NY: Benjamin Blom, 1965.

Herm, Gerhard. *The Phoenicians*. NY: Wm. Morrow and Co., 1975.

Herodotus. *The Histories*. Trans. Henry Cary. NY: D. Appleton and Co., 1899.

Herzberg, Max. *Myths and Their Meaning*. Boston, MA: Allyn and Bacon, 1928.

Hicks, Jim. *The Persians*. NY: Time-Life Books, 1975.

Highwater, Jamake. *Myth and Sexuality*. NY: New American Library, 1990.

Hinnels, John. *Persian Mythology*. NY: Peter Bedrick Books, 1985.

Hitching, Francis. *Earth Magic*. NY: Pocket Books, 1978.

Hollander, Lee M. *The Skalds*. Ann Arbor, MI: University of Michigan Press, 1968.

Hooke, S. H. *Babylonian and Assyrian Religion*. UK: Hutchinson, 1953.

_____. *Middle Eastern Mythology*. UK: Penguin, 1963.

_____. *The Siege Perilous*. Freeport, NY: Books for Libraries Press, 1970.

Huxley, Francis. *The Way of the Sacred*. NY: Doubleday, 1974.

Hyde, Walter Woodburn. *Greek Religion and Its Survival*. NY: Cooper Square, 1963.

Ions, Veronica. *Indian Mythology*. NY: Paul Hamlyn, 1973.

Izett, James. *Maori Lore, the Traditions of the Maori People with the More Important of Their Legends*. Wellington, NZ: self-published, 1923.

Jacobi, Jolande. *Complex, Archetype, Symbol*. Princeton, NJ: Princeton University Press, 1971.

James, E. O. *The Ancient Gods*. NY: G. P. Putnam's Sons, 1960.

Jobes, Gertrude. *Dictionary of Mythology, Folklore and Symbols*. 3 vols. NY: Scarecrow Press, 1962.

Jobes, Gertrude and James. *Outer Space*. NY: Scarecrow Press, 1964.

Johnson, Robert. *He: Understanding Masculine Psychology*. NY: Harper and Row, 1989.

Jonas, Hans. *The Gnostic Religion*. Boston, MA: Beacon Press, 1963.

Joyce, P. W. *A Social History of Ancient Ireland*. 2 vols. NY: Arno, 1980.

Jung, Carl G. *The Archetypes and the Collective Unconscious*. Trans. R. F. C. Hull. NJ: Princeton University Press, 1990.

_____. *Man and His Symbols*. NY: Dell, 1968.

_____. *Psychology and Religion: West and East*. Princeton, NJ: Princeton University Press, 1969. Originally 1938.

Jung, Carl G. and Kerenyi, C. *Essays on a Science of Mythology*. Princeton, NJ: Princeton University Press, 1973.

_____. *The Myth of the Divine Child*. Princeton: NJ: Princeton University Press, 1973.

Keightley, Thomas. *The World Guide to Gnomes, Fairies, Elves and Other Little People*. NY: Avenel Books, 1978.

Keuls, Eva C. *The Reign of the Phallus: Sexual Politics in Ancient Athens*. NY: Harper and Row, 1985.

Kirby, W. F. *Kalevala*. Dent, 1907.

Kmietowicz, Frank A. *Slavic Mythical Beliefs*. Windsor, ON: self-published, 1982.

Knight, Richard Payne. *A Discourse on the Worship of Priapus*. NY: University Books, 1974.

_____. *The Symbolical Language of Ancient Art and Mythology*. NY: J. W. Bouton, 1892.

Koch, Rudolf. *The Book of Signs*. NY: Dover, 1955.

Kramer, Samuel N. *Cradle of Civilization*. NY: Time-Life Books, 1967.

_____. *History Begins at Sumer*. NY: Doubleday and Co., 1959.

_____. *The Sumerians: Their History, Culture and Character*. Chicago, IL: University of Chicago Press, 1963.

Kulikowski, Mark. *A Bibliography of Slavic Mythology*. Columbus, OH: Slavica Publishers, 1989.

La Barre, Weston. *They Shall Take Up Serpents: Psychology of the Southern Snake-Handling Cult*. NY: Schocken Books, 1974.

Lawson, John Cuthbert. *Modern Greek Folklore and Ancient Greek Religion*. NY: University Books, 1964.

Lederer, Wolfgang and Don D. Jackson. *The Mirages of Marriage*. NY: W. W. Norton and Co., 1968.

Legge, Francis. *Forerunners and Rivals of Christianity*. 2 vols. NY: University Books, 1964.

Lehane, Brendan. *Legends of Valor*. Alexandria, VA: Time-Life Books, n.d.

Leland, Charles Godfrey. *Gypsy Sorcery and Fortune Telling*. NY: University Books, 1962.

Lethaby, W. R. *Architecture, Mysticism and Myth*. NY: George Braziller, 1975.

Levi-Strauss, Claude. *Myth and Meaning*. NY: Schocken Books, 1979.

Lindsay, Jack. *The Ancient World*. NY: G. P. Putnam's Sons, 1968.

Lindow, John. *Myths and Legends of the Vikings*. Santa Barbara, CA: Bellerophon Books, 1979.

Loewe, Michael and Blacker, Carmen. *Oracles and Divination*. Boulder, CO: Shambhala, 1981.

Loomis, Roger S. and Laura H. *Medieval Romances*. NY: Modern Library, 1957.

Luck, Georg. *Arcana Mundi*. Baltimore, MD: Johns Hopkins University Press, 1985.

Lurker, Manfred. *Dictionary of Gods and Goddesses, Devils and Demons*. NY: Routledge and Kegan Paul, 1987.

MacCana, Proinsias. *Celtic Mythology*. NY: Peter Bedrick Books, 1983.

MacCulloch, J. A. *The Celtic and Scandinavian Religions*. Westport, CT: Greenwood Press, 1973.

_____, ed. *Mythology of All Races*. Boston MA: 1928.

MacKenzie, Donald. *German Myths and Legends*. NY: Avenel, 1985.

MacKenzie, Norman. *Secret Societies*. NY: Holt, Rinehart and Winston, 1967.

Malory, Sir Thomas. *Le Morte de'Arthur*. 2 vols. UK: J. M. Dent and Sons Ltd., 1961.

Marriott, Alice and Carol K. Rachlin. *American Indian Mythology*. NY: New American Library, 1972.

Martello, Leo Louis. *Weird Ways of Witchcraft*. Secaucus, NJ: Castle Books, 1972.

Maspero, Gaston. *Popular Stories of Ancient Egypt*. NY: University Books, 1967.

Massa, Aldo. *The Phoenicians*. Geneva: Editions Minerva, 1977.

Matthews, John. *Robin Hood: Green Lord of the Wildwood*. UK: Gothic Image, 1993.

Merivale, Patricia. *Pan the Goat-God*. Cambridge, MA: Harvard University Press, 1969.

Miles, Clement A. *Christmas Customs and Traditions*. NY: Dover, 1976.

Moore, Robert and Douglas Gillette. *King, Warrior, Magician, Lover: Rediscovering the Archetypes of the Mature Masculine*. San Francisco, CA: Harper and Row, 1991.

Morgan, Keith. *The Horned God*. UK: Pentacle Enterprises, 1992.

Mottram, E. *The Book of Herne*. UK: Arrowspire Press, 1981.

Muller, Max. *The Upanisads*. NY: Dover, 1962.

Murray, Alexander S. *Who's Who in Mythology*. NY: Bonanza Books, 1988.

Murray, Margaret A. *The Divine King in England*. UK: Faber and Faber Ltd., 1954.

_____. *The God of the Witches*. UK: Oxford University Press, 1981.

Mylonas, George. *Eleusis and the Eleusinian Mysteries*. Princeton, NJ: Princeton University Press, 1961.

Neumann, Erich. *Amor and Psyche*. NY: Harper and Row, 1956.

_____. *The Great Mother: An Analysis of the Archetype*. Princeton, NJ: Princeton University Press, 1963.

Nicholson, Irene. *Mexican and Central American Mythology*. NY: Peter Bedrick Books, 1985.

Norman, Dorothy. *The Hero*. NY: World Publishing Co., 1969.

Oates, Joan. *Babylon*. UK: Thames and Hudson, 1979.

O'Flaherty, Wendy Doniger. *Hindu Myths*. UK: Penguin, 1975.

_____, ed. *Textual Sources for the Study of Hinduism*. Totowa, NJ: Barnes and Noble, 1988.

Oinas, Felix J. *Essays on Russian Folklore and Mythology*. Columbus, OH: Slavica Publishers, 1985.

Osbourne, Harold. *South American Mythology*. NY: Peter Bedrick Books, 1984.

Oxenstierna, Eric. *The Norsemen*. Greenwich, CT: New York Graphic Society, 1965.

Page, Michael and Robert Ingpen. *Encyclopedia of Things That Never Were*. NY: Viking Penguin, 1987.

Pagels, Elaine. *The Gnostic Gospels*. NY: Random House, 1979.

Parrinder, E. G. *West African Religions*. UK: Epworth Press, 1949.

Parrinder, Geoffrey. *African Mythology*. UK: Paul Hamlyn, 1975.

_____. *African Traditional Religion*. UK: Hutchinson House, 1954.

Patai, Raphael. *The Hebrew Goddess*. Ktav Publishing House, 1967.

Pegg, Bob. *Rites and Riots: Folk Customs of Britain and Europe*. UK: Blandford Press, 1981.

Perowne, Stewart. *Roman Mythology*. UK: Paul Hamlyn, 1973.

Perry, John Weir. *Lord of the Four Quarters*. NY: Macmillan, 1966.

Piggott, Juliet. *Japanese Mythology*. UK: Paul Hamlyn, 1975.

Pfiefer, Charles F. *The Dead Sea Scrolls and the Bible*. NY: Weathervane Books, 1969.

Poignant, Roslyn. *Oceanic Mythology: The Myths of Polynesia, Micronesia, Melanesia, Australia*. UK: Paul Hamlyn, 1975.

Potter, Stephen and Sargent, Laurens. *Pedigree*. NY: Taplinger, 1974.

Pritchard, James B. *The Ancient Near East*. NJ: Princeton University Press, 1958.

Puhvel, Jaan. *Comparative Mythology*. UK: Johns Hopkins University Press, 1993.

Rank, Otto. *The Myth of the Birth of the Hero*. NY: Vintage Books, 1959.

Rawson, Philip. *Erotic Art of the East*. NY: G. P. Putnam's Sons, 1968.

_____. *The Art of Tantra*. Greenwich, CT: New York Graphic Society, 1973.

Ray, Benjamin. *African Religions*. NY: Prentice-Hall, 1976.

Rees, Alwyn and Brinley. *Celtic Heritage*. NY: Grove Press, 1961.

Reinach, Salomon. *Orpheus*. NY: Horace Liveright, 1930.

Richardson, Alan. *Earth God Rising: The Return of the Male Mysteries*. St. Paul, MN: Llewellyn Publications, 1992.

Ringgren, Helmer. *Religions of the Ancient Near East*. Trans. John Sturdy. Philadelphia, PA: Westminster Press, 1973.

Rippin, Andrew and Jan Knappert, eds. and trans. *Textual Sources for the Study of Islam*. Totowa, NJ: Barnes and Noble, 1987.

Robertson, J. M. *Pagan Christs*. NY: Dorset Press, 1966.

Rose, H. J. *Religion in Greece and Rome*. NY: Harper and Row, 1959.

Ross, Anne. *Druids, Gods and Heroes from Celtic Mythology*. NY: Schocken Books, 1986.

Ross, Anne and Michael Cyprien. *A Traveller's Guide to Celtic Britain.* Harrisburg, VA: Historical Times, 1985.

_____. *The Pagan Celts.* Totowa, NJ: Barnes and Noble, 1986.

Ross, Nancy Wilson. *Three Ways of Asian Wisdom.* NY: Simon and Schuster, 1966.

Sadeh, Pinhas. *Jewish Folklore.* Trans. Hillel Halkin. NY: Anchor Books, 1989.

Scott, George Ryley. *Phallic Worship.* Westport, CT: Associated Booksellers, n.d.

Sejourne, Laurette. *Burning Water: Thought and Religion in Ancient Mexico.* Berkeley, CA: Shambhala, 1976.

Seligmann, Kurt. *Magic, Supernaturalism and Religion.* NY: Pantheon Books, 1948.

Seznec, Jean. *The Survival of the Pagan Gods.* Princeton, NJ: Princeton University Press, 1953.

Shah, Indris. *The Sufis.* UK: Octagon Press, 1964.

Silberer, Herbert. *Hidden Symbolism of Alchemy and the Occult Arts.* NY: Dover, 1971.

Simek, Rudolf. *Dictionary of Northern Mythology.* Trans. Angela Hall. UK: D. S. Brewer, 1993.

Simons, G. L. *Sex and Superstition.* NY: Harper and Row, 1973.

Singer, Milton, ed. *Krishna: Myths, Rites and Attitudes.* Chicago, IL: University of Chicago Press, 1968.

Sjoo, Monica and Barbara Mor. *The Great Cosmic Mother: Rediscovering the Religion of the Earth.* San Francisco, CA: Harper and Row, 1987.

Skinner, Hubert. *Readings in Folk-Lore.* NY: American Book Co., 1893.

Smith, Homer. *Man and His Gods.* Boston, MA: Little, Brown and Co., 1952.

Smith, Morton. *Jesus the Magician.* San Francisco, CA: Harper and Row, 1978.

Spence, Lewis. *The Minor Traditions in British Mythology.* UK: Rider, 1948.

_____. *The Myths of the North American Indians.* NY: Dover, 1989.

Squire, Charles. *Celtic Myth and Legend, Poetry and Romance.* NY: Newcastle Publishing, 1975.

Steenstrup, Johannes C. H. R. *The Medieval Popular Ballad.* Seattle, WA: University of Washington Press, 1968.

Stewart, R. J. *Celebrating the Male Mysteries*. UK: Arcana, 1991.

_____. *Celtic Gods, Celtic Goddesses*. UK: Blandford, 1990.

_____. *The Underworld Initiation: A Journey Towards Psychic Transformation*. UK: Aquarian Press, 1985.

Sturluson, Snorri. *The Prose Edda*. Berkeley, CA: University of California Press, 1954.

Talbott, David N. *The Saturn Myth*. NY: Doubleday, 1980.

Tannahil, Reay. *Flesh and Blood: A History of the Cannibal Complex*. NY: Stein and Day, 1975.

_____. *Sex in History*. NY: Stein and Day, 1980.

Thomas, P. *Epics, Myths and Legends of India*. Bombay, India: D. B. Taraporevala Sons and Co., n.d.

Thompson, J. Eric S. *Maya History and Religion*. Norman, OK: University of Oklahoma Press, 1970.

Tompkins, Ptolemy. *This Tree Grows Out of Hell*. San Francisco, CA: Harper and Row, 1990.

Titchenell, Elsa-Brita. *The Masks of Odin*. Pasadena, CA: Theosophical University Press, 1988.

Trachtenberg, Joshua. *Jewish Magic and Superstition: A Study in Folk Religion*. NY: Atheneum, 1984.

Turville-Petre, E. O. G. *Myth and Religion of the North: The Religion of Ancient Scandinavia*. Westport, CT: Greenwood Press, 1975.

Vermaseren, Maartten J. *Cybele and Attis*. UK: Thames and Hudson, 1977.

von Hagen, Victor W. *World of the Maya*. NY: New American Library, 1960.

Waddell, L. Austine. *Tibetan Buddhism*. NY: Dover, 1972.

Walker, Barbara. *The Woman's Dictionary of Symbols and Sacred Objects*. San Francisco, CA: Harper and Row, 1988.

_____. *The Woman's Encyclopedia of Myths and Secrets*. San Francisco, CA: Harper and Row, 1983.

Warner, Elizabeth. *Heroes, Monsters and Other Worlds From Russian Mythology*. NY: Schocken Books, 1985.

Warner, Rex. *The Stories of the Greeks*. NY: Farrar, Straus and Giroux, 1967.

Watts, Alan W. *Myth and Ritual in Christianity*. NY: Grove, 1954.

Webster, G. *The British Celts and Their Gods Under Rome*. UK: Batsford, 1986.

Wendt, Herbert. *It Began in Babel.* Boston, MA: Houghton Mifflin, 1962.

Werner, A. *Myths and Legends of the Bantu.* UK: Harrap, 1933.

Whitlock, R. *In Search of Lost Gods.* UK: Phaidon, 1979.

Whittick, Arnold. *Symbols: Signs and Their Meaning and Uses in Design.* Newton, MA: Charles T. Branford, 1971.

Williamson, John. *The Oak King, the Holly King, and the Unicorn.* NY: Harper and Row, 1986.

Wimberly, Lowry Charles. *Folklore in the English and Scottish Ballads.* NY: Dover, 1965.

Woodroffe, Sir John, trans. *Mahanirvanatantra.* NY: Dover, 1972.

Woods, William. *A History of the Devil.* NY: Putnam, 1974.

Wright, Thomas. *The Worship of the Generative Powers During the Middle Ages of Western Europe.* NY: Bell, 1957.

Zimmer, Heinrich. *Myths and Symbols in Indian Art and Civilization.* Princeton, NJ: Princeton University Press, 1946.

Zimmerman, J. E. *Dictionary of Classical Mythology.* NY: Bantam Books, 1978.

Znayenko, Myroslava T. *The Gods of the Ancient Slavs.* Columbus, OH: Slavica Publishers, 1980.

INDEX

Abyss, 14, 17, 22, 25, 33, 128, 147, 175
Aciel, 130, 145, 187
Addad, 48, 145, 179, 181-182, 185-188
Adonai, 112
Adonis, 14, 31-34, 111-112, 114, 145, 152, 168, 177-181, 183, 185, 187, 197, 209
Adrastea, 16
Adroa, 51, 145, 179-182, 186
Aegir, 104, 146, 178, 185-186, 188
Agni, 14, 90, 113, 128, 146, 168, 177-188, 199
Ahriman, 25, 49, 110, 128-129, 146, 160, 179-180, 187
Ahto, 104, 186, 188
Ahura Mazdah, 25, 49, 82, 84, 110, 127-129, 146, 157, 181-182, 185, 187
Airmid, 149
Akshobhya, 51, 187
Alchemists, 73, 96
Aleyin, 34, 129, 157, 183

Aluluei, 104, 188
Amen, 51, 83, 125, 146, 169, 177, 179-181, 184-185, 188
Amida-Nyorai, 115
Amphitrite, 102, 159
Anahita, 14
Anath, 103
Anemone, 31, 112
Angelic voices, 22, 114
Angurboda, 70
Angus mac Og, 39, 146, 178, 183, 188
Anointed One, 108, 110, 112, 145, 150, 177
Anqet, 37, 51, 155
Antlers, 15, 59, 142, 148, 194
Anubis, 12, 83, 126, 146, 172, 177-183, 185-188
Apep, 126, 179-180, 186-187
Aphrodite, 19, 31-32, 123, 145, 150
Apollo, 10, 14, 16-17, 24, 27, 44-46, 64, 66, 73, 80, 90, 147-148, 152, 169, 171-173, 178-179, 181-185, 187-188, 195
Apsaras, 36, 154

Apsu, 48, 147, 188
Arabs, 96
Arawn, 123-124, 147, 179, 185, 187-
    188
Arcadia, 17, 191
Archetypes, 9-10, 31, 212, 214
Ares, 19, 31-32, 89, 147, 178-179,
    181, 185, 188
Arianrhod, 95, 115
Artemis, 24, 46, 80, 169-170
Arth Vawr, 115
Arthur, 24, 95, 115-116, 123, 151,
    179, 186, 188, 191, 198, 203, 207,
    209, 213
Asagaya Gigaei, 52, 147, 187
Asclepius, 64-66, 147, 169, 179, 181,
    183, 185-186
Asha, 49, 84
Asherat, 34
Ashes, 66, 113, 141, 168, 198
Asshur, 48, 147, 180, 187-188
Astarte, 49, 128
Asvins, 66, 181, 183, 185
Atargatis, 103, 149
Atea, 40, 147, 183
Athene, 58, 80, 89, 123, 147, 165
Atho, 59, 151
Atius Tirawa, 52, 147, 183, 186
Atonement, 107, 113-114, 168
Attis, 33, 112-114, 126, 167-168, 174,
    183, 185, 190, 209, 217
Avalon, 116, 203
Aya, 84, 161
Aztecs, 40, 61, 76, 117-118, 130, 169,
    194, 204-206

Ba'al, 34, 49, 103, 116, 127-129, 147,
    157, 179-183, 185-188
Ba'al-Hammon, 34, 183
Babylon, 33, 48-49, 84-85, 99, 111,
    114, 126, 129, 157, 167, 214
Bacchantes, 38, 108
Bacchus, 14, 38, 65, 108, 147, 175,
    180-181, 184, 188
Badger, 70, 187
Balder, 47, 71, 84, 116-117, 125, 148,
    178, 181-182, 185-188, 199
Balefires, 117
Baptism, 21, 134, 191

Bards, 94-95, 162
Bel, 44, 49, 116-117, 148, 150, 177,
    180-181, 183, 185-187
Beli Mawr, 44, 148
Belit, 84, 150
Beltane, 24, 44, 117, 148, 173
Bes, 37, 148, 177-185
Bethlehem, 31, 112
Bisexual, 25, 51, 70, 154
Black God, 49, 130, 148, 189
Black Sun, 126, 129-130, 145, 169-
    170, 175, 195, 200
Boar, 32, 109, 114, 157, 168, 197
Bragi, 96, 148, 178-180, 183-185, 188
Brahma, 47, 148, 182-183, 186, 188
Bran the Blessed, 84, 148, 178, 184-
    185, 188
Branwen, 84, 148, 155
Bread, 109-112, 197-198
Brigit, 149
Brimos, 21
Buddha, 14, 23, 82, 98, 109-110, 115,
    148, 156, 160, 179, 186, 188
Bull, 15, 34, 49, 59, 90, 110, 145, 148,
    150, 152, 156-157, 159-160, 168,
    174, 193
Buto, 12
Byelobog, 49-50, 130, 148, 178, 182

Caduceus, 65, 73, 96, 156, 169
Cakes, 110-111
Camelot, 24, 95, 207
Castration, 32-35, 71, 111
Cave, 13-17, 19, 31, 73, 75, 83, 109,
    112, 143, 191, 195
Centaurs, 38, 108
Ceres, 39
Cerne Abbas Giant, 59
Cernowain, 59, 148
Cernunnos, 58-59, 61, 148, 151-152,
    171-172, 177-181, 183-188, 194
Cerridwen, 94
Chandra, 82, 179, 183-186
Chaos, 6, 17, 25, 45, 48, 69, 103, 158,
    161
Chernobog, 49, 130, 148, 179-180,
    187, 189
Chimalman, 118
Chimati No Kami, 40, 149, 183

Chiron, 64
Christmas, 10, 214
Christos, 108, 110, 112, 198
Chu-Jung, 130, 187
Cinteotl, 118, 149, 181, 186
Confucius, 14
Consort, 3, 6, 15, 19-20, 34, 39-40, 44,
    46, 48-49, 51-52, 59, 61, 81, 83-84,
    96, 103-104, 108, 115, 122-123,
    128-129, 168-170, 172, 175, 193
Coyote, 76, 149, 153, 160, 187
Cremation, 117
Crete, 10, 15-16, 45, 168
Crone, 25, 84, 94, 103, 128, 131
Cronus, 16, 44-45, 101, 149, 160-161,
    171-172, 177, 179, 181, 185-186
Crook, 111, 167
Cross, 36, 96, 109, 111, 113, 117,
    167-168, 174, 197-198
Crucified, 112-113, 167-168
Cu Chulainn, 89, 181
Cupid, 19, 37, 179, 183-184
Cwn Annwn, 170
Cybele, 33-34, 80, 112, 217

Daevas, 128-129, 189
Dagda, 59, 89, 95, 124, 149, 178-188
Dagon, 103, 149, 188
Daramulun, 40, 149, 183
December, 14, 33, 81, 157, 160, 190
Delphi, 16, 80
Demeter, 21, 122, 150, 159, 165, 172,
    191
Demons, 46, 109, 128-129, 146, 152,
    159-160, 191, 204, 213
Devil, 25, 123-124, 199, 218
Dharma, 82, 128, 165
Dia, 109
Diancecht, 65, 149, 181-183, 185
Dikte, 16
Dionysus, 10, 15, 20-22, 35, 38, 58,
    65, 73, 80, 90, 96, 107-108, 126,
    147, 149, 159, 171-175, 177-185,
    187-188, 190-191, 197, 207
Dis Pater, 123, 177, 179, 185, 187
Disciples, 97, 109
Dithyrambos, 20, 108, 149
Divine Potter, 37, 51, 155
Dodona, 81

Dolphin, 16
Don, 5, 17, 63, 95, 121, 137-138, 213
Doomsday, 72, 117
Dorje, 36, 170, 192
Dumuzi, 33, 129, 150, 177, 180-181,
    183, 185, 187-188
Durga, 35

Ea, 33, 48, 84, 99, 103, 150, 178-181,
    183-186, 188, 193
Easter, 10, 31, 112
El, 49, 129, 150, 168, 186
Eleusinia, 191
Eleusinian Mysteries, 21-22, 58, 98,
    108, 149, 171, 173, 214
Elphin, 94
Emma-O, 130, 150, 179, 185, 187
End of the world, 25, 49, 110, 117,
    129, 160
Enki, 70, 99, 103, 150, 183, 187-188
Enlil, 84, 150, 158, 174, 178-182, 184-
    186, 188
Ereshkigal, 33, 129, 158
Erl King, 123-124, 188
Eros, 19-20, 37-38, 150, 165, 179,
    183-184
Eternal life, 22, 51, 107, 109, 111,
    125, 154
Etna, 122
Etruscan, 90, 156
Eucharist, 197

Fa, 85, 182
Faery Queen, 58
Father of Lies, 70, 155
Faunus, 56, 58, 150, 177, 179-185,
    187-188
Feathered Serpent, 118, 155, 160
Februus, 122, 159
Fenris, 70, 84, 89
Fire, 47, 50, 52, 80, 90, 96, 98, 109,
    117, 122, 124, 128, 130, 146, 148,
    151-155, 159, 164, 180
Firstborn, 10, 22, 38, 84, 114, 155,
    190
Flayed, 113-114, 117, 164
Fool, 55, 69, 171
Forseti, 84, 182, 184
Fountain of Wisdom, 83, 116

Fox, 70, 171, 187
Frankincense, 14-15
Freyja, 39, 72, 88, 96-97, 104, 114, 116, 150, 152, 158, 168
Freyr, 39-40, 104, 114, 150, 168, 171, 173, 177-178, 180-181, 183-185, 187-188, 190, 192
Frigg, 47, 96, 148, 152, 158
Furka, 167

Gaea, 16, 44, 149, 163
Ganesha, 81-82, 151, 177-178, 182-186, 188, 191
Gerda, 39-40, 150
Gibil, 85, 180, 182, 185
Gidja, 85, 151, 179-180, 183, 185
Gnostics, 93
Goat-foot God, 18, 159
Goddess, 3, 5-7, 10-16, 18-27, 29-37, 39, 41, 43-50, 52, 56, 58-61, 63-66, 69, 71-73, 75, 80-85, 88-89, 91, 94-96, 98, 101-104, 108-109, 113-117, 119, 121-123, 126-129, 131, 134-135, 146-158, 160-164, 168-170, 172-173, 175, 190-192, 194, 196, 198, 200-201, 210, 215
Goidniu, 124, 151
Good Shepherd, 109, 111-112, 114, 122, 125, 128, 152, 159, 167, 197
Gopi, 36
Govannon, 95, 151
Great Goddess, 3, 13-14, 25, 35, 56, 58
Great Mother, 22, 51, 66, 168, 170, 199, 214
Green Man, 55, 58-60, 151-152, 180, 188, 203
Gucumatz, 52, 151, 177-178, 186-187
Guineveres, 115-116
Gwion Bach, 94
Gwydion, 95, 151, 178, 180-183, 186-188
Gwyn, 115, 186
Gwynn ap Nudd, 124, 151-152, 179, 187
Gwythur ap Greidawl, 115

Hades, 45, 102, 122, 129-130, 152, 177, 179, 181, 183, 185, 187, 200

Hahbwehdiyu, 52, 186
Hahgwehdaetgah, 52
Hammer, 47, 49-50, 72, 88-89, 99, 159, 161-162, 164, 193
Hammurabi, 84
Hapi, 103, 177, 180-181, 185, 187-188
Hay-Tau, 34, 152, 183
Hecate, 122, 126
Heimdall, 24, 88, 96, 152, 178, 180-183, 185, 188
Hel, 70, 116, 124, 170, 209
Helios, 45, 152, 169, 187, 190
Hell, 26, 52, 85, 109-110, 118, 124, 126, 130, 147, 151, 154, 160, 163, 165, 200, 217
Hephaestus, 50, 80, 96, 122-123, 126, 128, 152, 178, 180-183, 187-188, 199
Hera, 20, 24, 73, 96, 123, 165
Hercules, 44, 109, 116, 158, 178, 182, 184-188
Hermaphrodite, 96
Hermes, 10, 14, 17-20, 65, 70, 73-75, 95-97, 99, 111, 122, 152, 156, 163, 167, 169, 173, 177-187, 198
Hermes Trismegistus, 96-97
Herne the Hunter, 59, 152, 177-180, 187-188, 193
Heruka, 13
Hodr, 116, 125, 187, 199
Holy Grail, 95
Horned God, 55, 59, 108, 148-151, 159, 170, 177, 180, 187-188, 191, 194, 214
Horus, 11-13, 15-16, 27, 65, 98, 112, 125, 152, 168-169, 171, 174, 178-179, 182-186, 188, 199
Hou-Chi, 118, 152, 186
Hounds of the Hunt, 124
Hsuan-T'ien-Shang-Ti, 98, 152, 183
Hu Gadern, 59, 180
Huehuecoyotl, 76, 153, 187
Huitzilopochtli, 130, 153, 179, 182, 187
Hupasiyas, 49
Hurukan, 52, 153, 177, 179-180, 182, 186, 188

Ichthys, 103, 188
Ida, 16
Idunn, 71, 148
Iliad, 21, 209
Illapa, 52, 186
Illuyankas, 49
Ilma, 47, 153, 186
Ilmarinen, 98, 177, 183, 185
Ilmatar, 47, 88, 153
Imhotep, 65, 153, 181-184, 188
Inanna, 49
Incas, 52, 85, 118, 130
Indra, 34, 46, 73-74, 153, 177-178,
    180-183, 185-188
Indrani, 46, 74, 153
Inti Raymi, 52
Ioskeha, 26, 153, 181, 187
Ishtar, 33, 49, 65, 150, 161-162, 169,
    174
Isis, 11-13, 27, 37, 50, 83, 98, 125-
    126, 152, 169, 172, 174-175
Ithome, 191
Itzamna, 52, 153, 177-178, 180-181,
    185-186, 188
Itzcoliuhqui, 130, 153, 187
Ixchel, 52, 153
Ixion, 109, 185
Izanagi, 51, 153, 179-180

Jade Emperor, 51, 155
Janus, 81, 154, 178-188
Jerusalem, 31, 33, 108, 112, 129, 157
Jester, 69
Julunggul, 51, 154
Jumala, 47, 154, 187
June, 50, 52
Jupiter, 14, 45-46, 50-51, 101, 146,
    154, 159, 173, 177-178, 181-188

Kaka-Guia, 130, 154, 179, 187
Kalevala, 88, 212
Kali, 103, 114, 127-128, 161, 168,
    172, 175, 196
Kalki Avatara, 110
Kama, 36, 154, 179-184
Kamadeva, 34, 183, 192
Kannon Bosatsu, 85, 154, 182
Karma, 64, 85, 91, 113, 182
Keys of heaven, 109

Khepera, 51, 154, 178, 185
Khnemu, 37, 51, 155, 177-180, 182-
    183, 185-186
Khors, 50, 187
Kiakra, 36
King of Kings, 108, 111, 159
Kingu, 48, 84, 182
Kolyada, 189
Krishna, 14, 22, 24, 34, 36, 74, 109,
    113-115, 155, 167, 179, 183-184,
    186-187, 216
Krukis, 61, 181
Kuan Ti, 85, 155, 178-179, 181-183,
    185, 188
Kuan Yin, 85, 154
Kubera, 128, 155, 177, 180-182, 185,
    187
Kulkulkan, 85, 182
Kupala, 50
Kupalo, 50, 180-181, 183, 185-187
Kupila, 118, 186
Kuretes, 16-17
Kusor, 99
Kybalion, 97

Ladon, 57
Lakshmi, 47, 153, 164
Lancelot, 39, 89, 183
Lanceor, 39
Lao-Tien-Yeh, 51, 155
Last Supper, 109
Latpon, 99, 183
Legba, 70, 75, 180-183, 185, 187
Lei-King, 85, 182, 185
Leshy, 61, 155, 180-181, 187-188
Liber Pater, 38, 147
Libera, 147
Light of the World, 109
Lightning, 13, 20, 36, 45-46, 48, 50,
    52, 90, 145, 162, 164-165, 168,
    170, 174-175, 182, 192-193
Lir, 95, 103, 155-156, 178, 180, 183,
    185-186, 188
Lleu Llaw Gyffes, 44, 155, 187
Llyr, 95, 103, 155-156, 183, 186, 188
Logos, 22, 75, 198
Loki, 70-72, 75, 88-89, 96, 125, 149,
    155, 179-180, 182, 185-187, 208
Lono, 61, 177, 181

Lord of Death, 7, 49, 83, 114-115, 121, 123-131, 143, 156, 161, 165, 169
Lord of the Dance, 34, 127
Lord of the World, 47, 150, 161, 169
Lud, 104, 155
Lugh, 44, 65, 84, 89, 115, 151, 155, 177-178, 181-188
Lunasa, 44, 115, 156, 198
Luonnotar, 47, 153
Lupercalia, 56
Lupercus, 56, 150, 180
Lykaion, 191

Maat, 83, 98, 126, 146, 195
Macha, 89
Mader-Atcha, 47, 154
Maenads, 10, 38, 58, 90, 108
Magi, 13-15, 129, 190
Maia, 14, 17, 96, 122, 164
Mama Quilla, 52, 153
Manannan mac Lir, 95, 156, 178, 180, 183, 185-186, 188
Manawydden ap Llyr, 95, 183
Manitou, 52, 155, 181-182, 186, 188
Mantis, 70, 187
Mara, 98, 128, 154, 156, 179, 182-183, 185, 187
March, 33, 112-114, 168
Marduk, 48, 79, 84, 103, 127, 156-157, 174, 177-185, 187-188, 193
Margawse, 24
Mari, 33, 60, 103
Maris, 39, 90, 113, 156
Mars, 39, 80, 89-90, 113-114, 156, 168, 177-179, 181, 185, 187-188
Martiya, 39
Maruts, 114
Masks, 114, 168, 205, 217
Mass, 12, 110
Matriarchies, 4, 6
Maui, 23, 75-76, 156, 179-180, 185-188
Maya, 14, 23, 148, 163, 206, 217
Mayas, 52, 85, 113, 168
Meditation, 53, 57, 74, 113, 137-144, 161
Medusa, 159

Menat, 37
Mercury, 73, 95, 99, 156, 177-187
Merlin, 24, 95, 157, 178-188
Messiah, 110, 190
Mexico, 117, 204-205, 216, 220
Mictlantecuhtli, 130, 157, 187
Mielikki, 61, 162
Mimir, 83, 157, 178, 182-184, 188
Min, 37, 157, 183
Mistletoe, 116, 125
Mithraic Mystery, 13
Mithras, 13-15, 22, 82, 109-110, 157, 168, 171, 177-188
Mixcoatl, 52, 186
Modranect, 190
Modred, 24, 179
Morrigan, 65, 149
Mot, 34, 129, 157, 187
Mut, 83, 98, 146, 154
Myrddin, 157
Myrrha, 14, 31
Mystery Religions, 107, 123, 191, 210

Naaman, 192
Nabu, 84, 157, 172
Nana, 33, 112
Nanna, 49, 84, 148, 161
Narayana, 114
Native Americans, 194
Nehmauit, 98
Nephthys, 12, 37, 83, 125-126, 172
Neptune, 45, 101-102, 104, 155, 157, 175, 177-178, 180, 186, 188
Nereus, 103, 157, 188
Nergal, 129, 158, 174, 179-180, 183, 185-188
Net, 48, 103
Ningal, 49, 162
Ninhursag, 84, 150
Ninip, 81
Ninlil, 48, 147
Njord, 39, 71, 104, 158, 177-178, 180, 182, 185-188
Nodens, 66, 155, 170, 181
Nuada, 65, 104, 155, 177-178, 180-181, 183-184, 186, 188
Nut, 36-37, 50, 125, 161, 173
Nymphs, 16, 20, 36, 56, 58, 73

O-Kuni-Nushi, 67, 99, 158, 180-181, 183, 186
O-Wata-Tsumi, 104, 159, 186, 188
Obelisk, 37, 50, 173-174
Oceanus, 102-103, 158, 188
Odhinn, 39-40, 45-47, 70, 72, 80, 83-84, 88, 95-97, 113, 116, 123-124, 155, 158, 167, 170, 175, 177-188, 199
Ogma, 44, 158, 178-180, 182-188
Ogun, 90, 158, 178, 180-181, 184-185, 188
Only Begotten Son, 109
Only One, 36, 50, 65, 160
Ops, 81, 160
Oracle, 80-81
Orion, 190, 210
Orpheus, 90, 109, 123, 171, 181, 195, 206, 210, 215
Orphic Mysteries, 38, 90, 123
Osirian Mysteries, 37, 90, 111, 125-126, 159, 164, 172
Osiris, 11-13, 15, 37, 82-83, 97-98, 109, 111-113, 125-126, 146, 159, 167-168, 173-175, 177-187, 190, 197, 205, 209
Ouroboros, 81

Pachacamac, 85, 159, 178, 180-181, 184-185
Pales, 112, 168
Palestine, 112, 168
Pan, 18-19, 37-39, 56-60, 64, 74, 80, 150, 157, 159, 173, 177, 179-185, 187-188, 192, 204, 214
Parvati, 35, 81, 151, 161
Pater Patrum, 15, 110
Pellervoinen, 61, 181
Persephone, 31-32, 122, 145, 150, 152, 191
Perun, 50, 159, 177, 180-182, 184-188
Petra, 13, 110
Phorcys, 103, 157, 188
Phrygia, 33, 172
Pluto, 45, 102, 122, 152, 159, 177, 179, 181, 183, 185, 187
Pomegranate, 33-34, 49, 112, 160
Poseidon, 45, 102-103, 158-159, 168, 175, 177, 180, 186, 188, 196

Prajapati, 22, 34, 60-61, 179
Priapus, 32-33, 64-65, 159, 181, 212
Prince of Peace, 109
Prometheus, 80, 184, 195
Psychopomp, 10, 111, 122, 126, 128, 169, 171-172
Ptah, 65, 126-127, 160, 177-179, 182-183, 185, 187
Puchan, 128, 160, 177, 182-187
Purgatory, 110
Python, 24, 80

Quetzalcoatl, 85, 99, 118, 130, 155, 160, 162, 178, 180, 183, 186-188, 205

Ra, 37, 50, 82-83, 97, 160, 169, 177-181, 183, 185, 187
Rabbit, 70, 187
Radha, 36, 115, 155
Ragnarok, 72
Rainbow Snake, 51, 154
Ram of God, 14
Ram-Bearer, 17, 122, 152
Ran, 33, 104, 124, 146
Rati, 36, 154
Rauni, 154
Raven, 76, 97, 148, 156, 160, 187, 196
Rebirth, 16, 33, 67, 95, 107, 111, 116-117, 124, 143-144, 146-147, 150, 156, 158, 167, 185
Red god, 114, 160
Redeemer, 22, 114, 155
Reincarnation, 22, 59, 85, 90, 148-149, 153-154, 156, 158-159, 161, 163, 185
Rhea, 16, 19-20, 44-45, 73, 101, 149
Ride of Death, 123
Rimmon, 49, 160, 187
Robin Hood, 55, 59-60, 124-125, 180, 188, 214
Rome, 15, 110, 126, 171, 199, 204, 206, 215, 217
Rudra, 60, 64, 114, 128, 160, 177-182, 184-186, 188

Saishyant, 110, 160, 185
Sakyamuni, 115, 160
Samana, 82, 128, 164

Sanskrit, 45, 49, 70, 82, 189-190, 197
Sati, 37, 51
Saturn, 56, 63, 81, 129, 160, 177, 180-183, 185-186, 188, 195, 200, 217
Saturnalia, 81, 195
Satyrs, 20, 35, 38, 108, 114
Seb, 36-37, 50, 161, 179-180, 183
Sebek, 126, 161, 179-180, 187
Sekhmet, 126, 160
Selene, 58
Semele, 20
Set, 11-12, 19, 25, 37, 40, 57, 60, 65, 72, 75, 81, 90, 94, 96, 98, 111-112, 118, 125, 129, 138-139, 143, 161, 167-169, 173, 179-180, 183, 185-186, 199
Shakti, 192, 203
Shala, 48
Shamash, 49, 84, 161, 174, 178-179, 182-183, 185-188
Shamrock, 36, 175
Shango, 99, 161, 183, 186, 188
Shen Nung, 67, 181
Shepherds, 13, 22, 56, 65, 111, 114, 167
Shiva, 22, 34-35, 46-47, 66-67, 72, 81, 103, 126-127, 161, 168, 172-173, 175, 179-184, 186-188, 207
Shou-Hsing, 85, 161, 179, 182-183, 185
Shu, 37, 50-51, 186
Siddhartha, 23, 115, 198
Sif, 47, 162
Sigyn, 72, 155
Sin Bearer, 22, 155, 198
Sinai, 49
Sinn, 48-49, 161, 174, 180, 182-183, 185, 188
Sins, 14, 35, 82, 107, 110, 113, 155, 168, 173, 198
Skadi, 71-72, 104, 158
Skalds, 96-97, 116, 148, 193, 211
Slaughter of the Innocents, 24, 114, 191
Sleipnir, 70, 72
Smyrna, 31
Soma, 34, 46, 82, 183-184
Sommona Cadom, 14

Son of Man, 110, 114
Soter, 107
Spear, 59, 90, 116, 125, 174
Spenta Mainyu, 25
Spring Equinox, 10, 14-16, 109, 112, 145
Star, 22-23, 114, 160, 164, 190, 197
Sucellos, 59
Summer Solstice, 15, 58
Supai, 130, 187
Susanoo, 75, 162, 177-180, 185-188
Svantovit, 50, 162, 177-180, 187-188
Svarog, 50, 182, 187
Syrinx, 57

T'ai-Yueh-Ta-Ti, 85, 177, 182
Ta'aroa, 104, 162, 179, 186, 188
Tablets of Destiny, 79, 84, 150
Taliesin, 94-95, 162, 178, 180, 182-184, 186-188
Tammuz, 31, 33, 111-112, 114, 129, 150, 157, 168, 177, 183, 185
Tangaroa, 52, 162, 177-181, 186
Tapio, 61, 162, 181, 188
Tawhaki, 99, 162, 183, 186
Tawiscara, 26, 153, 187
Tegid, 94
Tekkeitsertok, 61, 162, 177, 180-181
Terminus, 55, 177-178, 180
Teshub, 49, 162, 187
Tezcatlipoca, 130, 162, 179, 181, 183-184, 186-188
The Lord, 6-7, 30-31, 34, 43, 45, 49, 52, 55, 59-61, 82, 85, 88, 105, 112, 114-115, 121, 123, 127-131, 140, 146, 165, 169, 172, 193
Thetis, 21
Third eye, 46
Thorr, 39, 47, 50, 71-72, 88-89, 99, 159, 161-162, 177-179, 181-182, 185-188, 193
Thoth, 12, 65, 82-83, 95, 97-99, 125, 163, 177-179, 181-188, 195
Thrice-born, 146
Thrud, 47
Thunderbirds, 85, 182, 185-188
Thunderbolt, 36, 45-46, 51, 64, 153, 157

Thyrsus, 38, 174-175
Tiamat, 48, 84, 103, 156
Titans, 10, 16, 20, 44, 93, 108
Tlaloc, 40, 61, 163, 180-181, 183-184,
    186-187
Trefuilngid Tre-Eochair, 36, 175
Trident, 35-36, 101, 103, 157, 159,
    175
Trinity, 47, 110, 146
Triple Goddess, 19, 35-36, 73, 103,
    113, 115-116, 127, 175
Triptolemus, 21, 108, 171
Tryambaka, 114
Tuoni, 130, 163, 179, 187
Twins, 24-27, 128, 175, 187
Tyr, 84, 89, 163, 168, 178-179, 181-
    182, 185-188, 195

Ukko, 48, 88, 163, 185-187
Uma, 35, 161
Underwater Panthers, 67, 181, 188
Uranus, 44, 163, 181, 186

Vainamoinen, 88, 181, 184, 187
Vajra, 36, 46, 175
Vajrapani, 60, 180, 182-184, 188
Varuna, 82, 103, 163, 178-179, 182-
    188, 195
Vatican, 15
Vediovis, 10
Velchanos, 122, 187
Vellamo, 104
Venus, 37
Vertumnus, 58, 163, 180-181, 186-187
Vesuvius, 122
Viracocha, 52, 118, 164, 179-180,
    182, 184-186
Virgin, 13, 31-33, 60, 88, 109-110,
    112, 118, 203
Vishnu, 36, 47, 114, 164, 168-169,
    177, 182-187, 198
Volos, 61, 164, 177, 181, 184-185,
    188
Vulcan, 96, 122, 124, 151, 164, 178,
    180, 182-183, 187-188
Vulcanalia, 122

Wepwawet, 90, 164, 175, 181, 185
Wheel, 37, 50-51, 109, 165, 169
White God, 49, 96, 115, 130, 148, 152
White Moon Goddess, 59
Wild Hunt, 84, 123, 151-152, 158,
    170, 175, 188
Windsor Castle, 193
Wine, 20, 38, 58, 65, 108, 147, 172,
    175, 188, 197
Winter Solstice, 10, 15-16, 52, 189
Wise Men, 14, 22, 114, 190
Wodan, 123, 188
Womb, 15-16, 19, 23, 25-26, 51, 96,
    101, 116, 122-123, 125, 127, 170
World Egg, 51
World Serpent, 70
World Tree, 113, 116, 167

Xevioso, 40, 183, 185, 187
Xipe Totec, 117, 164, 177, 179, 186
Xiuhtzilopochtli, 117, 186
Xolotl, 99, 130, 164, 183, 187

Yama, 82, 85, 115, 128, 164-165, 179-
    180, 182, 185, 187, 200
Yamantaka, 115, 128, 165
Yamm, 49, 128, 187
Yanauluha, 67, 165, 181
Yao-Shih, 67, 181
Yarilo, 118, 165, 185-186
Yeng-Wang-Yeh, 85, 130, 165, 180,
    182, 185, 187
Yima, 114, 128
Yule, 150, 190
Yum Caax, 117, 165, 177, 181, 185-
    186

Zagreus, 10, 15-17, 179
Zend Avesta, 84
Zeus, 10, 14-20, 24, 31-32, 44-46, 51,
    64, 73-74, 81, 96, 101-102, 108-
    109, 123, 127, 146-147, 165, 177-
    179, 181-188, 191, 200
Zodiac, 45, 109
Zoroaster, 14-15, 84, 110, 128, 182,
    191, 197
Zurvan, 25, 128, 191

STAY IN TOUCH...

Llewellyn publishes hundreds of books on your favorite subjects!

Order by Phone

Call toll-free within the U.S. and Canada, **1–800–THE MOON.** In Minnesota call **(612) 291–1970.** We accept Visa, MasterCard, and American Express.

Order by Mail

Send the full price of your order (MN residents add 7% sales tax) in U.S. funds to:

> **Llewellyn Worldwide**
> **P.O. Box 64383, Dept. K177–5**
> **St. Paul, MN 55164–0383, U.S.A.**

Postage and Handling

- ◆ $4.00 for orders $15.00 and under
- ◆ $5.00 for orders over $15.00
- ◆ No charge for orders over $100.00

We ship UPS in the continental United States. We cannot ship to P.O. boxes. Orders shipped to Alaska, Hawaii, Canada, Mexico, and Puerto Rico will be sent first-class mail.

International orders: Airmail—add freight equal to price of each book to the total price of order, plus $5.00 for each non-book item (audiotapes, etc.). Surface mail—add $1.00 per item.

Allow 4–6 weeks delivery on all orders. Postage and handling rates subject to change.

Group Discounts

We offer a 20% quantity discount to group leaders or agents. You must order a minimum of 5 copies of the same book to get our special quantity price.

Free Catalog

Get a free copy of our color catalog, *New Worlds of Mind and Spirit.* Subscribe for just $10.00 in the United States and Canada ($20.00 overseas, first-class mail). Many bookstores carry *New Worlds*—ask for it!